The
Brightest
Star

Betty Cody

The Brightest Star

BETTY
CODY

POOLBEG

Published 2022 by Poolbeg Press Ltd
123 Grange Hill, Baldoyle
Dublin 13, Ireland
www.poolbeg.com
Email: info@poolbeg.com

A catalogue record for this book is available from the British Library.

ISBN 978178199-471-9

www.poolbeg.com

About the Author

I was born in Cork City but moved to Dublin after my marriage. While my children attended school, I did a PhD in Psychology at University College Dublin.

Apart from my family, sport has been my main passion in life: table tennis, followed by squash, golf and now pitch and putt.

I have also written a golf psychology column in the *Irish Independent* and features, plus celebrity interviews, in *Irish Lady Golfer magazine*. My self-published book, *The Road to Perfect Golf*, sold out its print run.

Playing bridge is a new passion in life for me and I recently had the unusual experience of winning an event that allowed myself and my partner to compete in the Irish International Camrose Cup trials.

Over the past few years, during Covid lockdown, I wrote my first novel.

Acknowledgements

I want to thank the incredible team at Poolbeg for their leap of faith in publishing my first novel! In particular, I am indebted to my wonderful editor, Gaye Shortland, for her breadth of knowledge about everything, especially 19th century Ireland. I wish also to convey my deepest thanks to Poolbeg's Paula Campbell. As my first point of contact with Poolbeg, she has regularly kept me up to date regarding every aspect of the process towards publication. Her cheerful emails kept me entertained, as well as informed!

Over the years, I have received support also from many other women, while pursuing my writing. Penny Howard in London, Mary Stanley and Irene Graham in Ireland, and Lisa Clifford and Philippa Donovan in Italy.

Last, but by no means least, I want to thank my eldest grandchild, Lía Kirwan, who read the very first draft of the book and gave me positive feedback on the characters.

I wish to dedicate this book to my beloved family.

To my husband Michael, our children Gillian and Alan,

their spouses Ken and Laura, and our grandchildren

Chloe and Joe Cody and Lia, Jack and Louis Kirwan.

Part 1

Chapter 1

28th January 1816

The four green fields I long to see,
United in love with them and thee.
The yearning for you is deep in my soul
To watch a star from Irish soil.

As Jack Ryan walked along the quay to join the *Seahorse,* he was in good spirits. It would be his last time at sea. He had experienced the exotic beauty of Venice, had smelt the aroma of spices in India which would stay with him for life, and had even learned to swim which was unusual for an Irish city boy. But he knew that he wasn't cut out for a life at sea. He had just turned twenty-one years old and he had met enough old seamen in his travels to curb any desire to roam for life. He wanted his prints left on the soil of Ireland. He would never have left Ireland except for his drunken bullying father. Three years ago, his father had gone one step too far by taking his strap to Jack's head with such force that the buckle had made a deep gash above his ear. It happened on Jack's eighteenth birthday. This was because the family were happy and cheerful, eating cake made by Jack's grandmother, Sheila, for his eighteenth birthday. Jack's father, Septimius Ryan, was an ugly drunk. Drink didn't make him happy, it just turned him into a jealous sour-faced bully. Jack had had enough. Although he had loved the work in the family market garden in Friarsland near the city of Cork, he wanted to get away from anything to do with his father.

Returning to Ireland, he now intended to set his sights higher. He wanted to see his grandmother, his mother and his older sisters Hannah and Julia, but he was never going to work anywhere near his drunken father again.

The ship looked impressive in the still air. Jack could already imagine it at sea with its sails soaring right into the clouds. It was early morning and Jack was joining the ship at the Downs, a pretty sheltered harbour off the Kent coast. It was a merchant ship that had earlier set sail from Ramsgate, part of a flotilla taking soldiers from the Napoleonic wars back home to Cork. In just two days Jack too would be home.

Soldiers with their distinctive red coats and tall black hats milled around its decks. There were also some women and children waving excitedly to people standing on the quay.

Jack had been helped by his last captain, Matthew Bates, who had secured him a passage to Ireland if he helped out around the decks once the ship had sailed. He would not have sleeping accommodation but could bed down after dark in a quiet corner. That suited Jack just fine. He had his few possessions in a hemp bag and was wearing a warm heavy coat that he had bought in Finland eighteen months before, when they nearly got icebound off the coast.

Matthew Bates had told him he was to find a good mate of his called Corky and introduce himself. Jack smiled to himself now, recalling how his captain had explained why the seaman was called such a funny name.

"Unlike you," Matthew had said, "he never shut up talking about his home town of Cork. He nearly drove us all mad."

Jack knew it was true that he rarely talked about his home life when he was at sea.

Jack had no trouble identifying his ex-captain's good friend, Corky, as he had been given a full description. He had been told that Corky was an ordinary seaman and that he would be on the deck. Jack could see him standing at the top of the ramp, checking passengers onto the ship. He greeted Jack with a warm handshake and asked how his old friend Matthew Bates was keeping. Jack assured him that he was well and with a smile and a quick nod the crewman pointed along the deck to where Jack could find himself a corner to sleep.

"As you already know, the ship is fairly packed and there is no room for sleeping below deck. Sorry about that."

Jack assured him that it was no problem. "It will hopefully be my last time at sea and I'll enjoy it no matter where I sleep."

Corky nodded and told him that he would bring him some food and hot tea once they had set sail. Jack thanked him, shook his hand again with a grateful squeeze and made his way past the soldiers and their families to a quiet part of the ship.

As he walked along the deck, the mouth-watering aroma of cooking ham wafted up from the galley below. He dropped his bag in a small covered spot behind a waist-high bar, which was sheltered from the rain. With a smile he realised that he was really going home.

As they sailed out of the harbour, Jack sat on a wooden crate and watched the land recede, bidding farewell to his travelling days. He felt that having reached the age of twenty-one, this milestone was encouraging him to search for a more settled life. He thought about meeting someone, getting married and having a family. He felt it was time for that.

During the past three years he had often contemplated getting his mother to move away from his father. When he was a child, he used to dream of giving her a better life, but he had been too young then. Maybe he could do it for her sometime in the future. Lately he had a recurring dream of standing in the middle of four green fields looking at the stars. He knew that his future lay deep within his own Irish soil. He knew also that he was willing to learn new skills as he had proved at sea. He had always applied himself to any task given to him.

Jack Ryan always seemed at his happiest when helping

other people. He found at times that he seemed less comfortable when others did kind things for him. It was probably his upbringing, he thought. When he was growing up, he never knew from day to day whether his father would cuff him in the head or throw him a few pennies if he had won some money at cards. Jack often felt that the unpredictability of his father's actions had been his greatest fear when he was young. The feeling whereby he was so apprehensive about the possibility of a crack of a belt that he was never able to feel happy even when his father's mood was good. This apprehension was always there until he went to sea. The lads at sea had laughed when Jack refused even one glass of rum but he had stuck to his belief that if drink could make his father so crazy, it could do the same to him, so he wasn't giving it any opportunity to entice him into an alcoholic haze.

As he sat in thought, he heard a cheery laugh and his new friend appeared with a huge tin mug of tea and a tin plate with two chunks of bread and a good lump of cheese to put on it.

"I've brought you enough food for the journey. Keep it safe in your bag as the weather can get rough at times."

"I already have some food in my bag, but I'm very grateful, especially for the hot tea."

Corky told him he could stay where he was and didn't need to do any work during the voyage to Cork.

Jack wondered at this. It felt now as if his presence on the ship was almost clandestine. How far was Corky sticking his neck out to accommodate him? He hadn't thought to question Matthew Bates about it, just thanked him profusely for his help. Perhaps best not to bring the subject up now.

"Enjoy your time at sea," Corky said, smiling, before he returned to his duties.

As the evening shadows began to fall across the deck, Jack sat watching parents showing their children the waves and the other ships sailing in the distance. The families looked happy, especially the children. Many of them were probably on a boat for the first time.

A little girl of about seven years of age looked at him curiously and asked if he was a soldier. Jack smiled and told her that he was not – that he had been away on a big ship and was now going home to Ireland.

"My dada was fighting a big war," she said.

As her parents and elder brother arrived behind her, she turned to them.

"This man is not a soldier, Dada. He's been away on a big ship!"

Jack laughed and shook hands with her parents.

The soldier told Jack that he had seen enough of fighting and couldn't think of anything better than returning to Ireland with his family. Jack agreed and, before they left, he gave the children a sweet each, wrapped in shiny paper. He told them that the sweets had come all the way from India.

The little girl was delighted and, as she skipped away, she turned and with a smile said, "My friends call me Angel, but it's not my real name."

Jack smiled back and waved goodbye.

Angel had blonde curls under a pink bonnet. One day I'd love to have a little daughter like her, Jack thought.

Chapter 2

Jack's quiet corner allowed him to sleep in relative comfort. He used his bag as a pillow and the wooden slats that jutted out over his head meant he was sheltered from the winds.

He woke early and enjoyed his breakfast food. Suddenly little Angel peeped into his den and asked him what he was doing there. He told her that he was sheltering from the wind. Angel's parents arrived and told him that she insisted on coming to thank him for the sweet. She was such a lovely child with her soft golden hair and sparkling blue eyes, Jack thought. He again hoped that one day he would have a daughter with similar looks and a cheeky smile.

As the family went below deck, Jack stood up and walked to stretch his legs.

Later in the morning he ate an apple that he had brought with him. He kept the rest of the food for his supper. He enjoyed the next while strolling around the deck and happily leaning over the rail, watching other ships in the distance.

After some time he noticed that the sky had begun to darken. As the wind rose, the families who were walking about began to disappear below deck. There was now just the odd soldier or deckhand leaning on the ship's rail and maybe reflecting on what lay ahead.

Jack stood by the rails for a while, watching the waves begin to rise and fall rapidly as the wind blew and rain started to fall – slowly at first, but soon it was coming down in massive sheets of water, and the swaying movement of the ship had intensified.

He returned to his sheltered den and, as he sat down, he heard a loud thud followed by raised voices coming from further along the ship.

He heard somebody shouting, *"He's fallen!"*

The voices called, *"We have him, we have him, get him inside!"*

The voices ceased.

Jack knew that someone had been injured. He was not surprised as he looked up at the massive billowing sails straining in the wind.

Jack was grateful for his secluded corner safe from the high winds.

Later, Corky returned with another mug of tea and a welcome couple of oat biscuits. Jack thanked him and asked him if they could have a meal together when they reached shore, in Cork. They agreed to meet the following day and have a good chat. Jack laughed and promised to pay for that meal when they got back to dry land.

"That sounds like a good idea!" said Corky with a laugh.

As Jack settled into the corner, he watched the dark clouds as they scurried backwards and forwards above. He had sailed on ships all over the east, and had experienced some serious storms, but something about today's wind and rain spooked him. As he looked up, he felt a deep uneasiness in the pit of his stomach. He didn't like this feeling.

The long day dragged and, as night began to fall, the winds rose even more and rain pelted down. Jack began to fear for the safety of the passengers. How frightened the women and children must be, he thought. He was lucky to be in a sheltered corner. If not, he believed that he could easily be washed overboard. For some reason, he felt safer on deck as he could see what was going on.

He lost track of time. He was just moving back and forth with the constant heaving of the ship. He knew in his heart that this storm was going to test the skills of all the seamen and he found himself thinking of how much he had been looking forward to seeing his mother in Cork. His arms were exhausted from holding on tight to the slippery bar across the front of his den.

Was it a mirage or did he see something like light in the distance? It was just the first stirrings of dawn but the chinks of light from the east kept turning to black as the raging winds and rain refused to offer up a false dawn. This storm was going to have its say.

* * *

As morning finally broke without any respite from the weather, soldiers and crew began to sway along the deck and Corky came to check on Jack. He said that they had lost a mate called John Sullivan from Cork, who had a serious fall earlier when the gale first blew up. He told Jack that they were part of a convoy of three ships on course for Cork; the *Boadicea* and the *Lord Melville* were the other two ships. The *Seahorse* was now heading for shelter in Waterford.

The storm raged and another sailor informed Jack that they had dropped three anchors to try and steady the ship. There was a fear that if the anchors did not hold, the ship would hit rocks. Hundreds of people were by now milling around on deck.

The ship began to groan, making sounds like the cries of a seriously wounded animal. This was matched by the softer but more sorrowful sounds of women and children weeping. Jack noticed Angel's parents, with their two children, as they moved along, holding on to the rail. He stepped out to be close to them and try to reassure the children who were crying.

"Don't worry," he said, trying to offer them some comfort. "I'm used to ships and I'll stay with you."

He stood gripping the rail of the ship, looking in horror at the scenes that surrounded him. Women were by now beginning to scream, children were clinging wildly to their parents as sailors ran back and forth trying to calm hysterical people. The boat began to heave and dip and Jack almost froze with shock as he saw two soldiers remove their greatcoats and jump from the deck into the foaming seas below before they disappeared from sight as the boat listed yet again. A tall sea officer came in their direction, shouting to everyone to stay calm but that unfortunate man was quickly surrounded by fathers and mothers asking what he would do for their small children. For a moment Jack almost felt sorry for him as the anguish on his face was there for all to see. Jack knew that this ship would not win the fight against the strong forces of nature and he knew also that the men who jumped were more likely to live than the sad and terrified passengers clinging on to the hope that this ship would right itself and stay afloat.

He felt overwhelmed with the greatest burden ever placed on his shoulders. He turned his eyes, now filled with tears and not just sea spray, to Angel's father.

"I'll do everything in my power to save you all."

Angel stood at Jack's side while gripping her father's hand tightly. As Jack looked down at her little face, she took from her pocket the sweet that Jack had given to her.

"My brother ate his, but I'm keeping mine until I'm at home in Ireland."

Jack's stricken face turned to her father. The men locked eyes before Angel's father lifted his face to the sky.

"Only God can help us now," he said. "Will you please just pray with us?"

Jack began to sense the man's feeling of hopefulness and prayed with the family. For the first time in his life, he prayed for someone other than his own family. He prayed that these four people would live, even if his own life was lost. He would try to do everything possible to save them. He pulled off his now soaked greatcoat and threw it back on top of his hemp bag. He knew the coat wouldn't help if things got worse.

Angel's parents were holding the railings, sure that their lives depended on it.

Suddenly, the sound that Jack feared began to create a collective panic on deck – the sound of timber snapping, growing louder than the winds. The ship lifted and listed as the anchors tore away from the seabed. The shudder as the ship hit rocks sent it first towards the sky and then it dipped and dipped and dipped.

Jack reached towards the children but saw that they were being held close to the hearts of their parents. As the ship began to creak and groan, it again began to move towards the sky and somebody shouted "*Jump or you will end up underneath!*"

As Jack shouted to the family to stay near to him, the rail snapped fully and they all slowly fell into the churning waves below. Jack felt himself sink lower and lower into the depths of the sea before the shock left him and he swam to the surface. His head surfaced and he swam against the rough waves, not knowing where anyone was, then he was swallowed back into the sea again.

He surfaced again. All he could see was devastation and chaos around him, as he roared out, "*I'm coming for you – I'll get you out – I'm here, I'm here!*"

But he could not see the family anywhere.

No, no, no, this can't be happening! This can't be happening! he thought.

He frantically began to swim round and round in circles but he could see nothing but ink-black water and debris everywhere.

Chapter 3

1st February 1816

"No, no, no, I must save them, I must save them, where are they, where are they . . ." As he struggled to get up, Jack could feel somebody touching his face and squeezing his hand.

He heard a soothing voice washing over him.

"Hush, lad, hush, it will all be fine. You're safe now."

"Where are they? Where are the children?"

He heard a man say. "Hello, lad."

Jack's head was pounding and his chest pain made it difficult to turn.

"Could you let me know your name, lad?"

Jack turned his head very slowly.

"Where am I?"

He could see a lady with a tearful face sitting by his bed as a tall grey-haired man stood with his arm on her shoulder. It was she who was holding his hand.

"You're safe here with us now," she said softly.

"Do you remember what happened?"

A sudden shudder like a bolt of lightning went through Jack's body as he recalled going down and down past the shattered wreck that had been the *Seahorse*.

The lady patted his hand. "My name is Ellen Murray and this is my husband Cornelius," she said. "My son Henry lifted you from the water and put you on his cart. He brought you here to the cottage and we've been taking care of you for a couple of days."

"We believe that you've got a touch of pneumonia," said the man, "and our local doctor told us to keep you cool. We're to call him again if you aren't improving."

Jack was suddenly afraid that he could make trouble for his ex-captain Matthew Bates and his mate Corky who had made the apparently irregular arrangement on the ship for him. He couldn't think what to do.

"Where am I?" he asked again.

"You're in Tramore, close to Waterford," Cornelius answered.

"Is everyone safe?"

"Don't worry, lad. Everything will be fine. We're taking care of you now and nothing bad will happen to you. I'll go and make you a cup of tea and maybe you would try a bit of bread with it?"

He nodded at his wife and shook his head as he left the room.

Cornelius wondered how he was going to tell the lad that almost all the passengers on the ship had died. But that would have to wait for another day.

Their eighteen-year-old son Henry was in the kitchen and Cornelius told him that Jack was awake.

"He was a lucky lad that you were there to pull him out of the water, son, but I worry about the effect it will have on his mind when he realises that so many people perished on the ship."

"Did he not ask?"

"He did, son. He asked if everyone was safe."

Henry grimaced. "That's bad."

"I'm going to make him a cup of tea. When you have milked the cow and fed the chickens, you might sit and chat with him for a while. But say nothing about the loss of life."

"That won't be easy, Dad."

"I know."

During the following weeks, as Jack's fever began to abate, he slept mostly during daylight hours because at night he woke frequently, shaking from the terror of his nightmares.

He knew people had called to the door and had wanted to know his name, but he hadn't told the Murrays his surname yet. As well as not wanting to get Captain Matthew Bates and Corky into trouble, he was afraid he himself might be jailed for sailing on the ship without full authority.

Henry sat with him each evening and one evening Jack told him of his fears. He explained that he was probably not properly registered to be on the ship.

"Don't worry. Nobody would have a problem with that

but, if it worries you, we won't tell anyone your name. My parents have told the authorities that your memory isn't back yet."

With relief, Jack once again fell into the happy oblivion of sleep, hoping that when he next woke up the whole nightmare would somehow be over.

As Jack began to get some physical strength back, he felt blessed that he had met such kindness. He knew deep down that sometime soon he needed to know everything about the fateful day when his ship sank into the ocean. The family seemed to know that he couldn't face talking about it and they had thankfully respected his wishes. He knew also that many people still called to the house to offer their good wishes. But he wasn't yet ready to face the wider world.

He began to take slow steps around their smallholding. He even helped with feeding the small number of chickens in the backyard. It reminded him a bit of the backyard of his own home but there the market gardens had stretched out a long way. These kind people had only a smallholding. Henry told him that it gave them ample food to live on and enough to take to market once each week.

Jack was so grateful for their kindness that he spent time with Henry, teaching him some of the secrets of the market garden that he had learned in his days back in Friarsland. He did anything he could to stop having to think. He also knew it was nearly time for him to move on. His time in the cottage where this lovely family had kept him safe for almost a month, away from the world, needed to end.

Yet, he still didn't know what happened to the *Seahorse*. In truth, he was afraid to ask. Plus, the fact that the Murrays had never ever mentioned the shipwreck in his presence made him fear the worst. During his night terrors he kept seeing the face of Angel smiling at him, before he woke each time sweating and screaming.

I'm a mess, he thought. I can't face this and I don't know what to do about it. But I know I can't stay hiding away any longer. I'll have to leave.

The following morning, he looked out the window of the small cosy bedroom that felt so warm and welcoming and watched the winter sun rise over the distant horizon. Having made the decision to go, he knew there was no right time to leave but he just knew that it was finally time. He would tell the Murray family that evening.

When he sat down for tea with Ellen, Cornelius and Henry, he told him of his decision. He needed to move on soon.

Ellen and Cornelius looked at each other and nodded. They had already decided that it was time he knew the truth. He needed to know the full story of that fateful day at the end of January when three ships sank and the majority of their passengers died in the Atlantic Ocean.

Ellen took hold of Jack's hand and Henry sat beside him as Cornelius, as gently as possible, told him about the day the ships perished on the rocks. Jack's head fell lower and lower into his chest as he listened, in horror at the devastation that had occurred in the now calm seas close to the cottage. The pain he felt in his chest was so acute that he curled up in a ball and Ellen had to soothe him as Cornelius and Henry lifted him into his bed.

Henry stayed in the room with him for the whole of that night and calmed him every time he shouted out in terror. It was different to the previous nights but Henry knew that Jack would have to leave the horror that surrounded him in Tramore, if he was ever going to regain his health.

As the days passed, Jack slowly began to move out of the fog. He agonised about Corky who gave him food and drinks. Would he ever meet him again? Mostly he kept remembering little Angel. It was as if she was standing in front of him, with her blonde curls and cheeky, smiling face. He now knew that she had not survived. He knew also that he had to place her in a small corner of his heart. He believed that to keep her there and tell no one about her would allow him to get out of this nightmare that had been his life over the past month. He would never forget her and he hoped that someday he would have the strength to place some flowers on the beach at Tramore, in her memory.

At six o'clock on a spring morning in early March, Jack stood with the little bag that Ellen had filled with food and some of Henry's clothes. She had also put some stitches to a coat that had been in the house since her father died. She had kept the coat because it made her still feel close to her father even though he was dead ten years. But she now knew it was time to let it go.

Jack looks smart in the black wool coat, she thought. He had bathed and washed his hair in the tin bath in the kitchen on the previous night. He was tall and broad-shouldered just like her father, and his now clean-shaven face and shining black hair showed what a handsome lad he was. But he had a haunted look on his pale face that almost broke her heart. She had grown to love taking care of him but knew it was time for him to move on. She had packed enough food to keep him going for a few days, as Jack had little appetite that morning.

Henry got the cart ready and put the bag into it, as Jack said goodbye to Ellen and Cornelius. Ellen hugged him and said he must return someday, while Cornelius pressed a half-crown coin into his outstretched hand. What Jack didn't know was that the villagers had sent around some pennies to Cornelius to support the survivor of the shipwreck.

The men looked at each other and silent tears were shed.

Before he climbed on the cart, Jack looked at the family who had been so good to him.

"My full name is Jack Ryan and I come from Friarsland in Cork city. Please keep my name a secret until I can find the courage in the future to tell someone else what happened to me last month. When I get my head to make sense of it all, I will return to thank you for your kindness."

Henry drove Jack to the Cork Road and told him that he might be lucky and get cart rides, as it had many farms along the way. He also told him to watch for an inn about thirty miles away where they gave a bed and a fine breakfast for a small charge.

Before Jack stepped down, they embraced each other like brothers and promised to meet sometime in the future. Henry waited until Jack was out of sight and then, with a worried sigh, he took up the reins, turned the horse around and drove back in the direction of Tramore.

Chapter 4

The morning was bright but the sunshine did not light up the dark shadow that lay like a black ghost across Jack's mind. He had lost the warmth of the Murray family home and he had hidden the blackness that had descended on him when he heard the full extent of the tragedy he had been a part of. Why was he alive and others were not? He felt it was desperately cruel that children, especially the little girl Angel he had befriended, and their families, died while he lived. It didn't make sense to him. He walked the roads like a madman, moving so fast that he had to sit very often to rest.

He ate the food from his bag throughout the day, trying to hold on to his limited supply of money. As darkness descended, he spotted an inn and paid the small amount asked by the owner. He gratefully entered a small attic room. As he lay on the narrow bed, he prayed that he wouldn't waken people with his nightmares and hoped to enter a deep sleep, as he knew he had another long walk ahead of him tomorrow.

The sound of birdsong in the trees outside woke him, just as light began to appear over the horizon. The chirpy sound gladdened his heart. He set out and walked, listening to nature waking as he enjoyed Ellen's chunk of cheese and bread.

He was lucky that morning as he got a ride in a milk cart going two miles to deliver a churn to an inn. The farmer was chatty and Jack told him he was going back to see his family in Cork.

"Goodness, lad, you have a lot of miles to do – maybe you could pick up a coach from the inn?"

Jack thanked the farmer but knew he needed to keep walking to exhaustion because he didn't want time to think. He bought himself two cooked eggs at the inn and a hot oatcake. He didn't linger and, after what seemed hours on the road, he was glad to get a lift from another farm cart. Jack thought the driver must be the last cart-driver's brother because he gave the same advice about taking a coach to get him to Cork.

"It's a long way, lad," he said, shaking his head. "You'll have to keep walking all day for the next couple of days to get there."

Jack thanked him but knew he needed to keep moving. He ate another chunk of cheese and vowed to walk again until it got dark. But, as dusk arrived, his feet were so blistered and sore that he knew he needed to slow down.

Shortly afterwards he saw a cottage and knocked and asked them if he could pay to sleep in one of their sheds.

The farmer's wife took pity on him. 'I'll let you stay in the hayshed. It's nice and warm and there's no charge, lad. We're glad to help people who pass this way,' she said kindly. "Wait there. I'll be back."

When she returned with a large slice of bread with ample butter on top and a tin cup of warm milk, tears sprang to his eyes as he thanked her.

"Go over to the hayshed now, lad, and I'll bring a bowl of water over to you. You look as if you need a little wash."

As he thanked her, he made a solemn promise to himself to help people in need in the future. He knew that somehow he would have to pull himself together and stop feeling so sorry for himself.

After she brought the bowl of warm water, he bathed his sore feet, reflecting on the many kind people he had encountered since the ship sank.

I'll have to start being more positive, he thought, as he burrowed into the hay.

He slept fitfully and woke early. He was grateful that there was still no rain. He walked through the town of Youghal and beyond. His feet began to really hurt again and he was grateful for another cart-ride.

As the driver dropped him off, he told him he should be able to reach the town of Midleton before dark. There he would find a lovely place to stay called the Haven Inn.

Jack bade farewell to yet another kind person, thinking he just might be able to afford a night at the inn. He ate the last of his food and set out for Midleton.

Chapter 5

Eliza Turner stood patiently in the parlour of their farmhouse near Midleton. It was a calm day with more than a hint of spring in the air. She was waiting for her sixteen-year-old sister Lily, as she had to do almost every time before they went to the town of Midleton in the horse and trap. Eliza, who had turned eighteen in January, felt like she was ten years older than her giddy sister. Lily always wanted to have her bonnet straight and her blonde curls peeping through, in the hope that she would be admired when they shopped in the town. She had no need to worry because her peaches-and-cream skin and wide smile drew looks from most of the young boys when they ventured out. Eliza was tall with dark hair held up at the sides with fashionable clips, yet her more serious expression did not hide the allure of her midnight-blue eyes.

Their father Robert was very proud of his two

daughters. They were his life since their mother had died of a raging fever that had hit many people in the town just two years after Lily's birth. Young Meg Jackson, who had been employed as a nursery maid and helped Robert's wife Kathleen with the cooking, became nanny, housekeeper and surrogate mother to the girls. Meg was then just eighteen years of age. Robert sometimes felt guilty that he might have stopped Meg's chances of having a family of her own, but she was a light in all their lives and looked after the girls' every need over the years.

Eliza asked Lily to hurry up as their father Robert was already sitting patiently in the trap. Finally, they left the house, with Meg handing them extra shawls for fear it might get too cold on the way.

As the girls climbed onto the trap, Robert called to Meg. "Don't forget to get Sam to feed the cattle and mend the fence at the side of the stable while we're in town. He'd sit all day in the kitchen with you feeding him cups of tea if he could!"

Sam was their resident farmhand who loved the animals and going for a drink in the inn each evening. Some people thought him a bit quiet, but Meg knew he had an intelligence that was all his own and a kind heart.

She smiled and with a laugh promised that the jobs would be finished by the time they got home. "Get going now," she said, "or you won't be home in time for tea!"

The girls laughed as they waved their goodbyes and Robert smiled, content in the knowledge that his home was a happy place for everyone. He slapped the reins on Snugs the horse's back as a signal to move and they set off down the laneway.

Lily looked at her sister with a cheeky grin.

"I wonder if Toby Ramsay and Oliver Frankland will be at the Regency Room today? Toby was looking at you all the time last Saturday!"

Eliza lifted her eyebrows. Lily was so indiscreet – she should know better than to talk about such things in their father's company. As for Toby Ramsay, although she had been flattered by his attention recently, she was unlike Lily in such matters. She was the more cautious older sister.

"I heard that he's related to an earl," said Lily.

Eliza laughed and said she heard he was a distant relative only. Apparently, the earl had paid his college fees. And that's where he had met Squire Frankland's son Oliver.

"I'm perfectly happy with my life and my work and have no interest in men at the moment," she added primly, as she pushed her sister playfully.

They arrived at the square in Midleton and agreed to meet their father in the Regency Room after they had spent some time shopping.

"Can you hurry up, Lily, please, or father will arrive at the Regency Room before we even get there."

Lily was fussing over some lace trimmings that Meg would have to sew on a new dress Lily had bought. She couldn't decide what colour was best.

"Why don't you get both and I'll use the one you don't

want?" said Eliza, beginning to lose her patience. It was the same every week. Eliza bought necessities for herself and the house and her sixteen-year-old sister just bought frivolous baubles.

"Thanks, sister, I'll buy them both, and don't look so crossly at me!"

Eliza knew she could never be cross for long with her beloved sister and, as they left the shop, they linked arms. They walked towards the Regency Room, smiling at the prospect of a chat with friends while eating some of the gorgeous array of cakes baked to perfection by Mrs. Sexton.

Eliza and her exuberant sister loved the Regency Room at the inn. Eliza delighted in its calm ambience, whereas Lily adored its opulence. The Regency Room had been the brainchild of Lord Beconsford in the days when he was younger and had held huge parties and balls at the Big House, as Beconsford Manor was known. In the past, when party guests were staying at the inn, His Lordship needed a place for them to drink and relax in exclusive surroundings. To achieve his aim, he paid for an annex overlooking the river at the rear of the inn. He transformed it into a place befitting his affluent friends. Now that he spent most of his time holidaying abroad, the room was used regularly by his children Isaac and Helena as well as the gentry of the area. As friends of Helena, the girls took tea with her there each Saturday.

The girls walked around to the back of the inn where they entered the Regency Room through the highly polished mahogany door.

The room, as always, stirred Eliza's senses. Its rich cream embossed wallpaper gave it a sense of space. As she walked further in, her gaze always moved to the view from the large back window. She could see the green pastures dropping gently towards the quietly flowing river below. The tranquillity felt on first entering that room when she was just twelve years old, was still palpable today.

The girls waved to their father who was in a window seat, in the company of their friend Helena. Then they were greeted, as always, by the smiling Mrs. Sexton who owned the local bakery beside the inn. Throughout the town she was renowned for her hot crusty bread. Of more importance to the girls were her exquisite tea cakes and fruit pies with fresh cream.

She pointed to two young men taking coffee in a corner of the room.

Lily smiled knowingly at Eliza.

"Don't worry, ladies," said Mrs. Sexton. "Just like last week, if your father has to go and do business in town before those two gentlemen leave, I will be in attendance keeping an eye on them until he arrives back to take you home!"

The girls laughed at Mrs. Sexton's now serious face.

"So long as the cakes are as appetising as ever, we are delighted to have you stay with us, Mrs. Sexton," said Eliza.

Since Mrs. Sexton had acquired two extra helpers in the bakery, she had taken on the role of attending at the Regency Room with her culinary delights whenever members of the Big House were present. She enjoyed the extra bit of excitement in her life. She especially delighted in serving young Isaac and Helena and their friends. It made a great change from their father, the overbearing Lord of the Manor, and his friends. As she watched the girls going to their seats by the window, she wondered, as she often did, how the unpleasant Edward Beconsford had such delightful children.

Eliza and Lily were lucky to have grown up close to the Beconsford Estate. The estate tutor, Mr. Lucas, had taught them from childhood together with Isaac and Helena, as well as the children of the estate managers. Many years before, Mr. Lucas had persuaded the reluctant Beconsfords that it was important for Isaac and Helena to mix with other children. Lord Beconsford thought they were a cut above the majority of the Irish but the more rounded education was agreed upon and it had made Isaac and Helena popular in the county.

Eliza, who had acted as a monitor helping Mr. Lucas with his class for the past two years, had been teaching the young children of the farming families in the district since the harvest had ended last September. Lily said children were boring and thought her sister was mad to work with them. Helena, who was a rather shy and quiet girl, thought it was a wonderful thing to do. Helena was likely to travel abroad this summer. As was the way of the rich, these travels were likely to end in marriage for Helena with an 'Honourable' or, at the very least, a gentleman of means.

As the girls chatted, they each glanced surreptitiously in

the direction of Oliver and Toby who were looking in their direction.

After a few minutes, the boys sauntered over and proffered their hands in greeting to Robert, who had not met them the previous Saturday. He knew, of course, who these young gentlemen were.

"Mr. Turner, I am Toby Ramsay and this is my friend Oliver Frankland. We are friends of Miss Helena." He bowed to Helena who smiled in response.

"Sir," said Oliver, "I'd like to invite you and your two lovely daughters to our estate in Youghal for our spring ball. Of course, Lord Beconsford and his family will attend, so you will be among friends."

Robert, who was not easily impressed by monied people, smiled at the boys and agreed to go, but only if his daughters wished to attend.

Lily answered yes immediately, while surreptitiously kicking her sister under the table for fear she might demur.

Oliver thanked them as Toby stood by smiling and not taking his eyes off Eliza. Oliver added that an invitation would be posted to them shortly.

When the young men had left the Regency Room, Robert went to join a farming friend. Helena smiled and spoke in her usual quiet way.

"I like Oliver but my brother Isaac says he's not so sure about Toby Ramsay. He says he's too brash and full of his own importance."

"Well, he seemed very charming just now and he is so

handsome, is he not, Eliza?" Lily said, beaming at her sister.

Eliza had to agree, but felt vaguely uncomfortable about the way he kept looking at her in an intimate way when she didn't even know him well.

"A trip to the estate will be great fun anyway as I've heard that Squire Frankland gives great parties," said Lily with enthusiasm. She had always found that her sister was never as impressed with glamorous people as she was.

The girls continued to enjoy their usual gossip about everything that went on in the district that they couldn't talk about while the adults were around.

At three o'clock, Robert insisted that it was time to leave as they needed to get onto the boreen that led to their farm before darkness fell. They carried their parcels to the trap and chatted happily as they made their way home.

Chapter 6

Dusk was beginning to fall and the sun was sinking deep into the horizon as Robert Turner drove the trap up to the crossroads.

Suddenly Snugs began to neigh and lifted her front legs. The trap began to shake as Robert jerked the reins. A man had stepped out in front of them, so quickly that he seemed to have tripped over something, and had fallen head-first onto the road. The horse's hooves came down just inches away from his head.

Robert, who never swore, let out an expletive as he jumped to the ground. The girls were not far behind him. As they reached the man, he slowly turned over to display a nasty gash on his forehead, and the contents of his bag were beginning to spill onto the road. Although he was unshaven, and his coat looked a little too big for him, he looked to be a young man and not at all what they expected. He didn't look like a vagrant.

He tried to sit up.

"I'm so sorry, I'm so sorry, it's all my fault. I think I must have fallen asleep or something. I never heard the horse at all. Are you all uninjured? Is the horse alright? I was trying to get to the Haven Inn for the night."

"Slow down, lad, slow down, we need to take care of that cut in your head."

The young man put his hand to his head and looked surprised to see the blood.

"Let's get you back to our farm and we'll fix you up. What's your name, lad?"

"It's Jack, sir," he replied.

"I'm Robert Turner and these are my daughters Eliza and Lily. Girls, will you help put Jack's stuff back in his bag and put it in the trap? Jack, when we get to the farm, I'll have our housekeeper Meg take a look at that cut. We'll be there in no time."

He gave Jack a hand to mount the trap while the girls gathered up the scattered things.

Then the girls scrambled up into the trap and Robert told Snugs to move on.

As he sat in front, opposite their father, the first thing Eliza noticed were Jack's large, sad eyes. She noticed his shoulders were slumped and despair was evident. Tragedy has struck him, she thought.

As they slowly drove the cart up the lane to the Turners'

home, Jack was surprised to see the large farmhouse standing in the distance. It was a rather grand two-storey house covered with ivy and Jack recognised that this family was not poor. The house had two windows at each side of the large oak door with five windows across the second floor above.

As they reached the house, Meg, who had been watching for their return, ran outside when she saw the young man with blood on his face sitting in the trap. Robert got down and explained to her what had happened.

Sam came around to take Snugs and the trap to the stables at the back of the house. He helped the girls down and Jack slowly followed, feeling slightly dizzy as he did.

"I can see that this young man needs help," Meg said. "Let's get him into the kitchen and I'll attend to him."

There, she got out her mystery box of medicines and bandages, which also included needles for fear anyone ever needed a little stitch in a cut. Meg knew as much as many medical men. She helped cure the various minor illnesses and small accidents that sometimes happened around the farm.

The girls had placed Jack's bag near the chair where Meg had asked him to sit.

Meg got warm water from the kettle and a clean cloth and within seconds she was smiling as she patted Jack's arm.

"Well, you're not going to die, lad! It's not deep, I'll clean it up and put a small covering on it for tonight. And it won't affect your beauty, when a lock of that nice head of hair falls down and hides it. You'll be grand in a few days."

As she tended to the cut, Robert sat down next to Jack, while Eliza and Lily set the table for dinner.

Robert could see that Jack looked drained and exhausted.

"You will join us for dinner of course, Jack, and as you were looking for an inn you are more than welcome to a bed in our home for the night."

"Thank you, sir. You're all very kind."

"Girls, set up another place at the table for Jack," said Robert.

When Meg had finished treating the cut, Robert took Jack to clean himself up and soon they were all sitting at the table, with the others grateful that Jack's colour seemed to be returning to his face.

"Have you much further to travel?" Robert asked.

Jack explained that he was a market gardener and was returning home having being away for some time. He said he wanted to go back to Cork city in order to see his mother but that he had future hopes of getting some gardening work in a large estate because he wanted to learn more and expand his knowledge of plants and vegetables.

Lily piped up enthusiastically.

"They're looking for some new staff over at Lord Beconsford's estate! It's not one of these really large estates, but they have lovely cottages for workers!"

"Slow down, Lily," her father said. "Jack has his own plans, no doubt."

"A job like that sounds wonderful," said Jack, wondering if religion might be important if he was looking for a job in some landed estate with their "big houses", as they were called in Ireland. For some reason, he felt that it was necessary to explain to the Turners that his mother was a member of the Church of Ireland, but his father was a Catholic.

Eliza noticed that a scowl came briefly over his face as he mentioned his father.

He said that his grandmother's family had good land in West Cork and held no animosity towards people of any religion. He went on to explain that, like his grandmother and mother, he too was a member of the Church of Ireland. When young he had always gone to church with his grandmother. He added that on many a Sunday morning he was called names by the young Catholic boys, but his Granny Sheila always said to take no notice of them.

"She is the wisest woman I know," he added. "She always said that we are all Christians and that I was never to take notice of bigoted people. She even had my mother educated by Nano Nagle, the renowned Catholic nun and educator. Granny Sheila had great respect for anyone who was interested in educating everyone. As for me, I never take religion into account and only judge people by the way they behave." He said nothing about his time at sea but he was remembering people in the Far East who had little knowledge of Christianity.

"Well said, lad," agreed Robert. "We are of the same faith but believe, just like you, that it's how people behave towards others that matters most. I work for Lord Beconsford's son Isaac three days each week. I mainly look after the books and the accounts of His Lordship's estate. Isaac is such a broadminded young man that his workers are all sort of religions or none! The problem, lad, is that some people want power over others, whether it's saying their religion is better, or that they are richer and that makes them more important. How these people behave is that they abuse the power they have. People like Isaac Beconsford are grateful for what they have but I must tell you, lad, that he's in the minority as many of the so-called large landowners, including Isaac's own father Lord Edward when he ran the estate, would scrape the last coin out of their tenants' pockets if they could get away with it. Many of them are absentee landlords who live in England and care nothing about conditions on their estates as long as they produce enough rents and crops to keep them in luxury. We can all but do our own bit to help others and someday maybe everyone will be treated more fairly in life. Now, Lily, I must remind you that you can't always be offering solutions to everyone's life off the top of your head."

As Robert smiled indulgently at her, Jack noticed with envy that he was a very loving father to his daughters.

Lily still chatted on excitedly, telling Meg about meeting Squire Frankland's son Oliver and Toby Ramsay and the invitation they had received to the spring ball. Jack noticed the smile on Eliza's face as she shook her head, acknowledging the exuberance of her younger sister.

Robert continued to chat to Jack and explained that his farm had been large but a couple of years before he had decided to sell a major part of the land to his neighbour and good friend Bart Cummins. Bart had two grown sons and wanted to keep them both in farming, while Robert reasoned that as he had no sons and neither of his daughters had an interest in farm work, he would keep a couple of acres where himself and Sam, his farm hand, would grow produce and have a few cattle. Meg had also wanted to continue with the chickens.

"I decided when Isaac offered me the position in the Big House to make more time for all the family to enjoy the farm but not to be consumed by it. I might even take a few more holidays!"

The girls smiled indulgently at their loving father who just wanted to be around the comfort of the farmhouse with the family and to indulge in his newly acquired hobby of painting the rich scenery around Midleton.

"What he's not telling you, Jack, is that all he wants to do now is paint!" said Eliza. She pointed to Robert's first picture which was of their own house and now hung proudly on the wall.

"It's wonderful," Jack said, adding hesitantly that he too loved to sketch and draw.

For the next while the men talked happily of art paper, drawing pens and paints.

Jack's eyes kept returning to Eliza's alluring and serene face. She really is lovely, he thought, even though she doesn't have the blonde cheeky good looks of her young sister. Suddenly Jack had a strange feeling. For the first time in a month, he felt contented. He continued looking at a lady who had been a stranger to him until a few hours ago. He realised that he might never see her again but he was grateful for the fact that for a few moments he felt normal. After all, he thought, even if I were living in the area, how could I possibly compete with the likes of Oliver Frankland and Toby Ramsay?

The dinner was one of the best he had eaten in a long time – large slices of pork with potatoes and butter and vegetables as good as he had ever grown in Friarsland. Robert had offered him some ale but Jack explained that he never touched alcohol. Robert said that abstinence was very commendable, while the girls looked at him, intrigued.

When dinner finished, Meg cleared up and she then showed Jack to a room behind the kitchen.

"We keep this room to house some extra help at harvest time. It's always warm. I'll get bedclothes and put a hot stone in for comfort. And I'll bring along some shaving material. You might like to freshen up."

"Thank you, Meg."

She turned at the door. "And when you are finished you can join us for some music. We play in the parlour whenever we have visitors. Lily plays the piano and Eliza sings."

When Jack entered the parlour later, he was dressed in the fresh clothing that Ellen had placed in his bag before he left Tramore.

Lily was playing some relaxing music while Eliza stood

by the piano turning the music sheets. Eliza watched Jack move across the room and thought that he was quite handsome since he had spruced up. Robert waved at Jack to take a chair and gave him a glass of apple juice which was wonderfully refreshing.

As Jack sipped, he began to relax. He watched Eliza's graceful countenance. She was tall and elegant, with her shining ebony hair swept up with clips and just a few soft tendrils touching her high cheekbones. Then she began to sing. Jack was momentarily taken aback at the magnificent sound of her voice singing an Irish love song well known to him. Such a lovely sound he had not heard before and he was so enthralled that when the song ended he clapped vigorously as the family laughed and joked that they only clapped after a few songs to encourage her to keep on singing!

Eliza continued with a funny song about a jumping goat and she ended with a sad lament that made him close his eyes as he knew he was very close to shedding tears.

Jack slept peacefully that night, both from exhaustion and the relaxation of being in a loving family home.

The following morning Meg knocked at his door and left some hot water outside his room, for washing. She had breakfast ready for him when he later appeared in the kitchen. Robert had breakfasted earlier, but sat with Jack as they both enjoyed a cup of tea.

"I will not take no for an answer, Jack. I have no need for the trap today so I'm going to get our Sam to take you into Cork. It's the least I can do after nearly knocking you down last evening."

Jack again felt like shedding a tear and he thanked him so much that Robert laughed.

"It's very little really, but I also want to say to you that if you're thinking of looking for work, come back to me first and we'll talk it through. At the moment you look like you need to get your strength back, so let your mother look after you for a while."

Jack's silence at this made Robert feel that all was not well at Jack's home. He remembered how Jack had looked uncomfortable during dinner when his father was mentioned.

Chapter 7

The Turners all came out to say goodbye to him. Meg reminded him to look after himself and Robert gave instructions to Sam while warning him to come straight back to the farm and not to go wandering about Cork city.

But Jack's eyes kept returning to Eliza who looked so graceful in a blue gown that matched the wonderful colour of her eyes. What incredible luck to have met these people, he thought. Today, he felt he had more energy, having slept so peacefully in the warm bedroom, and he realised how much he was looking forward to seeing his mother again.

They all waved as the trap moved off and Lily shouted *"Come back soon, Jack!"*

Sam and Jack chatted on the road to Cork. Jack asked him if he knew Beconsford Manor. Sam proudly informed him that he had grown up in a cottage on the estate and he had nothing but praise for young Isaac and the way he treated everyone.

"Since Isaac is now looking after the estate, the Lord and Ladyship spend most of their time in London and taking holidays. Many people disliked Lord Edward as he had a quick temper and had thrown people out of their homes. But that is now in the past."

Jack discovered that Sam had attended school for a time while he was young but always had difficulty with reading and writing. He talked about how Miss Eliza assisted Mr. Lucas with the teaching and how next September she would be teaching his young niece.

"I love working for Robert Turner and I want to work for the Turners forever," he said with a smile.

Jack found him such a likable man that he was almost sorry when the journey finally came to an end. He got Sam to turn back when they got to the edge of the city. As he bade him farewell, he told him to thank the family for their kindness.

Jack picked up his bag and walked along the pathway by the wall of the River Lee. As he made his way through the city, he saw many ragged children, to whom he would love to have given a coin but at this time he just had the few pennies left from the kindness of Cornelius Murray in Tramore. He began to think that he now had a very uncertain future ahead of him and he didn't like the way that made him feel. He felt regretful that he had left his money in the coat that went down with the ship and he was now penniless. Yet he also knew that he had so much more than those poor beggars on the streets of Cork.

It took him half an hour to get to the end of First Avenue, which was a couple of miles south of the river. It was an unlikely grand-sounding name for a lane that led up to his family home and market garden. The fields beyond the city where they grew produce for sale could be seen from the left side of the lane. Low hedgerows grew along the edge of the field, looking uneven as if they had not been tended for a long time. To the right there were two small cottages. His sister Julia and her husband Jarad lived in the cottage closest to the family house and the second cottage was rented to a local labourer until such time as it was required by another member of Granny Sheila's family. Each cottage had a back yard and small garden where chickens ran free and where vegetables could be grown. Thankfully, the one thing that the Ryan family could always do was feed themselves. Jarad, his brother-in-law, was employed driving a cart to deliver turf around Cork and he got a bag of turf each week as part of his wages. Those two cottages, with their thatched roofs, were always warm.

Jack's mother, Molly, was able to read and write as Granny Sheila had spent hard-earned pennies many years ago making sure that her daughter was schooled. However, Jack hadn't written a letter to his mother since he had sent her a Christmas gift of money. It was at the start of the new year that he had finally made up his mind to come home and he had intended to surprise her. He also did not want his father to know that he was coming.

He was already beginning to sweat at the prospect of

going into his old home again. On impulse, he decided to call on his sister first, as he didn't have the energy to face his father just yet.

He gave the knock that his sisters all knew from their childhood. Seven quick knocks and then stand to one side of the door, pretending there was no one outside!

There was a flurry of steps from inside and Julia called out *"Is that you, Hannah?"* When there was no reply, she opened the door, laughing.

She looked shocked when she saw him standing there. She put her arms around him and hugged him. There were tears in her eyes as she moved back to look at him again. He was younger than her and would always be her baby brother.

"You're alive! Thank God! Have you seen Mam yet?"

Jack shook his head.

"Come in quickly," she said. "Has any of the family seen you?"

"No."

Julia looked relieved.

"Stay here until Father goes to the alehouse later and I'll go up and let Mam and Granny Sheila know you're here. We heard around the city that lots of boats sank in the storms last month and we were so worried – Granny Sheila hasn't stopped praying since! I was afraid that you'd never get to see your first niece or nephew!" She smiled as she patted her slightly plump stomach.

Jack was so delighted for her that he took her in a hug and didn't want to let her go.

"Did you have a good crossing?" she asked as she held him away from her. Then she noticed the gash on his forehead. "Oh! What happened to you? Did you have an accident?

"Yes, kind of, but I don't want to talk about it." He had no intention of telling them about the shipwreck if that was possible. "I just want to know if you're all well."

"We're all grand, apart from our drunken father who is worse than ever. If it wasn't for Granny Sheila keeping a tight hold on the purse-strings, we'd all be on the side of the road. As it is, he drinks enough to feed two families every week! And our Hannah is finally courting a friend of my Jarad's from over the north side of the city. He's a grand lad, is Ted, and she can't wait to marry and move across to the north side. His mother is a widow and they'll live with her. Now, let us have a cup of tea and some nice soda cake I baked and then I'll go up and talk to Mam. She'll be over the moon when I tell her!"

Before Julia left to tell his mother that he was home, she handed him a letter that had arrived recently for him. She had kept it so his father wouldn't open it. He was astonished but waited until she was gone to sit by the turf fire and read it.

It was from Captain Bates, his old skipper, saying that his friend Corky who had been so kind to him on the *Seahorse* had died in the storm. As he hadn't seen Jack's name on the list of the dead passengers, he hoped he was safe and well and had not travelled on that ship. Jack sat rigid and could feel his chest constricting. He began to sweat profusely. He never wanted to relive that deeply

51

painful day again, if he could possibly avoid it. His hands began to shake and he remembered Ellen sitting by his side in Tramore telling him to breathe long and slow and when he did that he always felt better. He began to breathe deeply and tell himself to stay calm and the terrible heat began to leave his body.

He knew he had to concentrate on the present and that his immediate problem was his father. Did he want to see him at all? Did he want to stay around? Or did he want to just see the family and go away? But he had nowhere else to go at the moment until he got himself a job.

To take his mind off his dark thoughts, Jack thought about seeing his mother and the other love of his life, his Granny Sheila, whom all the local people called Granny. He recalled the stories she had told him when he was young. How Jack's mother Molly had been born in Friarsland. Back in the past, Sheila and her new husband Alex Cotter had both come up to the city from Ballydehob in West Cork when Alex Cotter came into some money. He had inherited it from his single Uncle Hector whom he had helped care for before he died. It was agreed that Alex's older brother would work the family farm in Ballydehob. Therefore, when Alex started to court Sheila Kingston, he was happy to take his new bride to the city of Cork and buy a few acres of land that already had a solid house and a few small cottages. He built up his market-gardening business to a high standard with the help of his wife who worked every bit as hard as he. Their happiness was complete after the birth of their only child Molly. She was adored by her mother and indulged by her happy father. But during a hard and cold winter when Molly was just six years old, her father caught a bad cold in his chest and by the week's end it had turned to a fever that raged for days until the effort of trying to stay alive failed. Alex Cotter was just 30 years of age when his eyes closed for the last time. Granny Sheila became a young widow and the owner of the market gardens. Jack remembered how he had usually shed tears when his granny spoke of her husband's death.

Jack was dragged away from his thoughts and had to put a smile on his face when his happy sister brought him the news that his mam and granny were almost in shock, they were so relieved he was safe and well and had come home.

"You always were their favourite," she said with a laugh. "If they had a fatted calf, it would be cooked in the next few hours to welcome you! So, do you want the good news or the good news? Well, I'll tell you anyway! While you are home, you're going to stay with myself and Jarad so you don't have to sleep or eat up in the house when he's around and you will be glad to hear that he'll be going out to the alehouse tonight for a long time because Granny Sheila is going to give him extra money when he asks for his usual wage advance. That should keep him away until after midnight and by then you'll be asleep in your bed here!"

Jack took her hand to thank her warmly and knew that if he could just get some rest in Julia's home, he'd be ready to face his father.

Chapter 8

That evening he enjoyed the meal cooked by Julia. It consisted of fresh chicken and delicious vegetables, all supplied by Granny Sheila. The meal was made even better by the arrival of his twenty-two-year-old sister Hannah, who had passed up the family meal by saying she was going over to Ted's house for supper. It was a happy hour for all, while Jack caught up on all the news about the neighbours. They asked him about his travels and he told them of his journeys to Sweden and India and named countries that none of them had ever even heard of. Leaving gaps in his story, he told them that he now wanted to go back to work in gardening and he hoped to get work in some "big house" in the future. He had seen many exotic plants and different vegetables around the world and he wanted to learn as much as he could about what could be grown in Ireland.

"Well, at least you're staying in the country," said Hannah.

"Don't go too far away," warned Julia. "We want to see our little brother more often in the future."

Jack assured them that he wanted that also.

After the meal, Jarad went to the front window to keep watch for his father-in-law. At half past seven, he saw him strutting down the lane, whistling as if he hadn't a care in the world. Jarad thought he looked pathetic with his ever-widening beer belly. Maybe in his small mind he didn't know the destruction that he had wreaked, especially on his wife and son, he thought. Julia had told him that Septimius had taken out most of his anger on Jack, maybe because Jack could read and write at an early age and had a wonderful way with the plants and vegetables. He may have been jealous but maybe it was just that with his violent temper he needed someone smaller than himself to hit. But it was hard to work out the thoughts of a bully like Septimius, whose friends in the pub thought he was "a great fella" who always bought his round, although Jarad had heard that many of them said they wouldn't like to get on the wrong side of him.

At eight o'clock, Hannah and Julia linked arms with Jack as they walked to the top of the lane. The house was straight in front of them. It stood three storeys tall when you included 'The Loft' which was a very large attic that stretched the length of the house. Granny Sheila had moved into this warm and comfortable space on her daughter's marriage to Septimius Ryan. She had allowed them have the three small bedrooms on the first floor and the kitchen and parlour on the ground floor, as their home. She had made the loft into a grand bedroom and parlour for herself and it had a window view that let her see way beyond the end of their holding. However, Sheila had promised herself to keep tight control of the house and market gardens because she had a feeling that Septimius had a nasty streak in him. That was confirmed when she saw how much ale he could sup. Sheila and her husband had made a good success of their business and they had made money for their future which was still well hidden in a place that Septimius would never find.

For a time after his marriage to Molly, Septimius had been working for a farmer close enough to Friarsland to allow him walk to work each day, but it wasn't long before he got fed up of the walk and he suggested that he'd make a great success of the market garden. Molly asked her mother to give him a chance. Sheila agreed a wage with him but often said later that she "did it for her sins". As she expected, on any given day he never put more than half a day's work into the gardens. As Molly had given birth to four children, one a stillborn baby boy just a year after Jack's birth, Septimius began to complain more and more of a bad back that stopped him from working much. Yet it never stopped him collecting his wages and going to the alehouse whenever he had money in his pocket. Luckily Sheila had always enjoyed working the land and with Molly's help and two good local lads who were glad of the work, she continued to make enough money to feed a growing household.

As they reached the front door, Jack was pleased to notice that the ivy on the front wall and the flower beds at each side of the front door were still well tended. Snowdrops and pansies were competing with each other for space and his mother's favourite Lily of the Valley still stood tall and white in the corners. He wanted so much to tend, grow and nurture exquisite flowers wherever he worked in the future. An image of Eliza's face came into his head as he feasted his eyes on the flowers.

At that moment, the girls pushed him forward and the door opened.

His mother, with Granny Sheila behind her, stood in the doorway. Molly's arms were outstretched and she cried tears of pure joy at the sight of her beloved son. He held her in his arms – or was she holding him, because that's what it felt like.

"*Shush*, Mam, *shush*, this is supposed to be a happy time."

She held him away from her. "It is, son," and with tears streaming down her face she added, "It's the happiest day of my whole life."

With that she hugged him again and Jack could see also the big broad beam on the face of his granny, as he put his right hand out and brought her into the hug. All crowded into the narrow hallway, crying and laughing in turn. It was the happiest Jack had been for some time and he wondered how he could hold on to that feeling.

Jack walked into the long kitchen, with windows which gave a view of the acres of market garden stretching from the back of the house. The long wooden kitchen table was filled with the best china which was usually kept for visitors and the smell of cakes baking brought back memories of his childhood.

They spent the next hour laughing and reminiscing and the teapot kept being filled and plates of cakes consumed. Jack recalled sneaking tea cakes after his mother took them from the oven. Tonight she informed him that she always saw him taking them, which made the girls laugh, as she had always stopped them taking any!

"Irish mothers and their sons!" said Julia, laughing.

At last Granny Sheila said she wanted to get ready for bed and asked Jack if he'd come up to her later and have a chat. Jack was delighted, remembering the good advice she had doled out in the past.

Everybody who knew her called her Granny Sheila. She was in her sixties, but still energetic and sprightly. The hard work seemed to suit her and she always had an agile brain. As she waited for Jack in the loft, she thought of her life since her beloved Alex had died. She had a tough but good life rearing Molly alone. She was always a strong, wiry woman but her black hair had slowly turned to silver after the death of her beloved Alex. She knew she would never find another love like his and she had put all her energy into raising her daughter.

She gave generous donations to a fund that was set up by the nuns to help educate and feed poor children. She believed that everyone improves their chances of avoiding poverty if they have an ability to read, write and do their sums.

Molly was a pretty young child with a quiet placid nature that at times worried Sheila who thought she was too easily led and tended to let people who were of a more forceful nature turn her head. When she was fifteen, Molly took over the cooking from her mother and cooked also for the market-garden workers. Her cooking skills had been learned in Nano Nagle's school where all the girls learned domestic skills alongside their reading and writing. Then, when Molly was eighteen, her head was turned by Septimius Ryan. Sheila never took to him but didn't try to interfere as Molly was so happy to be seen walking out with the handsome and strong Septimius.

When Jack entered the loft, he sat in his favourite chair and Sheila sat opposite in her comfortable chintz-covered armchair with its armrests covered in white linen. Nothing had changed in years and her prized grandfather clock, which was her pride and joy, stood in the corner making its comfortable tick-tock.

Sheila was smiling as she looked at Jack.

"I'm not going to ask you how you got the injury to your forehead and I can see that you have pain in your ribs by the way you sat down. I'm also not going to ask you why there is a sadness in your eyes. I just want to talk to you about the future. All the rest can wait until you feel ready to tell me."

Jack visibly relaxed, in awe at his granny's ability to say what he wanted to hear.

"I'm going to stay with Julia for a while and, when I feel ready, I'll help around the gardens and I'll start with tidying and trimming the hedge up the lane."

"That's great, lad, but after that have you worked out what you want?"

Jack nodded forcefully.

"I'm going to look for a job in some Big House and I want to study more about plants and vegetables. You know from my letters in the past how fascinated I was by the marvellous trees and plants I saw when I went to some of the hot countries. I also want to visit the big glasshouses and see the exotic plants up in the new Dublin Society Gardens. Not that I'd necessarily grow them myself or anything but I'd love to see how it all works."

Sheila nodded approvingly at Jack's enthusiasm.

"Well, lad, I'm going to help you with all of that. Maybe someday in the distant future you will come home here, but I think that your ideas are better suited to a bigger place. I have quite a bit of money saved that your father is never going to get his hands on. I gave a bit to Julia when she married and the same will be given to Hannah shortly. Just to make them feel secure. But I have a bit more to give to you because in the future you have to find work and because you will likely marry and have a family."

Sheila got up and went to the press in the corner. She opened it with a key and took out a velvet drawstring purse.

"There are a few guineas and crowns in this for you, Jack. I always keep some tucked away for fear of an emergency. I've been saving since before you were born, and most of it is safe in the Bank of Ireland down in the city. I'm giving you a sum that should set you up to follow the path in life that you want to take. This purse is just to start you off, but I am going to advise you to keep most of your money in a banking house. I'll go with you to my bank tomorrow and have the rest of the money transferred into your name."

Jack looked into the bag and gasped. "I can't take even this amount of money from you, let alone money that you have spent a lifetime saving in the bank!" he said, as he endeavoured to hand the purse back to her.

She shook her head and pressed the money back into his hand.

"Jack, it belongs to you. You take it and do good with it. Help others when they need it. Sure, it's just a nest-egg to get you started on the journey that you're about to take. I will call to Julia's tomorrow and the two of us will walk into the city to the bank."

They both had tears in their eyes as they sat back quietly, listening to the ticking of the clock.

When Jack returned to the kitchen, his mother had put some cakes in a bag along with some of his own clothes which he had left when he stormed out of the house three years before. Jack took them from her and put the velvet purse in with the clothes as his mother nodded and smiled at him.

"I'll tell your father tonight that you are home and you can take it from there yourself."

Jack nodded. "Tell him I'll see him at six o'clock tomorrow here. I'll be staying around for a bit and I'm going to start tidying up the hedges in the lane the day after tomorrow – I need to go into town tomorrow."

His mother gave him a knowing glance.

He hugged her tightly before he set off down the lane with Julia.

Chapter 9

Jack didn't wake until eleven o'clock the following day. It was the first good sleep he'd had in what felt like a lifetime and he felt the better for it. Julia had his breakfast ready and told him his father still didn't know he was home because their mother was in bed when he rolled in from the alehouse the night before and he hadn't got up yet. She said Molly would serve Septimius dinner at two o'clock after Sheila had left the house and would tell him then.

Jack enjoyed his breakfast and, as he looked around the small cottage, he was happy that his sister had such a cosy home.

Later, when Granny Sheila arrived at the door, Jack thought she looked a picture in her bonnet with lace trimmings and her blue dress the colour of cornflowers. Her unlined, smiling face did not look like that of most of the women of her age. He believed that her spirit and optimistic nature had seen her through any hard times in her life.

They set out for the bank, arm in arm, both exhilarated at the thought of the business before them.

At the bank, they were shown into the manager's office. Sheila got a great welcome from the middle-aged Mr. Granger, manager of the southern region. He was a tall man, slightly stooped, who had a merry twinkle in his eye. He welcomed Jack to the bank and said he would be seen as a very valued customer.

After the money was transferred to an account in Jack's name, Mr. Granger explained to him that they had banks around the country that would allow him withdraw money even if he moved far from Cork. He also suggested that Jack should take an amount to tide him over the next couple of months. He would give it to him in bank notes and some coins. He advised that he should hide this amount securely and spend it cautiously until he obtained regular employment.

Jack nodded but was embarrassed that he couldn't explain why he had no money, having been away at sea for so long. Nobody knew that the money he had earned to set himself up in Ireland was now at the bottom of the Atlantic Ocean.

Granny Sheila and Jack left the bank, with Jack's money tucked into a pocket inside his coat. They strolled along, arm in arm, until they reached the grand Patrick Street, where they walked to the river. There they stood and admired the scene. They could see the spire of St. Anne's Shandon church, famous for its bells, on the hill that rose beyond the river on the north side of the city. The church looked impressive, with its red sandstone taken from the old Shandon Castle and its limestone from the Franciscan Abbey. On top of its spire was the "Goldie Fish" – a salmon-shaped weathervane, eleven feet three inches long and gilded in gold leaf.

Sheila then decided that they needed to go to a hotel to celebrate. Jack laughed as he told her that he would pay! She agreed with a smile. So they turned and walked towards the newly opened Imperial Hotel on the South Mall.

The city was bustling with shoppers and merchants moving around with their carts. They also passed many hungry-looking children and beggars looking for help along the way. Jack and Sheila both quietly had a word with some of these and slipped a coin into their hands. The city authorities never seemed to do enough for the needy, Jack thought. It was a fine city with the River Lee helping to ship its butter and meat to Britain in the tall ships moored at the quayside, yet crushing poverty was always around for those who found it hard to get work. Jack reflected on Robert Turner's wise words about not judging people and promised that he would always watch out for those in need who would cross his path during his lifetime. He began to feel a stirring of hope within him as he drank the tea that his granny insisted was the best in the world. He would beat his demons.

After tea, Sheila insisted that they hire a horse-drawn

carriage to take them home and it gave Jack a chance to see more of the city that he loved, which seemed to have expanded enormously in the past years while he'd been away. He had even heard many more people speaking French in the hotel and on the streets. Many were Huguenots who had fled their homeland because of religious persecution. Jack felt that they added great character to the city and it again brought memories of the various port cities he had visited around Europe and Asia.

Jack had had a great day but he wasn't looking forward to the confrontation with his father. He was going up to the house at six o'clock. He was glad he had about an hour to think. He knew one thing. He had no control over his father's reaction to seeing him. What he did have control over was his own dislike for the man and how he dealt with his own reactions. He made a pledge to himself that he would never again suffer the indignity of running away like he did when he was eighteen.

He left Julia's house just before six. It would only be himself, plus his mother and father sitting down for tea. Although Jack smiled as he thought of Granny Sheila listening to every word from the top of the stairs.

Jack knocked at the door and almost immediately it was opened by his mother. She was silent as she hugged him, squeezed his arm and preceded him into the kitchen. Septimius was sitting at the table stuffing a large sandwich of ham and bread into his mouth.

As Jack sat down, Septimius wiped his mouth with his sleeve and laughed out loud.

"So, here's the rich sailor home from the sea. I met my pal Joe Gargan this afternoon and he tells me that he saw you coming into the city yesterday, looking like a tramp! *Ha*, so after all your high-falutin' talk about your travels all over the world, you're back expecting us to feed you again!"

Jack clenched his hands to stop himself getting angry as Molly spoke up.

"Septimius, you have no right to talk like that to your adult son."

"A son, a son? He's just a sop, an excuse for a man who couldn't hold his own if he was in a fight with anyone. Did they teach you to fight when you were at sea, or did they all just laugh at you too?" Septimius gave a belly laugh as he stuffed more food into his mouth.

Molly put her hand on Jack's shoulder, silently begging him not to react.

Jack, who was seated facing his father, stood up and smiled.

"Go on, if you're such a big man," he said. "Why don't you take off your belt again and try to surprise me by beating me like you did three years ago? This time I'm ready for you."

Septimius began to splutter and rise up.

"*Sit down or I swear I'll hit you!*" Jack roared at him and Septimius fell back on his chair. "We'll then see how big a man you are!"

Septimius roared, *"Get out of my house or I'll kill you!"*

Jack lowered his voice and said quietly, "Sit down and just listen to me for once in our home – not yours, its ours, thanks to Granny Sheila. I put up with your bullying for far too long when I was young, but I had seen the way you belittled my mother and I thought you might hit her and instead I took all the beatings. But, while I was away, I realised that you wouldn't hit her because you had a soft life doing very little work and drinking with your so-called friends and that the soft money could end like the click of a finger if Granny Sheila kicked you out. So, I have not come back to eat your food. I'm staying for a short while with Julia and Jarad to help clear up the market garden and get it ready for the spring planting. Then I'm off though I won't be leaving Ireland again. But I'll have people watching for fear you ever step out of line again and make life difficult for my mother or granny. Julia's husband and Hannah's boyfriend Ted are good lads and they will help keep an eye on you. And, by the way, some of your so-called friends in the boozer would have enough decency in them to keep you in line, if you know what I mean, if you make life difficult for Mam and Gran. So, think in the future before you act. And, for the record, I don't actually even hate you, I just feel sorry for you. I had a good mother and sisters when I was growing up and I know that you had few people you could trust and you didn't see much love."

Jack walked to the door and called to Sheila to come down to the kitchen and join him for tea.

Septimius scraped his chair on the floor as he stood up.

"*You bloody good-for-nothing!*" he roared. "*I don't ever want to see you in me sight again! I'm going to the pub where I'll meet civil drinking men and not little uppity pups like you. Clear out of me way, and I hope I never see you again!*"

With that, he barged past Sheila who was coming into the room and slammed the front door behind him.

Jack went back and sat before his legs would give out on him. He hadn't thought of what he'd say to his father but when the time came, he had spoken from the heart, and he was happy he did. His father was a pathetic excuse for a man. He just felt sorry for him now. He promised himself that he would never ever turn into a man who would make so many lives a misery.

"Good lad yourself, Jack, for standing up to him like that," said his mother.

"You're right, you know," said Sheila, with a satisfied look on her face. "He wouldn't touch us because he knows which side his bread is buttered on. Molly, sit down and we'll all have a nice tea together and we'll talk to Jack about the jobs he can get done while we still have him around."

Jack stood again and put an arm around each of their shoulders.

"You know, if either of you ever have any problems with him, I'll only be a letter away. But you will know where I am as soon as I'm settled and, because of your help, Granny, I will always be able to provide you both with a home in the future should you need it."

Chapter 10

Jack spent well over a month working around the market gardens. He was getting his strength back while preparing the ground for sowing. As spring brought some warmth in the sun, he felt calmer and began to think of the future. He kept out of his father's way and Sheila told him that Septimius wasn't as nasty with his tongue as before. Maybe Jack was right to feel sorry for him, she said, but the drink had such a hold that she couldn't see any road back to normality for him.

It was almost the beginning of summer when Jack decided to leave the city. The sun had finally begun to spread a little warmth over the previously damp and cool spring landscape.

He had bought a wooden trunk in a market. In it he placed Mrs. Murray's coat to return it to her when he made his promised visit back to her lovely family in Tramore. He then went into the centre of Cork and bought a good coat, a tall hat, two pairs of breeches, a new fashionable stiff-necked white shirt and necktie, and a pair of knee-length boots in fine glossy leather. He also bought two good cutaway tailcoats and an embroidered waistcoat in pristine condition from a second-hand stall. He would keep all these purchases for Sundays and any interviews he might have in the future – and a return to Midleton. He had never owned such fine clothes before. The rest of his purchases were for a working man: heavy boots, jackets, plain shirts, trousers and some flat cloth caps. His family would provide him with knitted wool socks. He had thought of growing a moustache to look a little older, but felt more comfortable with a clean-shaven face.

When Jack left his old surroundings at last, his family walked down the lane with him. Thankfully his father was still in bed. He was walking to the city centre where he would take a carriage to Midleton. He was hoping that he could stay at the Haven Inn which, according to Robert Turner, was a reputable establishment open to taking in long-term guests.

He hugged the four women in his life who had always looked out for him.

"Write as soon as you settle," said Granny Sheila.

"I want you to write to me tomorrow," his mother demanded, while smiling and giving him a final hug. "I want to know where you are staying as soon as possible. I never knew where you were for three years but from now on, I want you back in my life."

Jack left them, with a warm glow in his heart as he set out on what he hoped was the start of a journey towards his new life. His family kept waving until he turned a corner and was out of sight.

In the carriage, he settled down to watch the city as they wound through the narrow streets and over a bridge until they were finally on the road to the east.

The weather had again turned a bit miserable, typical of the changeable Irish weather, but a low watery sun shone. Watching the animals in the fields and the birds in the hedgerows gave him the feeling in the pit of his stomach that he was going to a place where he could heal. His head was full of thoughts of how he could get the kind of work he loved but for now he would let himself slowly move into his new life.

Midleton was a market town and Robert had told Jack that Walter Raleigh, who had brought the planting of potatoes to nearby Youghal, had lived close by for a time in Barry's Castle in Cahermore. The potato had since become the most widely used vegetable in Ireland and was in fact the staple diet of the millions of poor people.

As he passed through the town, he spotted some poor and ragged children playing by a slum-like row of cottages. It reminded him that he had seen worse, such as the massive poverty in India, while he was on his travels. It's everywhere, he thought, but I need to make something of myself before I'm of use to people less fortunate.

***

The Haven Inn was situated in a very pleasant square in the middle of the town. Inside, he was greeted by a small plump lady with a glorious smile on her face.

He placed his trunk on the floor and offered his hand.

"My name is Jack Ryan. I'm a friend of Robert Turner and he recommended your inn. I'm looking for some lodgings for about a month."

The small woman held his hand warmly as she introduced herself.

"I am Laura Jennings. My husband Liam and I run this establishment. Any friend of Robert's is a friend of ours, and you are in luck, Jack. A land agent from Dublin was in our best single room for the last two weeks and he left yesterday."

Jack was relieved to hear this.

She told Jack the cost of the room which included breakfast and said that he could have an evening meal whenever he wanted at a special rate for guests. She took a key from behind the bar.

Jack picked up his trunk and prepared to follow her.

"It's at the back of the house so that you have no noise from the bar area," she told him as she nimbly took the stairs ahead of him.

She opened a room at the end of a corridor and smiled as she let him step in first.

"It's a splendid view, isn't it?" she said. "And you have a little writing desk here also."

Jack stood, looking around the room. The single bed was against the far wall. It was covered with a rich-red bed covering. But it was the view from the larger than expected window overlooking fields that Jack was drawn to. A forest was visible in the distance – the estate forest, he thought.

"It's perfect," he said to Mrs. Jennings as he placed his trunk on the floor close to a cupboard and washstand.

He asked her if he could have a meal that evening and she offered hot pork and potatoes, which sounded good to Jack.

When the landlady left, Jack moved the writing table until it was in front of the window. He knew he'd enjoy every moment he had looking out at that view and he might even sketch it. He sat on the chair provided. He was delighted to find the inn had supplied some ink, a quill and a few sheets of parchment, probably because the room was used by people of means. He wrote a letter with his address to his mother but sent it to Julia's address to keep it out of the clutches of his father.

Then, with his elbows on the desk, he sat and gazed at the fields and forests. With a smile on his face, he began to plan his future.

Chapter 11

By the following day, word had got to the Turner family that Jack was back in Midleton. They sent Sam with a card to the Haven Inn, inviting him to have a meal with them on the following Sunday. Jack was delighted. He went into the local market and bought some small gifts for the girls – a handkerchief with E embroidered on it for Eliza and pretty hair ribbons for Lily. Purchasing the gifts gave him a small sense of normality. He already had purchaced some sketching pencils for Robert in Cork, plus he had splashed out on a small silver brooch for Meg.

He got up early on Sunday and dressed in the clothes he had bought for special occasions. As he tied the knot of his necktie, he felt a little uncomfortable as he saw himself in the mirror in his fancy waistcoat and smart tailed coat, but as he walked around the room he began to ease into his new look.

He was meeting the family after they had all attended church in the town. He got to the church early and sat at the back, where he could see the family when they arrived. He smiled as they passed.

Lily gave him a big beam and her eyes widened as she whispered to Eliza. Eliza nodded more serenely at Jack, but her eyes were shining. Jack prayed that she was truly glad to see him and he continued with this prayer until the service ended.

Waiting in the crowded churchyard, Jack saw Lily hurrying over, with Eliza following close behind her. He greeted them warmly and immediately handed them his two little gifts.

"I hope these tokens don't in some way offend you but they are just to thank you for your kindness to me."

Exuberant Lily squealed in delight. "Thank you for your gift, Jack! I'll wear these ribbons when I next go to town and we are all looking forward to having you come to our home again."

"Thank you, Miss Lily," said Jack, giving a little bow.

He turned to Eliza. "I hope I find you well, Miss Turner," he said rather stiffly.

"Please, Jack, my name is Eliza to all my friends and I count you among them."

As she lifted her gaze to Jack's eyes, his stomach almost did a somersault with nerves. She's captivating, he thought, and I now know that I'd walk over hot coals to reach her if she said she loved me.

"Are you alright, Jack?" Eliza asked, looking at him curiously.

"Yes, yes, just lost in thought and so pleased to see you all again. Is Meg here?"

"Yes, but she likes a natter with some of her relatives on Sundays and we usually have to drag her away!"

"My mother Molly sent a gift of a tablecloth for the family, to say thank you."

"How kind of her!" said Eliza. "Let's go to the trap and wait for Meg and Father to join us."

Some hours later they sat replete, having enjoyed a wonderful meal, with the new tablecloth adorning the table and Meg wearing her brooch.

Jack told them of his hopes for work. They all agreed that he should apply to the Beconsford Estate but Jack said that he wanted to get more knowledge of plants and vegetables before he'd try for work. He told him that his granny had given him a "male dowry", at which they all laughed, and that he wanted to visit the Dublin Gardens that had been founded twenty years before by the Dublin Society which was founded in 1731 with the aim of seeing that Ireland thrived culturally and economically. He wanted to meet some tutors who knew so much more than he did.

"I'd also like to see what plants and flowers are used for healing illnesses," he said. "Some while ago I was at sea and visited countries abroad. It appeared many people relied more on herbs and plants as cures than they did on the medical men."

Robert noticed a pained expression cross Jack's face

when he spoke of being at sea, and he wondered why.

"Oh," said Lily, "you know we have a man in the town whom lots of people say has healing powers and he uses herbs and plants. They call him Old John Darcy, even though he's not yet old! I don't know why they call him old but it may be because since he was young he always talked about old cures, and what the older people taught him. He's quite a character in the town."

"I'd like to meet him," said Jack.

"Your landlady, Mrs. Jennings, will show you his cottage," said Eliza. "I believe he does very good work, although some people laugh at him. Others respect him – after all, he is a seventh son of a seventh son and so was born a healer. He has healing powers in his hands, as well as using his herbs and plants."

"Another man worth talking to is Maurice Howard, the estate's senior manager," said Robert. "He's old and wise and, although one or two of his underlings are whippersnappers, he knows how to keep them all in line."

The afternoon continued with lots of chat until Eliza was persuaded to sing, accompanied by an ever-willing Lily, who seemed to love the limelight.

Jack sat back and, as he listened, he truly believed that he had never felt happier.

Eliza's voice soared as she sang.

"The peaks, the sky, so out of reach,
Like young love's pain, so bitter sweet
So, hold your heart and spread your wings,

And dream your dreams of greater things!'

As the song finished, Jack looked at Eliza and held her gaze. He knew that his feelings for her soared as high as her voice. But he would never be good enough for such a lady, who moved in such high places, he thought as everyone clapped.

A little while later he got ready to take his leave. He thanked them profusely and promised that he would keep them posted on what he was doing.

Robert offered to take him to the inn in the trap but Jack said he would enjoy the walk.

They accompanied him to the front door and, as he turned on the doorstep, he again held Eliza's eyes as he told them, "I won't say goodbye, it's only farewell."

They all smiled and they stood in the doorway waving until he reached a crossroads where he turned and could see them no more.

Chapter 12

Jack extended his stay at the inn, in pursuit of knowledge about gardens. His biggest problem, unfortunately, was still with him. He was still plagued with night sweats and woke in the middle of each night shivering, even as the warmer weather arrived.

The first time he went into the public area of the inn was when he arranged to meet Old John Darcy there. Jack didn't frequent this area as he preferred to have main meals in the dining area of the Inn. He was still uncomfortable meeting lots of strangers for fear that the shipwreck would be discussed.

He spotted a tall, broad-shouldered man enter the room.

Laura Jennings brought the man to Jack's table and introduced him as Old John.

Jack stood and held his hand out as he said, "I heard from Lily Turner that you are not old at all and she was right. She thought it was because you know all the natural cures the old folk used in the past."

Old John shook Jack's hand, laughing.

"No! It's because I had a cousin called Young John so I had to be called Old John!"

As they sat down, Jack looked at the man. He had a shock of black hair, with only a hint of grey. He noticed that he had kind eyes and the two men made easy eye contact with each other immediately. Jack liked what he saw.

"What would you like to drink?" Jack asked.

Old John lifted his hand in answer and called Laura Jenkins.

"I'm going to have to buy you a glass of Beamish beer, Jack, if you are to become a regular around the town," said Old John.

Jack declined the beer, opting instead for a refreshing apple drink.

Smiling, Laura went to fetch the drinks.

Old John Darcy was a revelation to Jack, he held such knowledge about plants and cures. He lived in a cottage by the side of the estate and seemed to earn enough money from the better-off people who bought his medicinal plants and creams to allow him help the poor who would otherwise go without.

On several occasions, after that first night, Jack invited John to have a meal at the inn as he refused to take money in exchange for all the knowledge Jack was so deeply grateful for.

***

Eliza was enjoying getting to know Jack but Toby Ramsay was pursuing her, since dancing with her during the evening of the spring ball. He sometimes joined them for tea at the Regency Room on Saturdays. Yet, even on the night of the ball, she had felt wary of him. Handsome he was and a few inches taller than Eliza, which she appreciated as she was tall herself. But it was the way he looked at her. He was always gazing at her body and she found that he seemed always to be trying to impress her. He also spent too much time talking about how connected he was to the aristocracy. Now that she had met Jack, she spent time comparing them and she knew at least one thing and that was she never felt uneasy in Jack's company, as he was a gentleman, if not a rich one.

Robert initiated a visit for Jack to the Beconsford Estate to meet Maurice Howard, the estate manager.

Jack was growing to love the area around Midleton and he was delighted to finally have an opportunity to see the Beconsford Estate.

As he was greeted by the gatekeeper at the gate lodge and given permission to enter the estate, he noticed a strange feeling in his stomach, but this time it was not worry but excitement. The long winding gravelled driveway was lined with majestic pine trees. Beyond them were fields stretching in all directions towards a forest and a river. He had a heightened sense of coming home so that he dared to dream that one day he could work in such an estate.

The imposing house in the distance impressed him. It had turrets on four corners and tall windows at either side of the massive oak door. The upstairs windows were large and wide, giving an impression that great shafts of light would offer brightness to the house. A terrace snaked its way around the exterior of the house. Jack liked this idea because whenever the sun shone there would be a section of the house where it could be enjoyed by just stepping from the house through the large glass windows.

As he made his way up the stone and gravel roadway, admiring the majestic pine trees, he was greeted by the sound of laughter from the terrace close to the front door. Lily and Helena were sitting on high-backed chairs, enjoying tea and delicacies.

"Hello, Jack!" called Lily.

"Father and Isaac are in the office and are expecting you," said Helena.

Jack waved a greeting to the giggling girls and smiled yet again at Lily's exuberance.

When he arrived at the front door, it was opened, not by a butler, but by a happy-looking young maid with a bright smile.

"I'm Jenny and Mr. Turner said to bring you to his office."

Jack smiled and followed her into a large room with a view of the forest.

83

He was greeted by Robert and was then introduced to Isaac, the son and heir who looked to be in his early twenties, tall and slim with blond hair. His expensive tailed coat and spotless white breeches were finished off with a perfectly polished pair of black knee-length boots.

"Any friend of Robert's is always welcome in the estate," said Isaac, as he extended his hand to Jack.

Jack liked his firm grip and said how much he was impressed with the size and architecture of the big house.

"It was built by my grandfather, the first Lord Beconsford," Isaac said with pride. "Let me show you around the ground floor."

Jack felt already that the terrace gave a sense of the building being a home and not just a house. It took away the feeling that people living inside such big houses were locked away. The long windows added much to the light that entered. Apart from the ballroom, the inside of the house had the feeling of a real warmth with rooms that were not overcrowded with heavy furniture. The best use was made of the space in each one.

Isaac explained that they had recently got rid of much of the oppressive furniture, especially in their living quarters. "My father was unhappy with the changes but I am now in charge and I want to simplify the running of the estate."

On completion of the tour, Isaac accompanied Jack as they went in search of Maurice Howard, the estate manager. They met him at the gates of his home which was situated beyond the landscaped gardens of the Big House and closer to the estate forest. Jack was immediately impressed by the manager's enthusiasm for the estate.

Isaac then shook hands with Jack and left, and the two men set off straight away in the direction of the forest.

"Isaac is really proud of his forest," said Maurice. "His father is a greedy man, unfortunately. When Isaac's grandfather was alive, like Isaac he was a gentleman. However, his son Lord Edward has always acted as if he is entitled to everything he wants. Thankfully, as Isaac was Edward's only son, he had to relinquish his power over the estate when Isaac threatened to go to England and not return again to Ireland. I admired his courage at the time as it was becoming impossible to please His Lordship who just wanted money to keep up his lavish lifestyle. But we are now slowly building bridges with the farmers and local communities."

Jack nodded, understanding the complexities of the relationship between the landed gentry and the locals in Ireland.

"We grow excellent oak trees that are always in demand for boat-building but we also have lovely pines and larch in the other part of the estate forest which is across the river," said Maurice. "It's wonderful the way Isaac now ensures that we replant new trees wherever it's necessary, unlike many of the absentee landowners who just sell off everything, to keep money coming in. I am so glad Isaac is not like his father. Lord Beconsford and Lady Ethel spend a lot of time now in England and Europe and usually it's

85

only Helena who goes with them. Isaac loves everything about the estate and wants to continue the vision of his grandfather. He is consistently saying that everyone should profit from the land and that includes the workers and the people in the town."

As they began to walk downhill, into a valley, Jack had his first view of the soft murmuring sounds of the River Owennacurra. It wound between the two parts of the forest, meandering through the estate in an S-bend and sparkling brightly as the rays of the sun hit its surface. He could hear its soft sounds as it moved slowly past. When they reached the river bank Jack discovered it was so clear that fish could be glimpsed below the surface.

Maurice pointed upriver to the bridge suspended above the water.

"That's how the planters and cutters go across to work on the other side. Beyond the bridge you can just glimpse the boat that is used to take heavy materials and trees that have already been cut and bagged for timber yards and fuel merchants. Once an area of forest has been clearfelled, the reforestation will then start in that area over the following two years."

Jack was very inspired by everything he heard and saw around him. He stood soaking in the peaceful surroundings as he watched the forest twigs floating past. On the bank the long grass weaved and swayed in various shades of green. It seemed as if it was dancing to the gurgle of the river.

I could happily live my life out here, he thought, as he

listened to the sound of silence that was broken only by the meandering of moving water.

As they parted, Maurice gave Jack the name of an important man in the Dublin Society, Gerry Harris.

As Jack thanked him, he thought how everyone he had met in Midleton seemed to be so helpful. Even the strong handshake of the Beconsford heir, Isaac, held warmth.

The happy mood stayed with him all the way back to the Haven Inn. The kindness he experienced was helping his healing and his night sweats were lessening although he continued to wake from nightmares when he would sit up in bed, shouting "*No! No! I must save them!*"

Chapter 13

At the end of July, Jack again went for his usual Sunday lunch with the Turner family. As they sat down at the now familiar dinner table, he told them he had some news for them.

"Since I came back to Midleton, I have learned so much from Old John and Maurice Howard. All of that is down to your kindness earlier in the year. I am very grateful for that help but in particular for your friendship. But it is time for me to look to my future. Maurice has given me an introductory letter to a head gardener named Gerry Harris at the Dublin Society Gardens in the north side of Dublin city. In the past Maurice and Gerry both worked in the Carden Estate in Templemore in County Tipperary. It is a huge estate and they both learned a lot from the Carden family. Sadly, it means that I'm going to be leaving Midleton. I'm taking the coach that leaves next Friday and I'm hoping to find a tutor to help with my studies, after

I've spoken to Mr. Harris in Dublin."

Robert and Meg said how sorry they would be to see him go while Eliza looked shocked.

Lily piped up, "Are you going to return to Cork in the future?"

Jack smiled and looked at the lovely face of Eliza.

"I have every intention of living my life near Cork. It's where my friends, such as your family and mine, all live. I love the county and the countryside and I will be back." He laughed. "You won't get rid of me that easily, especially if I can still come to eat Meg's Sunday dinner!"

After lunch, as the day was exceptionally hot, they served tea in the pretty garden at the side of the house. Meg had laid out a rug on which she placed a plate of cakes she had bought in Mrs. Sexton's bakery. They sat down and enjoyed the cakes in the warmth of the summer sun.

Jack admired the red and white roses in full bloom and the well-kept flower beds, set against the backdrop of the ivy plant climbing the high wall. The apples on the trees in the distance were just showing a bright pink skin and some had already fallen to the ground where the birds were having a little feast. As he sat listening to the sounds of nature, he turned his eyes to the soft white clouds moving quietly through the blue sky. He felt at peace and wanted this moment to last. He stayed quiet, happy to listen to the family chatting.

He eventually joined in, asking Eliza how her teaching was going.

"Very well indeed," she said. "I do enjoy it so much."

Eliza had told him previously that it was lucky she could speak some Gaelic as some of the children on the estate farms and the nearby village spoke only the Irish language. As she grew up, being taught on the estate by Mr. Lucas, she realised she wanted to become a teacher herself and decided she would teach the young children of the village and farming families in the district. Her father had thought this a worthy ambition and suggested she should learn Gaelic, as many of his workers over the years spoke Gaelic only. Robert found a woman in the village who was so happy to teach Eliza that she at first refused payment. He, however, insisted on paying her a fair sum.

Thinking of this, Eliza now added, "And I love having the opportunity to speak Gaelic."

"I'm glad of that," said Jack. He had learned Irish from Granny Sheila who spoke it when she had lived in the countryside but, as a lot of people in Cork city spoke only English, she insisted her grandchildren knew both languages.

"I'm also glad Granny Sheila insisted on us learning it. Though many a time we would have preferred to be out playing and dashing around!" He laughed at the memory.

Eliza nodded. "Lord Edward doesn't approve of Gaelic. Even though he was born in Ireland, he sees himself as English and describes the locals contemptuously as 'peasants'."

Robert nodded. "Isaac has changed all that and employs

as many locals as possible. I always say that we should remember that other people's ways are not necessarily wrong but just different."

When the conversation came to an end, Robert stood up, said he was too old to be sitting on the ground and went back to the house. Lily left also as she had to check some trimmings for her latest new dress.

Eliza looked at the man she had grown so fond of. He looked so handsome with his shock of black hair combed back to show off his dark but still sad eyes which were gazing at her intently. She thought that his serious countenance made him look older that his twenty-one years.

Jack broke the silence as he decided to be brave.

"Will, you miss me when I'm in Dublin, Eliza?"

She looked down at her dress for a moment and then lifted her eyes, where Jack thought he saw a hint of tears.

"Yes," she said and hesitated. "I will miss you."

Jack moved his hand and touched her fingers gently.

"Would you like me to write to you?" He held his breath.

"Yes, Jack, I'd love if you wrote to me."

He didn't remove his hand but squeezed her fingers gently and asked, "Will you write to me?"

Eliza put her other hand on top of Jack's and answered, "Of course I will."

Jack allowed himself to exhale deeply as he sat and looked into Eliza's radiant eyes.

Chapter 14

Jack arrived in Dublin and moved lodgings twice in the first week. He wanted to feel comfortable in his surroundings as he didn't know how long he would spend in the city. His final lodgings were in a house run by a Mrs. Maher, a widow whose family had left to marry and she had room for three guests.

He obtained a back room overlooking fields in the area of Glasnevin, close to the Dublin Society gardens. Breakfast and evening meal were supplied by Mrs. Maher. The two other gentlemen lodgers worked in office jobs. They were both decent men, who chatted at mealtimes, but Jack was happy to be left alone after his evening meal.

When he called to the office of the Dublin Society Gardens a week after leaving Midleton, he gave his letter of introduction to the clerk at the desk. He was brought to Mr. Harris's office where he was greeted warmly while being asked how Maurice Howard was keeping on the Beconsford Estate. Jack told him that Maurice was in good spirits and Gerry said that they had started out together on a large estate in Templemore in County Tipperary where they were both trained.

"Then Maurice went south and I went north," said Gerry.

He told Jack he could spend the morning looking around the gardens and at lunchtime they would talk.

Jack was overwhelmed by the beauty of the gardens and fascinated as he watched the gardeners working. He returned at lunchtime to Gerry, who took him around to a local inn where they ate a tasty meal of steak and kidney pie and potato. It was there that Gerry gave him the good news. He told Jack that the society would allow him to be trained in the gardens until Christmas time. He would not receive a wage but he would be tutored for two hours each day by one of the society workers, including Gerry. He would have to work from eight to six, with an hour for lunch. They would give him a Certificate of Learning at the end of his training and maybe even offer him a job if he proved suitable.

Jack was delighted with the offer. He had thought that he might have had to pay for training but this offer was so much better. He accepted on the spot and he and Gerry shook hands to seal the deal.

That night he sat in his room and penned his first letter since arriving in Dublin. He let his mother and sister Julia know where he was staying and he told them about his new training job.

He then set about thinking of what he would say in his first letter to Eliza.

It was Sunday, but Eliza couldn't settle in her room, where she was preparing work for a couple of children she was tutoring in the estate. Many of the children of the tenant farmers were helping their families with farming work and household chores. They would return in late September after the harvest had been gathered. But Maurice Howard wanted his two grandchildren to continue with their learning.

Eliza put down her pen. It was over a week since Jack left and she hadn't heard from him. She wondered if she had been mistaken that the touch of her hand by Jack meant something. Did he just want someone to write to? She felt that there was something about himself he wasn't telling her. He had spoken so warmly about his family but he had never spoken of his father. They never asked him, but wondered if his father might have left the family or maybe was in jail. They even wondered if Jack had been in jail himself or in some other serious trouble. Eliza rejected this idea – but why was he so silent about where he was before he came to them? It all disturbed Eliza and she felt her family might have difficulties being close to someone with such a past. But, on the other hand, she had always believed that you can't control what other people do or even what happens to them. After all, she and Lily were left without a mother when a winter flu left her with such difficulties breathing that she succumbed in the winter of 1802 when Lily was just two and she was four. Nobody could do anything about the fact that they grew up without a mother. Soon after, when Mrs. Kennedy, their housekeeper, retired to live with her sister in Tipperary, it was Meg, who was their nursemaid when their mother died, who became a second mother to them both. Meg was a wonderful person and Eliza and Lily had wondered over the years why their father didn't see that Meg loved him as much as them. Lily said that he spent too much time wrapped up in the farm and his work in the estate and there were even times when he still spoke of his wife as if she had just gone away for a holiday. Or, when they had their mother's sister over from Youghal for a Sunday meal, he often said, "Kathleen would have loved to hear you play that, Lily," or "Kathleen would have loved to hear you sing that song, Eliza".

Eliza felt sad for Meg, but could now understand more about such feelings since Jack had come into her life. Maybe it is related to his father, she thought, but could not get out of her mind the sight of the sad, unhappy man who fell on the road just months ago. He had looked at her that day in such a way that she felt as if she understood the troubled look in his eyes and she wanted to help him. He had such a different nature to the Toby Ramsays of this world and she was delighted that when he returned from Cork, he was healthier physically. But the sadness was still inside him.

Her mind returned to Toby Ramsay who seemed to flit in and out of Ireland but took every opportunity when they met to get close to her. This had happened again when they met at a musical recital at a country house nearby and he asked her to walk in the gardens during the interval. She had refused him because of nothing more than a gut feeling that he was a shallow man.

"Dinner is ready, Eliza!" called Lily. *"We have just had some great news from the Big House. Get down quickly as I'm bursting to tell you!"*

Eliza put her quill away and smiled as she always did when she heard the infectious voice of her sister. She made a promise to keep herself busy for the time being and put Jack to the back of her mind.

"What's happening that's so important?" she asked as she sat at the dining table.

"Just wait until Meg is sitting so that I can tell you all," Lily said.

Meg entered the room and sat next to Robert.

Lily drew a deep breath and announced, "The Honourable Isaac Beconsford is betrothed to a titled lady from Hertfordshire in England called Deborah Mitfield and I met her this afternoon when I was visiting the Big House!"

The family looked suitably astonished.

"And there's more – they are going to get married here in the estate chapel next June! They want good weather because they are going to put on a big outdoor party for everyone, including the estate workers! But the best news is that we are all going to be invited to the wedding!" She looked around the table gleefully. Then she noticed Meg looking questioningly at her.

"Of course you are coming, Meg – you are family."

Meg's usual happy face shed small tears.

"Why are you crying, Meg?" Lily asked.

"I'm just a little overwhelmed. Master Isaac is such a nice young man and he deserves a good lady to be at his side."

"She really is lovely, Meg. She is very pretty and has already been friendly and kind to myself and Helena. Helena is going to be a bridesmaid."

Robert agreed that Isaac deserved the best and the dinner continued with an excited happiness that was just what Eliza needed to take her away from her feelings of gloom.

Eliza was kept busy over the next few days. She met Deborah Mitfield, who impressed her with her kind manner. Lily was correct to say that she was beautiful. Her blonde hair fell almost to her waist and was plaited and held with a silver clip. Her creamy complexion and long neck were set off to perfection by the dress that flowed from her slim waist down to her expensive buckled shoes. Her strong handshake and spirited air led Eliza to believe that she would be well capable of dealing with Isaac's difficult father and highly strung mother. She was just two years older than Eliza and they both got on so well over tea in the Big House that Eliza believed they could become good friends.

Then on Thursday the Beconsfords' carriage took Eliza, Lily, Helena and Deborah Mitfield to take tea in the Regency Room. Toby and Oliver were also taking tea and, with Mrs. Sexton looking on, Eliza watched in amusement as Toby fawned over Deborah, telling her that his cousin the Earl was a good friend of her father.

Deborah had laughed when Toby and Oliver left and said she had never heard of the Ramsay family. The girls went on to discuss all the necessities needed for an upper-class wedding.

Eliza thought that Deborah was so lovely with her vibrant personality. Anything would look perfect on her, she thought. Deborah said that her gown would be made in London by her mother's favourite seamstress but that they would give as much business as possible to the local shops if that was possible. Eliza nodded her delight at Deborah's thoughtfulness and she went up even more in her estimation.

They showed her where they went shopping each Saturday but told her that she would need to go the City of Cork for elegant clothes and shoes.

When Eliza and Lily got home, they were greeted by a smiling Meg, who handed a letter to Eliza.

"Now, I wonder who that is from?"

"I bet it's from Jack!" Lily said, laughing as Eliza almost snatched the letter from Meg and told them both that she was going to her room to get school work ready for the following day.

Eliza sat by her desk in her bedroom as the sun streamed in through the window. She opened the letter and read Jack's words with trepidation.

Dear Eliza,

I must first apologise for not writing last week, but I had terrible difficulties finding accommodation to my liking. I had a room in an attic, followed by a room with a landlady who would want to know what you were doing all day! Finally, I found a lovely quiet room with a window facing a field of green close to the Dublin Society gardens. The other guests are two older gentlemen. The landlady, Mrs. Maher, is extremely pleasant and she provides breakfast and an evening meal.

But now for my exciting news. I met Mr. Harris today in the Dublin Society Gardens and he has agreed to train me in all aspects of horticulture. I will get a certificate of training from him when he is satisfied with my progress. I do not get paid, so I am deeply grateful to Granny Sheila for making this possible.

The gardens are magnificent and if you will permit me to write to you each week, I will delight in telling you all about their beauty. I miss you, and all of your family and I hope you will write to me. It is very lonely here, but I'm going to give all my time while in Dublin to make sure that I have a secure future.

Your respectful friend,
Jack

Eliza decided to go and sit in the garden and read the letter again. It seemed to have some hidden messages for her but she wasn't sure. It was certainly a letter that she could show the rest of the family and she felt also that Jack would know that the family would like to see his letters.

Eliza was in the garden rereading the letter when she was approached by Sam who had just finished feeding the animals nearby.

"Pardon me, Miss Eliza, but I need to say something to you. It's a message from my older brother who goes for a few pints in the local inn in the village where he lives."

Eliza looked at Sam with amusement as his face seemed to be getting extremely red with embarrassment.

"I'm a bit uncomfortable saying this but he heard Toby Ramsay talking. He was drunk and making funny remarks about how much he likes you. My brother didn't like his talk and asked me to let you know."

"Well, thank you, Sam, and it's always good to know what men say when they are drunk. I promise that I'll be fine and thank your brother."

When Sam left, Eliza sat thinking and was grateful for the protectiveness shown by Sam's family.

Have I encouraged Toby in any way, she wondered. But she certainly didn't feel threatened by him. As she sat back and reflected on the information, she recalled when she was younger overhearing one of the harvest farmhands talking about how his sister Dora had dealt with an attack by her employer where she worked as a maid. Her brother described what she had done and he said she had to disappear quickly from the area after that night and was now in Manchester where she had a good job in a millinery shop. Eliza wondered if she would have the same courage as Dora if she was ever faced with a similar situation. So, Toby Ramsay was back in Youghal. She wondered if he would contact her, but she wasn't concerned for her safety around him. Yet it made her think. Women aren't always safe around men.

That evening she wrote to Jack, expressing her delight at his news and asking him if he knew how long his training would take. She told him the news about Isaac Beconsford and how delighted they all were with an invitation to the wedding. She found it difficult to say much from the heart but she told him that she already missed his trips to the farm for his Sunday meal. She also promised him she would write back just as soon as she received his letters.

Chapter 15

Eliza kept herself busy as summer moved away and the harvest was over. Autumn leaves lay everywhere and she loved walking in the estate with leaves of red and gold crunching under her feet, just like she did when she was a child. She was now back teaching a big group of the estate children and was always proud whenever a child could read, write and understood how to deal with adding and subtracting small and large amounts of money.

She sat as usual at her desk and smiled as she opened Jack's weekly letter.

My dear Eliza,

I loved your news as always and was delighted to hear that Lily is having fun with Helena. The idea that they both want to go to Switzerland towards the end of next year to Helena's aunt made me smile. I'm sure your father will be persuaded to indulge her as she seems to see that nothing in life is impossible! Yet it is such a pity that Helena just wants to live away from her parents.

Since I have seen the sketches of gardens that are being created in the big houses and palaces in Milan and Florence, I too would love to visit such beauty. But I must be practical for the moment. As I told you recently, I am moving more in the direction of being able to create charming and restful gardens rather than staying only with plants and vegetables. I also think I'll let the healing plants to those who have a calling for medicine but I will always want to know how Old John is keeping and I write to him often.

I am enclosing one of my sketches of how a fine garden could be designed even in a small area and I have taken on the ideas from Italy of the importance of a water fountain. There is something so comforting about sitting next to a river or a stream and listening to the sounds and watching the movement of water. I have spoken of such things with Old John and he agrees that water has a positive effect on the calming of the body.

So now for the important news. Mr. Harris is delighted with my interest in creating beautiful spaces and he also said that my sketches and ideas are as good as they get from abroad (great praise indeed from the big man!), so he is suggesting that I should stay in Dublin until Easter next and that the level of my learning will be high enough to appeal to any of the big houses in Ireland or in Europe. Although I was expecting to leave Dublin by Christmas, he has agreed to pay me wages from January and that means I won't have to deplete my savings any more. I hope you agree that it is a good idea for me to stay in Dublin!

However, there is more good news! I am taking a break at Christmas and I would like nothing better than to spend that time in Midleton. If you think that's a good idea, could you ask Mrs. Jennings to reserve a room for me for about 10 days from Christmas Eve? I will have to return to Dublin at the start of January.

I hope I am not presumptuous in thinking that you, and your family would like to see me at Christmas time.

I await your reply,

As, always, your dear friend,

Jack

Eliza sat with her elbows on the desk and her head in her hands as she let Jack's news settle on her. She had conflicting feelings. She had been looking forward to him finishing his training by the New Year and perhaps coming back to Cork. However, she was so pleased that he was finding his true metier and sounding excited about his future. But she still wondered where she might fit into his plans. She would write to him tonight and let him know that she would love to see him at Christmas and she would tell the family that she was inviting him to Christmas dinner!

With her mind feeling more settled, she went to dinner and she had to give Jack's letter to Lily even before she got as far as the table!

Deborah came to Midleton in November and they took a trip to the city. Jack had told her how many poor people there now were in the city but she wasn't prepared for the enormous numbers of people crowding the centre. She handed out some coins to any of the poorer women who had a child in arms or held by hand. Children with no shoes and ragged clothes were evident in so many areas that Deborah and Eliza were glad to return to Midleton, even though they had also enjoyed a delicious afternoon tea in a hotel high up on a hill overlooking the city and the river below. Deborah had bought some early Christmas gifts in a shop that would have fitted comfortably into Mayfair in London.

Later, when she arrived home, Eliza again pondered on the poverty and wrote some of her thoughts to Jack that night. He seemed to always have interesting things to tell her about the architecture and gardens of Dublin. She wasn't sure how much interest he had in hearing the details of Isaac and Deborah's wedding. She realised that she knew very little about him and felt she needed that to change at Christmas time. He would need to open up his feelings and thoughts to her, if they were going to stay connected over the rest of the winter months.

Chapter 16

Winter had closed in and the golden autumn leaves were now but a distant memory, as Eliza made her way to her teaching job on a cold, crisp December morning. Chilling winds were blowing and making cheeks red but not from heat. She was warm, with her long crimson fitted coat covering her down to her buttoned boots. She was smiling as she thought of Jack's expected arrival before Christmas. She had already purchased a splendid sketching pad and some charcoals and even some paintbrushes and tubs of paint for him and her father. On a trip to Cork, she had discovered a specialist art shop while Lily, Helena and Deborah were enjoying the clothes shops. She hoped Jack would like his gifts. Her father seemed very pleased that Jack was joining them for Christmas dinner and they had also invited him to come and eat the leftovers on St. Stephen's Day.

Toby Ramsay had disappeared yet again and Eliza was

pleased as she had begun to get very irritated by his attentions. She had heard he had gone away to visit a school friend.

Deborah had by now returned to Hertfordshire to be with her family for Christmas. Eliza missed her as they had become good friends.

Her pupils were doing well at the school and she hoped that joyful things could happen this Christmas as she arrived at the school hut. She put Jack to the back of her mind as she greeted the children.

After her teaching day ended, Eliza decided to enjoy the afternoon sun that had chased the wind away. She decided to take a walk to the river before returning home. She always enjoyed watching the endless flow of the water as it meandered gently in front of her. As she stood by the river near the summerhouse, she heard a sound behind her.

As she turned from the river bank, to her surprise she saw Toby Ramsay walking towards her. She suddenly felt uncomfortable as he strode purposefully towards her with a frown puckering his otherwise handsome face.

As Eliza smiled politely at him, he came to her side and put a hand somewhat roughly on her shoulder.

"I need to talk to you urgently. I've been told that you are keeping in touch with a man called Jack Ryan."

Eliza shook his arm off and looked at him.

"What has that got to do you? He's a friend of mine and my family."

"You need to know, and I have it on authority from the Frankland estate, that Jack Ryan is nothing but a tramp of the road and a complete undesirable for someone like you to know. You need to cut all ties with such a man as you will be shunned by polite society if you consort with such people."

"Again, I'm asking what it's got to do with you?" Eliza asked in exasperation.

"Well, I was considering getting close to you and I don't want you around such people."

Eliza suddenly realised that Isaac Beconsford was right about Toby and for the life of her she couldn't work out why she had ever felt flattered by his attentions. How dare Toby Ramsay think that he just had to say the word and she would come running to him!

As he again tried to hold her arm, she aggressively shook him off. Then, as she looked into his face, she knew exactly who she wanted in her life.

He caught her arm again.

"How dare you belittle a friend of mine!" she said angrily. "And you might like to know that I would never want to get close to you in my life. *Now take your hand off my arm and leave me alone.*"

As Eliza glared at him, she saw his temper rise and he squeezed her arm so forcibly that she cried out, but it just seemed to make him angrier. As she tried to free herself, she suddenly found herself in an arm-lock and, as she began to panic, she remembered Sam's warning.

"What are you trying to do to me?" she asked, with tears in her eyes.

"I'm going to show you what it's like to enjoy the company of a real man and if you ever want to go back to that tramp you will be soiled goods!"

And he pulled her up the slope to the door of the summerhouse.

He stepped inside and tried to drag her in. She knew he was much too strong for her so she knew what she had to do. As he dragged her over the step she moved closer to his body, as if giving up.

"You will love what I want to do to you," he said with a smirk.

Suddenly she lifted her right knee and with all the force she could muster she thrust it up between his legs. A roar of agony made him lose his grip. As he let her go, she immediately put her hands on his chest and knocked him back onto the timber floor of the small summerhouse. As his heavy body hit the floor, she ran as fast as her legs could carry her.

She reached the edge of the estate without meeting anyone and she continued to run until she reached her own farmhouse gate where she sank to the ground, put her head in her hands and cried. She prayed that he'd be afraid to follow her and she now hoped also that nobody would see her before she composed herself.

At work that same day, Jack was in the office where he was showing sketches to Gerry Harris. They were part of an idea he had to plant herbs in a small area of the gardens by a sheltered wall. He thought it would be lovely if an area was enclosed where many seating benches would allow people to enjoy the beauty of the flowers and take in the heady smell of herbs such as lavender and camomile. He also had a sketch of a small water feature that would include the sight and sound of moving water flowing into a pond. He explained to Gerry that Old John in Midleton believed there was much healing for the soul in the sounds of rippling water while surrounded by perfumed smells.

Gerry saw Jack's face come alive as he explained the idea and told him that he would think about it. He praised Jack for his enthusiasm and his ideas and laughed as he said, "Lad, I think you will be loved by whoever gives you a job, but don't bankrupt them giving them ideas that cost them too much. We are still in our early days here and when we have enough money this will hopefully be the best garden in the country!"

Jack nodded in understanding and they both went for a walk to check on the work that needed doing over the winter months.

Jack had become good friends with his boss and had enjoyed good homemade food with him and his wife Theresa on occasions. In fact, Jack was looking forward to returning after Christmas, because he knew he had still a lot to take in and he was learning from the best. Yet, the highlight of his week was still the anticipation and the arrival of Eliza's letter.

***

Later that evening when Eliza had hidden from her family the trauma she had suffered at the hands of Toby, she made a decision to keep it a secret. She didn't believe that he would want anyone to know and she knew that if she disclosed it to her father, he would go wild and she didn't want to suffer even more by reliving it again. She understood enough about herself to realise that, being a private person, she would hate people talking about her. It was even possible that if people knew they would think she threw herself at the upper-class Toby Ramsay. She believed she was strong. She resolved not to let it affect her future and how she viewed other men. Thankfully, she had a great example of fine manhood in her beloved father.

Chapter 17

Christmas arrived and Jack found himself heading to Cork on a comfortable coach, with his bag full of small gifts for his family and the Turners. He would visit Cork on the 27th of the month and then return to spend his remaining time in Midleton, before going back to Dublin on the second day of the New Year.

The journey was uneventful, as the frosted roads had eased, with just a hint still left on the sun-sparkled surfaces. They stopped for food and sleep in Abbeyleix and Jack had time to spare to look at the beauty of the castle near the centre. Big estates had a beauty about them, but Jack thought that this type of beauty should be available in towns and villages also. It got him thinking. These days his mind was always working and he found that his sleep was improving and he was waking in fear less often. But he knew also that his life as it was at present was perfect, as he had no responsibilities and could indulge his passion for learning.

But his feelings for Eliza were part of this perfect time and, although he still knew that his situation might not match up to the expectations of the Turners, he was looking forward with hope to their meeting over Christmas time.

Jack arrived at the Haven Inn on Christmas Eve and was greeted warmly by Mrs. Jennings. She smothered him in a hug as if he were one of the family.

"I have your own room kept for you and I've set a fire and some hot water for washing. There's dinner waiting for you then and I can't wait to hear all your news of Dublin." She smiled as she drew breath and retrieved the key for his room from behind her desk.

As Jack followed her to the room, he had a smile on his face. He felt more at home in this inn than the toxic environment that his father had created for him in Friarsland. At that moment he knew that he would never go back to live at his childhood home on First Avenue.

At dinner, he told Mrs. Jennings all about his work in Dublin and she told him that she had met Eliza in the shops and she was looking forward to seeing him. She raised her eyebrows as she smiled at Jack. She could see the sparkle in his eyes when she mentioned Eliza. She hoped something good could happen for him, because she knew from the time he had stayed before that he had many nightmares. Now he looked much healthier and had put on some much-needed weight. He also looked smart in his good clothes which he had put on for dinner. She would say a prayer at Mass for him in the morning, she thought, as she patted his hand on the table.

"You must be exhausted, Jack, lad. Get a good sleep and promise yourself that you will enjoy your well-earned holiday."

Jack enjoyed a sound sleep and woke early. After breakfast, he spent a great deal of time brushing his clothes and shoes and carefully shaving his face. He had given his gift of a small marcasite brooch to Mrs. Jennings and he was now placing the gifts for the Turner family in a cloth bag that he would carry to church.

He waited outside for the Turners' horse and trap to arrive and to Jack's eyes Eliza looked a vision in her crimson coat and wide-brimmed bonnet.

Lily, of course, looked as happy as ever and was the first to run from the trap to Jack.

"You look very handsome!" she cried, before taking his hand and welcoming him.

Eliza came next as Meg and Robert got waylaid on their way to the church door. As Lily stepped back, Jack took Eliza's hand and placed his other hand over hers.

"Isn't he looking handsome, Eliza?" said Lily, grinning at her sister.

Eliza felt herself blushing. She felt almost tongue-tied.

"It's wonderful to see you, Jack," she managed to say.

"It's wonderful to see you too, Eliza."

He reluctantly let go of her hand as Meg and Robert approached. Robert shook his hand and Meg gave him a big hug as she greeted him.

"We are all happy to see you. You're looking splendid, Jack – they must be feeding you very well in Dublin!" she said with a smile on her face.

They all walked into the church together and Jack took his place at the wall side of the church bench, with Eliza beside him. He felt that he never wanted the service to end if he could continue to sit so close to her. She turned to smile at him on occasion and he tried to read what her eyes were saying. After church the whole community seemed in great humour as they wished each other Merry Christmas but Jack was glad when they left to go to the Turners' home.

As they entered the door of the farmhouse, the delicious smell of the roast greeted them. Jack felt the glow of merriment and happiness surrounding this family and this continued when Meg produced the banquet of food that they had been preparing for days. The table was laden with red meats, fowl, spiced beef, vegetables, basted potatoes, cold meat and salad dishes. The smell of the brandy on the rich fruit pudding for dessert was even better and a glass of mulled wine was also enjoyed by all, except Jack who enjoyed his refreshing apple juice. Today, they ate their dinner in the dining room where they ate on special occasions when guests were being entertained. The girls loved eating there and even Lily, who often found a reason for avoiding domestic duties, enjoyed laying the table on those occasions.

When the present-giving began, Jack gave a pair of woollen mittens to Lily and an embroidered table strip to Meg. He gave Robert a quill-holder for his desk and art brushes, and his present to Eliza was in a small carved wooden box which had velvet ruffled material on the inside. She was the last to receive her gift. Her eyes lit up when she opened it. A pendant of thin silver, with leaves of tiny silver pieces and a silver chain, sat on the velvet. Her eyes told him how much she loved it.

They all thanked him and handed him gifts of handkerchiefs and a necktie which he thanked them for. Then, when Eliza gave him the sketchpad and charcoal with the paints and a brush, he was close to tears. The gift was lovely and so clearly thought out that he wanted to hug her, but he just shook his head, somewhat embarrassed as he told her how kind she was. It's wonderful sitting with such a happy family, he thought.

They moved into the parlour where a welcoming fire blazed in the grate.

Lily and Eliza started the entertainment and Jack was again overcome when Eliza sang a lovely song to Lily's piano accompaniment.

"I watch the sky as darkness falls
The stars shine bright as if to call,
The brightest star shines just for me,
Telling me to follow my dreams."

Eliza looked at him as she finished singing and Jack hoped that her dreams included him.

Before he left, Jack was reminded that he should come for lunch the next day after which they were all invited to have tea at Beconsford House.

"Isaac asked for you to join us and said there is no need to bring any gifts with you. His parents are still in London, thank goodness," Eliza said with a laugh.

As Jack walked back to the village, a golden winter sun was slowly setting in the west. He was looking forward to spending the following day with Eliza.

Mrs. Jennings, who often sat with Jack at breakfast as most of the other guests at the inn were either couples or families, looked at him knowingly the next morning.

"You're sleeping better this trip, lad."

Jack saw the sympathy in her eyes and knew what she meant. He knew in himself that he had fewer night sweats and was pleased that he was now sleeping better.

He set out for the Turners' farm, thinking how lucky it was that the day was dry and bright. Rain would have created difficulties in transporting the ladies in their finery to Beconsford House. They would have needed to call on Isaac to send the carriage – which, indeed, he had already offered.

After a midday meal, every bit as enticing as the Christmas fare, the family got ready for the short trip to the

117

Big House. Lily, as always, took the longest time to dress and she had already checked that her friend Helena would not be wearing the same colours! Eliza shook her head with a smile and looked at Jack, who was smiling as ever at Lily's frivolity.

They all turned when Meg entered the hallway and collectively witnessed the pretty woman she still was. She wore a pale-blue gown, which showed off a still-narrow waist to perfection. The lace trimmings around the neckline were the same as adorned her wide-brimmed bonnet.

"Oh, you look lovely!" cried Lily.

"Well," she smiled, "I had to make an effort for our trip to the Big House, so I picked up some material in the town and I've been working on it whenever I had time." As they all exclaimed how well she looked, she added, "I'm glad you like it."

She donned her cloak and was smiling as she made her way to the trap and waited for Robert to help her step in. The three others looked at each other and Lily murmured, "Will he ever see how lovely she is?"

They arrived at the house and were greeted by the footman, who showed them into the drawing room where Helena was seated with Isaac standing by the fire.

Isaac came to greet his guests and shook Jack warmly by the hand.

They chatted for a long while, sipping their sherry from the best Waterford crystal. Isaac wanted to hear everything about Jack's garden designs and ideas about creating beauty.

Robert had already spoken to Isaac about Jack's progress, and they had both indicated an interest in it with a view to securing him for the estate garden. Jack responded to the questions with enthusiasm, telling him about the Dublin Society Gardens and how they were learning so much about garden architecture from Italian gardens.

Isaac was pondering and slightly hesitant as he asked Jack if he would consider creating a small garden for his wife-to-be, Deborah. He wondered if it would be possible to have one ready for the June wedding?

"And, if possible, I'd be happier if she didn't know about it," he said.

Helena giggled. "So, it's to be Deborah's Secret Garden?"

They all laughed and Jack said, "Well, that's a lovely name for a garden."

He was very taken aback at the offer but very grateful to have it made to him.

"I am somewhat overwhelmed, sir, and I think it would be possible. Could you give me a few days to consider a suitable plan and maybe much of the ground work could be carried out before I return in early April?"

"Yes, of course."

"My first assignment is 'Deborah's Secret Garden'," he voiced with a great feeling of satisfaction.

They later enjoyed a wonderful tea. Then the girls entertained the company, with Lily as always on the piano.

Eliza sang and watched Jack as she finished with a song that completely melted his heart.

"The words of a loved one from far, far away brings tears of joy to all

But the touch of a hand when they come back home, truly brings joy to the soul."

As everyone clapped, Jack knew he was hooked for life.

After an evening of music and many servings of the estate's best wine, the Beconsfords insisted on their carriage and driver being used to take all the guests home and Robert's horse and trap could be housed in the stables for the night.

As the guests said their goodbyes, Jack asked Eliza quietly if she could spend some time with him alone when he returned from his visit to Friarsland.

"We could walk around the estate and maybe it would give you some inspiration for the location of Deborah's Garden," she said.

He smiled and nodded. "I'll call for you after breakfast on Thursday," he said.

He helped her onto the carriage and then sat opposite her, where he was happy just to look at her.

Chapter 18

The following morning Jack took the coach to Cork and walked from the city to First Avenue. Yet again, he was sad to see the poverty so close to luxurious shops and in stark contrast to the ornate carriages making their way through the town. He passed some coins again to the women who seemed to look worn down just by existing.

When he reached Julia's house, she was watching out for him and ran out to meet him.

He embraced her and they went inside.

His mother and Jarad were seated at the kitchen table while Granny Sheila made tea.

Molly rose to hug him and exclaimed, "You're looking great, son! Someone has certainly been feeding you again. You're nearly back to the healthy-looking boy I reared!"

Granny Sheila greeted him with open arms.

"It's thanks to you all, but especially this wonderful

lady," Jack said as he hugged her and kissed the top of her silver hair.

"Hannah and Ted will be here shortly and you will have left before your father is around," said his mother.

"I left him his dinner for whenever he wakes."

Jack passed out gifts to all the family. He gave his granny a soft wool shawl, in pale pink, to put around her shoulders. She wore it straight away, exclaiming at the softness of the wool.

"I bought it in a fashion shop in Dublin and they thought it was for a girl," he said, laughing, "and I told them, yes, it was for a girl at heart!"

They all laughed and Sheila looked around, proud of the family her daughter had reared, in spite of their father.

Jack told them stories of his workmates in Dublin, but didn't say anything about his future plans. The day seemed to fly and it was soon time for him to say goodbye and return to the coach. He promised that he would keep writing when he returned to Dublin. He bade them a fond farewell, thankful that he had visited without having to endure any meeting with his father.

The following morning Jack woke early, in order to watch the sun rise, as frost still glistened in the fields outside his bedroom window. It is such a wonderful sight, he thought contentedly. He dressed and had breakfast as usual with Mrs. Jennings.

"You're looking very spruced-up this early in the morning, Jack," she said as she looked him in the eye.

"I'm meeting Eliza. We're going for a walk around the estate and I'm hoping to take her for tea to the Regency Room later in the morning."

"Will this be the first time you have been alone with her for any length of time?" she asked, with eyebrows raised.

He acknowledged that it was.

"Well, lad, you'd better make the most of it because a lass like Eliza won't be without a suitor for long."

Before he left, she brushed his coat and tidied his necktie.

"Thank you, Mrs. Jennings," he said with a smile.

"I think she likes you, lad, so make some progress before you return to Dublin. I know how you feel about her."

Jack entered the farmhouse and Meg greeted him.

"Have a cup of tea, she'll be ready in a few minutes," she said and poured him some tea.

"Thank you, Meg," Jack said as he sat.

"It's a lovely crisp day for a walk."

"Luckily. I'm hoping she'll agree to visiting the Regency Room for tea with me after."

"I've no doubt that she will!"

Eliza arrived, looking splendid in her crimson coat and her cream bonnet which covered her sleek black hair.

"Lily is still in bed and Robert is on the farm with Sam, so you can take the trap with you," said Meg.

Jack thanked her and, later, as he helped Eliza into the trap, he had never felt so apprehensive in his life.

They arrived at the estate and Jack gave the grateful estate stable lad a coin to look after the horse while they walked.

He offered Eliza his arm and she tucked hers into it.

"So let's take a look at parts of the estate that might be right for your garden, Jack," she said. "Then I want to show you inside the lovely summerhouse down a little valley but with a lovely view of the water. It may not be too cold because it has some glass panels that keeps some heat in during the winter."

"Yes, that would be grand," Jack answered.

Jack didn't mind where they went, provided her arm stayed tucked into his but he loved the feeling of being so close to so much nature. He thought how lucky for the Turner family and now him to have the freedom to walk in the grounds of the Big House.

He saw the sensible and practical side of Eliza when she moved him around the estate, showing him sections where the garden could get the best sunlight. He took good heed of her. His favourite position was close to the Big House which would make it immediately accessible for Deborah, near the side exit.

Later, Eliza took him to the river which was flowing high and she explained to him that the Owenacurra river sometimes flooded areas around the town, but the Big House and their farm were both at the higher end of the town, so they were spared that problem.

Eliza had deliberately brought him to this area. She needed to drive out the bad memories of the summerhouse as she always loved that place, by now going there with someone with whom she felt safe. She pointed to the delightful, small, ornate summerhouse, which had a spire-like roof and open door. Jack had missed that when Maurice Howard had walked there previously with him. They scrambled up the few steps and walked through the door of the quaint little building. They sat down on the curved cushioned bench, as Eliza caught her breath after the walk. Jack's heart on the other hand nearly stopped, he was so in awe of the setting of the small structure. The cleared area around the structure allowed a vista spreading from west to east, with views of the church to the west, and ahead the river flowed and weaved around the forest trees that bordered both banks. The frost on the grassy bank sparkled and the sun threw shadows and light across the flowing water.

Jack took a blanket from a basket that was situated in the corner of the summer house and placed it over Eliza's knees.

They sat for a while in companionable silence.

Then Jack took Eliza's hand and said hesitantly, "I want us to walk out together – I mean I want more than that – I want us to have a future together. I'm not saying this very well, am I?"

Eliza squeezed his hand and smiled.

"You're saying it fine."

There was silence for a while as Jack wondered what to say next.

Eliza broke the silence.

"I don't know you very well, Jack, do I? You know all about my family, my work and my friends. I just feel that you're holding things from me. You don't talk about your father, and we have never asked you why. If we are to have a future, I need to know such things. You never told us why you were so distracted-looking when we first met. I don't want to judge you, Jack, but I need more honesty before I agree to even walk out with you."

Jack took his hand from Eliza's and put his elbows on his knees as he held his head in his hands.

Eliza could see tears forming in his eyes and started to worry that she had opened some wounds too suddenly.

"It's all right, Jack – I don't wish you to get upset."

"It's not alright," Jack said as he began to shake his head and his knees began to tremble. "My father is a drunkard and I despise what he has done to me and my family with his bullying ways."

Eliza breathed a sigh of relief. She put her hand on his shoulder and said.

"That's fine, Jack. That's not your fault. I'm not going to judge you because of your father's actions. My family thought he might perhaps be in jail."

She kept her hand on his shoulder, until the silence was broken by Jack.

"There's something else I need to tell you, but I don't want anyone else to know about it. Even if you never want to see me again, I want you to promise me."

"Of course, I will give you that promise. Please trust me, Jack." But she felt great apprehension, wondering what this could be.

Jack stayed silent for a while before he unburdened himself of his horrific ordeal at sea just one year before. He told of his anguish for the lost children, their parents and his overwhelming grief for all the lives lost in that storm. He spoke of the unbelievable kindness and empathy of the Murray family. He told her of the shame of surviving when he wasn't supposed to even be on the ship.

Then he wept as he spoke of his broken spirit.

"I wanted to pretend it had never happened, but in the darkness of night the memories are always there."

Eliza's eyes filled with tears as she witnessed his anguish.

"I understand, Jack. Please don't cry."

"I felt all the time that I was deceiving you and your family in a way, by concealing all this when you were all so kind."

"Oh, Jack, we wondered if you had been involved in the shipwrecks off Tramore because everyone knew of the tragedies that happened at sea. We knew you had come from that direction and were surprised you never mentioned anything about it. Then we thought you had spent some time working in gardening in East Cork and that something very bad had happened to you there." She didn't mention that her family had speculated on whether he had been in jail – an idea she had rejected from the start. "At least it is good for me to now know that you spent all those years exploring the world." She smiled as she took his hand and kissed it.

Jack looked at her.

"You're not going to reject me?"

"I'm not," she said, "and we'll fight any demons that remain, together."

Jack looked at her in wonder.

"You know, Mrs. Jennings has told me that I have not had nightmares over Christmas. This morning she said I've been sleeping like a baby! I want to believe her because I wish to live a normal life. I wasn't going to tell you about myself but I now know you are right and it's important for me to be honest with you. Left to myself, I'm not sure I'd have had the courage to tell you."

He stood and drew her gently to her feet.

He held her close as his tears fell and he promised himself to be open with her in the future, whatever life threw at him.

Eliza wondered if she should confess to him what happened to her in this very place not too long ago. As she continued to let him hold her, she came to a decision. It was better to keep the actions of that horrible man Toby Ramsay a secret.

They walked back through the estate, holding hands.

Eliza looked at Jack's grey complexion and the haunted look in his eyes and just wanted to take him in her arms and make it all go away. Instead, she squeezed his hand and said with heartfelt feeling, "We're in this together, Jack, and you will come through it."

At her words, Jack brushed tears from his eyes yet again.

"I think you should go back to Dublin through Tramore," she said, "and talk again to the Murray family. That family saved your life and for that I am truly grateful. Maybe it will help to let them see how much better you are physically. We both owe that family a great debt. I would not have met you but for them. I'm sure they would love to see you."

Jack nodded his agreement and before they reached the edge of the town, he took her in his arms again and held her close.

After tea at the Regency Room, Jack took Eliza home. Having left her at the farm, he then took a detour along the road to the east of the Turners' farm and close to the Beconsford Estate. On one of his walks, he had seen a cottage set back from the road that had an air of neglect about it and he wanted to check it out. The garden gate had a chain to keep it locked but what he saw made him wonder. The garden had become a haven for wild flowers and the rose bushes under the two front windows lay limp and neglected. The roof had some moss but it looked in good shape and the name carved into the wooden front door read *Rose Cottage*. He could see that the stone garden wall went a good distance beyond the back of the cottage. He leaned his elbows on the gate and murmured to himself "*Rose Cottage*".

When he sat down for his meal with Mrs. Jennings that evening, he asked her about the cottage.

Her eyes widened and she gave him a knowing glance. "My goodness, you seem to be moving very fast after your morning's walk!"

Jack blushed which made her laugh.

"It was Mrs. Hadden's house," she said, "and when she died last year it took a while to track down her nephew who now owns it. I know his name is Gregory because he stayed with me when he came from West Cork to look at the cottage. He has a farm and I doubt he'd want to live in Midleton. I'm sure I can find out where he lives and I'll let you know, Jack."

"I'd be ever so grateful."

"There was great love in that house, Jack. May Hadden and her husband never had a family but they were very happy and always kept that cottage in splendid shape. Her husband was a cobbler in the town and he died five years ago and she was never the same afterwards. I think it might be true that you can die of a broken heart."

"Like the Hadden family, I'm falling in love with this area."

"You are indeed, Jack," said Mrs. Jennings, laughing, "and I think a certain young woman might be responsible for that!"

Jack didn't respond but nodded and a smile broke out on his face as he finished Mrs. Jennings' delicious apple pie and cream.

***

The following morning, Jack hugged Laura Jennings as he promised to return in the spring. He walked into the

Regency Room where he was meeting Eliza, with Lily and Helena, before taking the coach to Waterford to stay overnight with the Murray family. He had written to them and he hoped they had received his note.

He had purchased a small silver locket for Eliza and he slipped it into her hand while Lily and Helena chose cakes from the assortment placed in front of them by Mrs. Sexton.

"I'll miss you every day I'm away," he said quietly.

She opened the locket and discovered that Jack had sketched her portrait, opposite his, inside. She looked into his eyes as he touched her hand. They were both close to tears.

They joined the girls who had started into a large plate of fine pastries. They all then talked about the work that was already under way on Deborah's Secret Garden, as Isaac had been extremely pleased with the ideas Jack had proposed. Jack said that he would be writing to Isaac regularly, until he returned at Easter to take over the project.

As Jack waved farewell to the girls in the town square, he promised himself that when he next returned to the town, he would be stronger in mind and in body.

Late that evening the coach driver dropped Jack in Tramore, close to the sea road that was home to the Murrays. Cornelius Murray was watching out for him and the delight on their faces when he arrived brought him close to tears. As they sat at the kitchen table eating the tea prepared by Ellen, he tried to talk to them only of their kindness and to bring them up to date on the events of his life since he had left them almost a year ago. He did not want to remember the horror of the sinking of the *Seahorse*. He told them of his love for Eliza and that if she agreed to marry him, he wanted them to come to his wedding.

Ellen and Cornelius cautioned him not to rush into anything but assured him they would love to be guests whenever he wed.

Henry asked Jack if he wanted to walk to the village where the locals had erected some memorials to those lost at sea, but Jack found he couldn't do it.

"Not this time, Henry, but maybe in the future I'll have gained enough courage to do that." As Jack continued to reflect, he still couldn't understand his weakness in not being able to face what happened a year before. Yet the guilt he had felt, wondering why families died while he lived, had begun to lift, as he saw a future where he could make a difference to other people's lives, hopefully supported by his beloved Eliza. He felt that might atone for the guilt he felt as a survivor.

The four of them sat around the table for many hours and by the time they had all retired to bed, Jack was so exhausted that he fell into a deep sleep.

The following morning Henry took Jack to the coach stop, but on this occasion they said goodbye with hugs and smiles.

Chapter 19

Jack settled back into his Dublin lodgings and wrote to Eliza regularly. In his first letter he told her that he had visited his friends on the way back to Dublin and they were all in good health. He said he agreed with her that the trip had helped his healing. He knew he was sleeping better and each night he kept himself busy with letterwriting to Eliza and Isaac and his own family in Cork.

He had sent more detailed plans to Isaac and the estate manager as to how the garden should progress. He had also got an address for Mrs. Hadden's nephew from Mrs. Jennings. He wrote to him and hoped to hear back fairly soon.

Jack continued to gain great knowledge about gardening needs for Big Houses. He spent much of his time learning about trees and forestation – how to keep, clear and reseed forests. Gerry had good ideas in this regard from his time in the Carden family estate in Tipperary. Gerry told him that many Big Houses had forests attached to them and Jack realised the importance of this type of knowledge. His pet delight was seeing how water was used successfully in garden fish ponds and how fountains and small waterfalls could be installed where water wells were available. He learned how exotic plants could grow where heat was used and wished he could visit some of the gardens in the Mediterranean. He had sailed all around the Far East, yet he now longed to see the beauty of the architecture, paintings and gardens of Italy. His head was full of ideas learned from his training in the Dublin Society Gardens and from Gerry Harris's descriptions of his journeys through Italy. He would be eternally grateful to his mentor Gerry and to Gerry's wife Theresa who continued to feed him home-cooked meals, as he and Gerry endlessly talked about gardens.

The months seemed to fly and suddenly he was into his final week in Dublin. He received a Certificate of Training from Gerry Harris but the reference letter with the Dublin Society's heading was even more valuable to him. More important than anything else was an offer of employment on the Midleton estate from Isaac and his father.

The workers had also made a collection of their hard-earned pennies, to buy a miniature silver trowel that Jack told them, with tears in his eyes, he would cherish forever. On his last day they all gave him a big cheer as he left. After a goodbye meal with the Harrises, where he deighted

Theresa with a gift of a small framed painting of pretty flowers that he had purchased in Dublin, he took a ride to the city centre where he boarded a coach for his journey back to Midleton.

Eliza woke on the 5th day of April, 1817, with a warm fuzzy feeling inside. It was the day before Easter Sunday and Jack was returning from Dublin. She dressed with great care and barely ate her breakfast. Sam had the trap ready for the road soon after noon and the old mare Snugs slowly plodded her way into the town. Eliza spent some time buying material for a dress with some trimmings to match but was seated in the hallway of the Haven Inn far too early. She sat where she could see the coach arriving in the square and her excitement mounted when finally she spotted it. Her happiness grew as Jack stepped out, with his large new valise.

He looked around and smiled at a few locals before he walked across the town square and entered the Haven Inn.

Mrs. Sexton greeted him at the door like an old friend and pointed to where Eliza was waiting. Jack asked Mrs. Sexton to keep an eye on his bag and he all but marched with hands outstretched to clasp Eliza's hands. He sat down and gazed at her as if she might disappear.

They went into the Regency Room where a table was set by the window. Tea and cakes were placed in front of them.

Jack put his hand out to grasp Eliza's again.

"I can't wait, making small talk with you, before asking

the question I've wanted to ask for over a year. Eliza Turner, if your father approves, will you consent to let me love you and honour you and, yes, even obey you, if I ask you to marry me?"

Eliza's eyes opened and she smiled and chuckled with merriment as she answered with a big smile.

"I will, obviously, if you agree to obey me! I'd love to marry you, Jack Ryan."

Jack, whose heart had been beating too fast, let out a huge breath and could just manage to say, "Thank you, thank you, Eliza. This truly is the happiest day of my life. I know it is not a very romantic way of proposing, but I couldn't wait a minute longer!"

Finishing their tea in a hurry, they went back to Sam, who had been waiting with the trap, and were quickly on the road to the Turners' farm.

Jack was greeted with a big hug from Meg and Lily and a strong handshake from Robert. When Jack asked to speak to Robert privately, the others disappeared into the kitchen and Robert and Jack went into the parlour and sat down.

Jack sat on the chair, wringing his hands while also trying to slow his heartrate. That didn't work so he just plunged straight in.

"I want you to hear me out, Mr. Turner. I realise that you don't know me too well and that your family are held in high esteem in the county but I have fallen deeply in love with your daughter Eliza and I want to take care of her for as long as I have a breath in my body. Last week I received the news by letter that Isaac and his father have offered me a full-time position at the estate, starting next week. I have not told Eliza yet about the full-time job because my time in Midleton depends on my future with her. Mr. Turner, I'm asking for Eliza's hand in marriage."

As he hesitated for a moment Robert interrupted him.

"I heard from Isaac that you had been offered the job and I was very pleased for you, lad." It took just a second more before he smiled as he reached over and shook Jack's hand firmly. "Of course, Jack. I've seen how much Eliza's quiet nature comes to life when you are around. I'd be proud to have you as my son-in-law."

Jack's heart nearly jumped out of his chest in delight.

"Thank you so much and I promise that you will never regret this!" he said, smiling broadly.

Robert nodded, smiling.

"Now, listen, lad, about the job ... I want to give you a small warning. There are a couple of workers on the estate who might not take kindly to a young man being senior to them. The O'Leary brothers, Dermot and Brendan, are bad news but Isaac knows that their families would starve if they were let go. You see, many years ago their father had a small farm but he drank too much. Lord Beconsford refused to show sympathy and evicted him and his family. Since that time, they have been living in a slum area of the town. About two years ago Isaac gave the two boys a chance to work on the estate. Their mother was grateful for the offer but those lads drink too much like their father and the have to be watched carefully at work. Just keep your eyes open for them and let us know if they give you too much bother."

Jack only barely absorbed the information, agreeing that he'd keep an eye out for them. As they stood up, he asked Robert to say nothing to the family for about an hour as he had something to ask Eliza first. He asked if he could take her somewhere in the trap for a short time as he had something to show her.

Robert laughed and said that he'd better be back in time for tea or Meg would have words with them both!

Jack laughed and they went to the kitchen where everyone stood in anticipation. Jack asked Eliza if she would come for a short ride with him before tea. Looking puzzled, she agreed and he told the others that they would not be long. Eliza looked at her father anxiously, but he just smiled and patted her on the back gently.

"What's going on, Jack?" she asked, as they trotted Snugs out of the farm gates.

Jack laughed as he said, "I'm eloping with you but don't worry – I don't think Snugs would get us very far!"

As he turned east on the main road, Eliza became more puzzled.

"Where are you taking me, Jack?"

He grinned and didn't answer.

After a short ride he pulled up the trap and helped her to step down.

He put the reins over a tree stump and Snugs happily started to eat the verge grass.

Jack took Eliza's hand and almost pulled her towards the gate of Rose Cottage where he had halted.

"What do you think of it?" he asked with a smile.

"This is Mrs. Hadden's house," said Eliza. "When she was alive, myself and Lily brought her meat each week for her Sunday dinner." She looked at him, perplexed. "It's a delightful cottage but … why are you showing it to me?"

Jack put his arm around her shoulder.

"If you want this home to belong to Mr. and Mrs. Jack Ryan, just say yes and it will be ours tonight."

Eliza looked at him in astonishment.

"I have agreed to buy it, if my beloved wife-to-be wants us to live here after we wed! I'm meeting Mrs. Hadden's nephew's solicitor in the inn tonight to close the deal but of course that is if my Eliza wants to live here!" He finished and waited, with a wide grin on his face. Eliza responded by taking his face in her hands and he got his answer when her soft lips met his.

They returned to the farmhouse and when they imparted all their good news, they were both enveloped in the warmth of love and happiness. Robert and Meg were thrilled at the prospect of having Eliza still living close to them, as Lily was forever talking about going off to Europe sometime in the future. Robert insisted on the whole family drinking a toast to the happy couple.

However, when Lily began to discuss her bridesmaid's

dress Eliza told her to slow down, much to Jack's amusement.

"We're not getting wed tomorrow!" Eliza said, somewhat exasperated.

With a smile on his face, Jack said that he'd leave it to the women to discuss weddings and explained why he had to return to the inn. Everyone drank another toast to the couple's new cottage and as Jack closed the farmhouse gate, he did a small little dance of delight.

The warm feeling of happiness stayed with Jack when he returned to the inn. Having accepted the excited good wishes of Laura and her husband Liam, he waited for Gregory Hadden's solicitor to arrive.

After the cottage was signed and paid for, he wrote to his mother and Granny Sheila to tell them about the engagement and the purchase of the cottage. He was sending the letters via Julia and warned her, yet again, not to tell his father anything about him. He told Mrs. Jennings that he would stay in the inn until May and then he would move into the cottage alone, to get it ready, until he was wed to Eliza. She was so happy for them both and made a promise to fatten him up until he went off to live on his own at Rose Cottage.

Jack then walked back out to the farmhouse to let Eliza know that the cottage now belonged to them. She threw her arms around him in an unusually demonstrative way which made her father and Meg smile.

Jack returned to the village a very happy man. That night he fell asleep with a wide grin on his face.

***

Jack arrived at the estate office on the day after Easter and arranged to start his work the following day. He was delighted with the amount of work that had been completed in the Secret Garden, especially the walls, pathways and the shrubs and bulbs that needed to be in bloom for Isaac's wedding.

The estate manager Maurice Howard also brought Jack around to meet the rest of the estate staff. He was greeted warmly by some, but the O'Leary boys looked somewhat surly when he met them. He remembered Robert's warning and smiled and shook hands with everyone, although some dropped their eyes when he did so. A couple of young stable lads looked at the O'Leary men before they nodded at Jack. They are two bullies, thought Jack and he decided to keep a good eye on them.

He spent the rest of the month working on the water features, the seating and the different coloured flowerbeds that would look at their best in June. Thankfully Deborah was not going to return until it was time for the wedding, so Jack got on with the work. He had decided to add a short drystone walkway to the garden with wooden trellising at either side and a curved roof to keep the walkway dry. He created a further less elaborate pathway, from the side entrance to the house. This ended at the more ornate walkway that created a delightful entrance to the Secret Garden. He would intertwine flowers on the entrance trellising for the wedding and later grow ivy to keep a green walkway all year round.

In the evenings he worked on clearing the grounds of his cottage and, with the help of Sam from the farm, they had flowers planted at the front of the house that would bloom quickly. They put distemper on the walls inside the house to give the rooms a bright and airy look. Eliza had been happy for them to purchase much of Mrs. Hadden's furniture and serviceable mats and rugs. Even her china tea-sets, plus her linen bedding covers, were in such good condition that they would have little to spend after they wed.

The cottage had a large kitchen that looked towards the back garden and the parlour was large enough for the piano that Robert wanted to buy as a wedding gift for Eliza. The third small room downstairs could be used by Jack as a sketching and work room.

Eliza wanted an autumn wedding before Lily went on her travels to Switzerland with Helena. Jack was content with whatever made Eliza happy.

Chapter 20

On the first Sunday of May, Sam brought the farm cart to the inn and loaded Jack's trunk into the back. They drove to the farm for Sunday dinner before the whole family, including Meg and Sam, drove the short distance to Rose Cottage.

The sun had come out to greet them as Jack opened the newly oiled gate and led the family into the front garden.

After Eliza was given the key to open the door, it was her sister Lily, as ever, who was the first to run up the small cottage stairway that led to a large front bedroom.

"I can nearly see our farmhouse from here!" she cried as she looked out the window.

Then she tested the new bed and embarrassed Eliza by declaring that it was extremely comfortable. Everyone laughed as they heard her. Nobody could be cross with Lily for long.

Meg was impressed with the cooking pots and utensils

and agreed that the brick fireplace was going to work well for slow or fast cooking.

They all wished Jack well and later, having enjoyed a cup of tea, they left him with plenty of food to eat for the next few days.

As he put his belongings away, he reflected on a conversation he had with Mrs. Jennings before he left the inn. She had told him that she had overheard a few cronies of the O'Learys saying that the boys were going to give Jack his comeuppance for stealing a job from a Midleton man. She warned him to watch out and she'd listen out for anything being said. Jack didn't want to worry Eliza, or any of her family, but he began to keep an eye out for them while at work. He was afraid that they'd do something to the garden, although as that could affect their jobs they were unlikely to do that.

He turned his thoughts to happier things and agreed with Lily that the large bed was really comfortable and he slept without dreams of any kind that night.

Once the house was in shape, Jack had more free time to spend with Eliza. They met after work each day at the gate of the estate and walked back to the farmhouse, where a meal was always available for Jack.

On Saturdays, after an early finish at work, Jack met Eliza in the town, when she shopped for the family. On those occasions, they purchased items to wear for the upcoming wedding at the Big House, as Jack had now been added to the guest list. Eliza had made her own dress and, while she went in search of a bonnet to go with it, Jack called on Mrs. Jennings.

She took him aside and told him to be careful because the O'Leary boys were certainly planning something.

"They are in buying ale each night and bragging to their friends that you won't last much longer at the Big House."

Jack thought he'd better say something to Isaac and Robert, but was reluctant to tell Eliza.

When he arrived at work on Monday morning he went into the office and met with Isaac and Robert. Jack informed them of Mrs. Jennings' worries and the men agreed that the O'Learys were capable of stupid actions especially if they had drink in them. However, they agreed that accusing them of plotting might lead to a more dangerous situation.

Robert suggested that perhaps Sam could help keep an eye on them when he went for his nightly pint at the inn. Mrs. Jennings could keep her ears open and they might find out if they were planning anything. They all agreed that they needed to keep their eyes and ears open. Later, when Jack returned to work, he greeted the O'Learys when he passed them as if he had no knowledge of their deviousness.

During that week, everything was quiet and Jack was delighted as a few fine details were all that were left to complete the Secret Garden. He had a small replica of the summerhouse built close to the entrance. He explained to Isaac that it would allow Deborah, plus two more people, to sit watching the garden, even in wet weather.

Jack found time as the evenings began to lengthen to spend more time in the company of Eliza. She was already planning her own wedding, as her dress for Isaac and Deborah's big day was finished.

He also met with Old John one evening in the inn. They chatted about plants he had seen in the Dublin Society Gardens and he told Old John that Isaac was happy to let Jack set up an area in the estate that would be exclusively for healing plants and herbs. Old John went home happy that evening.

When Old John had left, Jack stayed to talk to Mrs. Jennings about the O'Learys. She said that Sam was keeping watch every night, while sitting in his favourite corner, and she and her husband Liam were keeping their ears open for any snippets of information.

It was the following Saturday night and Sam was enjoying his couple of pints of ale in the inn. He was chatting to Old John when suddenly Mrs. Jennings asked them loudly if they needed another pint. She then lowered her voice and muttered, "They're up to something. They're arranging to meet someone outside shortly. Old John, slip out and tell the law-and-order man he might be needed." Then, raising her voice, she said, "Two pints on the way, lads," and returned to the bar.

As she walked behind the counter, the O'Learys stood up and made their way to the door. Sam and Old John immediately followed Mrs. Jennings through the back door to the yard where Sam could better watch without being seen. Old John went in the other direction to get the law to help.

Sam saw a lad, who was the O'Leary's younger brother, handing them each a bottle that seemed full of liquid. The boy also handed Dermot an oil lamp and Brendan a bundle of cloth. That was followed by a cuff on the head for the young fellow's trouble. By now Sam was very worried and his heart was racing as he followed the two bullies as they started to walk out of the village in the direction of the main road. He watched as they skirted past the estate.

He saw Jeff Dickon, a good young lad, and whispered to him to get to the Turners' farm and tell Robert to get to Jack's cottage immediately. He warned him not to let the O'Learys see him. He slipped him a coin and the lad disappeared in a flash. Sam kept his distance from the thugs as he followed them and hid behind buildings, until they reached the crossroads.

Sam was right. They were heading in the direction of Jack's cottage. But darkness had now fallen. Sam knew the land and quietly stepped off the road and into a field so that he could keep moving without them seeing him. It was slow going in the dark and he didn't have the benefit of a lamp. He hoped he wouldn't trip up and he also prayed that help would come, because he'd stand little chance against two of them. Sam did his best to catch up with them and he was almost there when he suddenly heard a commotion coming from the cottage. He could hear shouting and a loud banging noise. When he reached the gate, he could still hear the men shouting something and he could see flames rising outside the front door. To his horror he realised that they were intent on setting fire to the cottage. He left out a roar and charged towards them.

Dermot rounded on him, kicking him and knocking him to the ground.

Inside the cottage Jack heard the commotion and raced to the front door. When he opened it, all he could see were massive flames rising up in front of him.

Then he heard Dermot roaring, *"That's a present from our family who were ruined by Lord Beconsford taking away our farm and by you taking a job that should have gone to a local!"*

As Jack struggled to close the front door, he heard glass smashing and he could hear another voice shouting, *"That's from Toby Ramsay who said your Eliza was no great shakes in his bed!"*

Jack got such a shock at the words that he almost froze. Then he sprang back into action, slamming the door shut against the flames. He ran into his parlour to find flames leaping from a rug that was on the floor close to the shattered window pane. A flaming ball of oil-soaked cloth had been thrown through the window. He ran towards the rug and tried to bundle it and the cloth out the window, but the flames ignited his shirtsleeve and he felt a searing pain in his lower arm. At the same time Sam's voice could be heard screaming for him to get out.

Jack tore his shirt off as the flames still rose up from the rug. He grabbed the heavy hearthug and threw it over the flames. Then he raced to the kitchen and lifted a bucket of water standing there. Running back to the parlour, he emptied the bucket over the rug. Then he heard a shrill whistle, voices and running feet.

He ran again to the kitchen and poured cold water over his painful arm, remembering Old John saying cold water was very important for burnt skin. When he returned to the parlour, the fire was out. He looked out the shattered window and saw that Sam had now lifted the burning rags with a shovel and was banging the flames out on the gravel path.

Jack went and opened the front door. Its paint was burnt off.

He went outside and slumped to the grass in relief. As he sat holding his painful arm, he offered up a silent prayer of thanks that Eliza was not in the house when this happened.

As he sat in a dazed state, a trap drew up and an anxious and angry Robert joined him. Shortly after the law-and-order man, Mr. Black, arrived in his cart with Old John.

In the meantime, Sam had ventured around the back of the house, but soon returned shouting that they had got away. Mr. Black calmed him down and asked if he knew who they were and nobody was surprised to hear his answer.

"It was the O'Leary boys, Dermot and Brendan. They were laughing as they ran away – because they weren't afraid of me."

Mr. Black congratulated Sam on his efforts and offered to take Jack to the doctor in the town, but Jack insisted he didn't need a doctor – he had Old John.

149

"You're coming to our house, where we will decide what needs to be done," Robert said firmly.

Mr. Black dropped them at the farmhouse where the door opened and a frantic Eliza ran out. She was in tears as Sam helped Jack from the cart.

Old John was already telling Meg to fill a basin with cold water. In the kitchen, he gently placed Jack's angry red arm into the water. He then said he needed to collect some medicines from his house.

Robert told Sam and Old John to go back to the cottage with Mr. Black and collect Snugs and the trap there. Then Old John could collect what he needed.

"I'll tell the doctor to call in to Jack, even though he says he doesn't want him," said Mr. Black. "As for the O'Learys, I'm not used to that class of disorder in this town against decent people and you won't have to worry about them again after the law catches up with them."

Old John arrived back with an Aloe vera plant lotion. He was happy that the water had reduced the redness but he could see Jack's pain as he applied the lotion.

Eliza sat by Jack's side, trying hard not to appear anxious.

"Don't worry, Eliza," Old John said. "Your young man is going to be fine. You're a lucky young man, Jack, that both you and your house are safe, after what I heard from Sam."

As he finished applying the lotion there was a knock on the door and Doctor Lynch came through.

Jack was in pain, angry and in shock but most of all his mind was in turmoil at what the O'Leary man had said about Eliza.

As a relieved Meg now went to make tea for everyone, the doctor confirmed that Jack was lucky because of his quick thinking and that his burn would heal in a short time.

Lily, as usual, tried to lighten the moment. "Thank goodness it's his left arm and he can still write and draw and I'm sure that he will still look handsome when he marries my sister in the autumn!"

They all laughed at this.

"You're staying here tonight, Jack," said Meg, "and we'll see what will happen when we wake tomorrow. Thankfully you're alive and that's all that matters." Then she left to get the back bedroom warm for him.

Chapter 21

The following morning Mr. Black arrived at the farm to tell them that the O'Learys had not returned home the previous night.

"I have been told reliably that they have gone to Cork and I've already sent a message to the authorities in Cork to look out for them."

Jack was relieved that they wouldn't be back to work on the estate and, although he had a restless night, his pain was subsiding and he felt that one weight had been lifted off his shoulders.

Jack stayed a further night but on the following day he asked Eliza to take a walk with him. He said that he needed to go up and check the cottage. When they arrived, he asked her to sit with him on the bench at the side of the house, as he wished to talk to her.

She sat and looked at him, concerned. He looked upset

and Eliza wondered what was making him so troubled when his injuries were minor and the cottage was fine.

He put his head in his hands, then turned to her and said: "One of the O'Leary brothers said that the bundle of cloth thrown through the window was from Toby Ramsay and that you were not much good in his bed. Do you know why he said that?"

It was now Eliza's turn to put her head into her hands. She was utterly shocked as she tried to digest what that nasty man had now done to her.

She turned to Jack and looked into his eyes.

"I'm beginning to believe that everyone in life has some secrets that they have to endure alone because they are too difficult to disclose."

As Jack began to slump on the bench, she continued.

"You had your secret and I needed to know it but I truly believed you did not need to know about that odious man Toby Ramsay. What happened between that man and me did not happen in his bed." She sighed, trembling. "Shortly before you came home for Christmas, he tried to attack me at the summerhouse up in the estate. He followed me to the summerhouse and was questioning your character and suitability for a lady. I told him I wanted nothing to do with him and that incensed him. Then he grabbed me and tried to force me into the summerhouse. He was trying to pull my clothing off. I actually attacked him where I knew it would hurt him most." Embarrassment made her drop her head. "I was lucky to fight him off and I just kept running until I reached home. I didn't feel that I had the words to explain it to anyone. I actually felt ashamed and blamed myself because I felt maybe I had encouraged him in the past."

Jack flushed with anger. "*Why didn't you tell me when it happened!*" he almost shouted at her.

"*Because I didn't think any good would have come out of telling you!*" she shouted back while tears began to stream down her cheeks. "*Tell me – if I had, what would you have done?*"

"*I would have bloody killed him, that's what I would have done!*"

Eliza made an effort to control her emotions. "That's exactly why I didn't tell you," she said, "and it's exactly why I didn't tell my father. He would have had him put up in front of the magistrates and you look as if you would have swung for him. What good would any of this have been for me? I had to decide to do what was right for me and I choose to tell nobody and I don't regret it. If you don't want to marry me after that, it is your problem, not mine!"

They both sat apart in strained silence until Jack at last spoke.

"Eliza, I'm sorry. Please forgive me. I should be proud of you for the strength you showed in dealing with it. What a despicable man! I hope he has left the country because I'm warning you – if he ever shows his face in Midleton again he'll remember it."

In relief, Eliza put her arms around Jack and assured him, "He won't be back. He's too much of a coward."

After checking that the cottage was secure and that no

damage was done except to the rug, the window and the front door, they slowly walked back to the farmhouse with Eliza gently squeezing his hand to assure him of her love.

They agreed never to mention Toby Ramsay again.

Jack decided to stay in Mrs. Jennings' until after Isaac's wedding.

"I want to supervise the rest of the work in the garden and I should be able to do some of the final planting this week," he told her.

Back at the estate everyone warned him to be careful and to take it easy, but Jack assured them that he was fine.

In fact, he thought, as he lay in his bed in the inn that night, I'm really feeling better than I have for a long time and it's all down to finding a wonderful girl who showed outstanding courage when that despicable man attacked her, and had the strength to keep it all to herself in order to spare her father and me.

He drifted into a contented sleep.

Chapter 22

When Jack got to the farm on the morning of the wedding, he found Lily wild with the excitement of wearing her new dress. Meg was calm, wanting only to look her best in a sleek pale-lemon gown with a low neckline and a demure white lace chemisette underneath.

Eliza was excited at the thought of seeing Jack's first project, which would be opened after the church service. All three ladies had diamante clips lifting their hair and allowing curls escape from under their elegant wedding hats.

Robert, who looked very smart in his new knee breeches and highly polished boots, congratulated the ladies on their beauty as he kissed each one on the cheek. Eliza and Lily looked at each other and smiled as he kissed the blushing Meg.

Sam had the trap adorned with flowers. They were picking Jack up from the inn. As they set off into the warm sunshine on this bright early June morning, they felt a collective sense of happiness and anticipation as to what the day ahead would bring.

Deborah entered the estate chapel on the arm of her father, to the strains of "Lumen Hilare".

The bride wore a gown of blue satin with beading and shimmering silver trimmings. The dress was nipped in at the waist and layers of satin flowed gracefully until it touched the white-silk-covered shoes. The sleeves were puffed to the elbow. The tiny silver trimmings on the bodice were picked up as colour from the glow of the sun through the stained-glass windows. Her hair was lifted and adorned with a tiara that had been in the Beconsford family for two centuries. It held her long white veil in place. Flower petals were dropped onto the ground in front of her by Deborah's niece, six-year-old Serena. Her veil was held by two young page boys. There were six bridesmaids, including Helena, who looked lovely in her cream satin dress with a band of blue lace.

The groom turned to watch his bride and Eliza shed a tear as she saw the happiness in the eyes of her good friend Isaac.

The service was rich with music and singing and Jack was so proud when Eliza added her fine voice to the proceedings as she had been asked to sing a prayer of hope for the couple. She sang her favourite song, which Jack had first heard at Christmas.

"The sun goes down and darkness falls

The stars shine bright from dusk 'til dawn
The brightest star throws out a beam
That lights the way to follow your dreams."

The service ended and, after the couple kissed, they moved into the sacristy with their witnesses to sign the marriage register, before walking slowly down the aisle as the musicians played a joyous hymn.

Outside the doors of the church the estate workers formed a guard of honour. Rose petals were strewn in front of the bride and groom and cheers of goodwill were shouted by the happy but boisterous crowd.

The church guests would feast with Lord Beconsford's family but a separate event was to be held in the grounds with food being served under a canopy erected for all the staff. Musicians had been hired so that everyone could dance later on the lawn.

As the happy couple disappeared into the house, the wedding guests knew that they were to go to the covered walkway that the workers had constructed, connecting the side entrance of the house along a paved pathway leading to the decorative archway at the entrance to Deborah's Secret Garden. Isaac had arranged to leave the house with Deborah when the guests had formed a guard of honour. His wife would then enter her own secret garden for the first time.

Eliza felt so proud as they stood by the covered walkway. She couldn't wait to see the gardens that had been described so well to her by Jack.

It wasn't long before Isaac led a bewildered Deborah through the clapping guests to the ornate garden gate with the excellently crafted carved name in a semicircle that read "*Deborah's Secret Garden*".

They could hear her infectious laugh as Isaac opened the gate with a flourish and walked her into the splendour of the garden. She stopped in her tracks as she turned to hug her husband and Eliza had tears in her eyes as she got her first glimpse of the magnificent space Jack had created.

The circular middle of the garden had a rockery, with a fountain of water flowing over the rocks into a large circular pond. The pond was full of thriving fish swimming gracefully in the clear shining water. Four seating areas surrounded the pond. Standing tall at the end of the enclosed garden stood another water fountain. At the front of the fountain a small sculpture, of a young man and woman looking at each other, stood. Jack had secured it through the Dublin Society, where it had been brought from Italy.

As the married couple reached the fountain, Isaac gave Deborah a coin and told her it would bring them good luck if she dropped it in the fountain. She threw the coin into the water as everyone again cheered.

When Isaac asked for everyone to be quiet, silence descended. He told Deborah and the guests how the idea for the garden started. Jack turned red when he was praised but Eliza was so proud as she looked around at the four flower gardens, each giving a different view when you changed where you sat. Around the walls Jack had added low brick seats where people could catch the sun whatever time of the day it was. His final triumph was to recreate the small summerhouse he had sat in with Eliza near the river at Christmas time. This he placed closest to the house where it could be accessed through the covered walkway in any weather, in a corner where the splendour of the whole garden could be viewed. The small summerhouse was a picture of beauty, as the sun shone and reflected on its glass windows.

At the end of the speech, Deborah's father came over to Jack and said with a smile that he'd give Jack a job in Hertfordshire if he ever wanted one.

Jack smiled and thanked him, adding jokingly that he'd keep it in mind.

They all retired to the house. Jack and Eliza had never before seen a sight like the banquet laid out in the ballroom. Glittering chandeliers with candles lit up the room. The fine Wedgwood china and porcelain ware sat happily with crystal glasses and elegant cutlery. Large silver trays with venison and various other freshly cooked meats were carried by staff and served to the guests while other staff members filled plates high with vegetables. Sauces were added to suit all taste buds.

Lily sat with Helena and the bridesmaids and Eliza and Meg laughed as they saw her and Helena pay great attention to the handsome groomsmen.

Meg, who had got many compliments from people she

knew as they had walked from the church, told Eliza that she had never expected to have a day like this in her whole life. Later, the cook's rich fruit wedding cake was cut by the bride and groom and each guest received a piece of it.

When the speeches were finished and everyone was replete, they drifted out to the gardens, while the ballroom was being prepared for music and dancing later in the evening. When the food was cleared the staff were now able to enjoy the festivities and were joined by their families for the dancing on the lawn. Many of the guests, especially those from abroad, were fascinated by the Irish music and dancing and they too began to join in.

Jack asked Eliza to dance and they both stared in amazement when they saw Robert bounding around to the music with a very happy Meg on his arm.

"I never knew your father could dance," said Jack.

"I didn't either," laughed Eliza. "But don't they make a lovely couple? You know Meg is only in her mid-thirties. She came to live in our house when she was only a young girl."

"Maybe all the talk around the house of weddings might shift your father," laughed Jack.

As the evening sun began to set, the workers cleared up after their party and made their way back to their cottages. The newlyweds were waved away in the carriage on their way to firstly visit Isaac's good friends the Carden family in their estate in Templemore. They would then continue with Deborah's family to spend time in Hertfordshire before visiting Paris.

After the newlyweds left the estate, the partying continued in the ballroom and Eliza told Jack that someday they too would go to Paris together.

Robert was relaxed and enjoying his day. "Maybe we could all go to Paris – someday," he said with a smile.

They all raised their eyebrows, including Meg and Lily, as Robert had never shown any interest in going abroad before. Of course, they knew he had taken a little more whiskey than usual.

He put out his hand to Meg and beamed at his daughters as Meg stood up.

"I want to dance with the most delightful woman in the room!" he said.

They could all see that Meg's cheeks were crimson with either embarrassment or excitement as the fine-looking couple took to the floor again and danced.

As the night drew to a close, Robert asked Jack to join them in the farmhouse for a cup of tea before he returned to Rose Cottage for the first night since the O'Learys tried to end his life. Sam, who had enjoyed the celebrations with the workers, had gone home earlier. Snugs was waiting with a stable boy and Jack, who was the only one who had not been drinking, drove them home to the farm.

They were all in a happy mood as they sat about the table, enjoying reliving the best parts of the day just gone, when Robert cleared his throat and asked for quiet.

They immediately fell silent and looked at him as he rose to his feet.

"As you know, when Eliza gets married and Lily goes off with her fine friends to Europe, myself and Meg will be the only people on the farm, apart from Sam and the workers who come and go." He cleared his throat again and continued. "What you all don't know is that Meg and I have been chatting a lot lately about the future when you girls are out, and tonight I walked her down to Deborah's Secret Garden and she consented to marry me!"

There was a stunned silence, followed immediately by an outburst of delight from the girls who rushed to kiss them both.

"Well, isn't it about time!" laughed Lily.

Robert turned to a very happy Meg.

"Didn't I tell you they would be delighted?" he said, taking her hand in his.

"Will the wedding be soon?" Lily asked.

"No – we won't wed for a while," said Robert, "so that everyone can concentrate on Eliza and Jack's wedding after the harvest."

Chapter 23

The year of 1816 had seen massive storms that caused many seafarers to lose their lives, most of the countryside suffering rain-soaked fields and there were poor harvests for many farmers. 1817 brought back the sun. This year the plants and vegetables needed regular watering and during the September harvest Jack was kept busy around the estate. He loved soaking up new knowledge and the estate manager was delighted to teach him everything that was necessary to know about keeping natural growth in balance across the property. The cattle and the forest trees were important, but so too were the chicken and egg collections.

The herb garden planted by Old John was a favourite of Jack's and he regularly joined in to help tend the plot. Isaac had suggested he place it in the Secret Garden, so that there would always be a heady aroma in that peaceful space.

Jack wrote regularly to Gerry Harris in Dublin. They

were always sharing ideas, which Jack loved. On the home front, he was concerned with information his sister Julia had sent by post saying that their father had been seen in a public bar in the city centre with a woman. She wondered if she should tell her mother, but Jack cautioned against it. Jack was now an uncle to Julia's little boy Freddy, whom Jack couldn't wait to see. Jack didn't want Julia put under too much pressure when she was minding her young baby. He included some money to be spent on Freddy and told her to find out more about their father and discuss it with Hannah, before they did anything about it.

A plan had been agreed for the upcoming wedding of Jack and Eliza which would take place in Midleton. Jack was adamant that he didn't want his father to know about it. They were sending a carriage to collect Granny Sheila, his mother and the girls plus their men, in the centre of the city, on the day before the wedding. Jarad's mother was going to mind little Freddy for the few days. They would stay away for two nights, telling Septimius that they had to attend to Granny Sheila's sister in the country, who wasn't well. Molly wrote and told Jack that they barely saw Septimius these days and he would hardly miss them.

Jack was also thrilled that the Murray family, who had saved his life and his sanity, were coming from Tramore for the wedding. He had booked all the rooms in Mrs. Jennings' inn and she and her husband were overjoyed to be invited guests at the wedding. They were to be married in the estate chapel and Isaac had insisted that they use the magnificent downstairs dining area in the Dower House to hold the wedding celebrations. The Dower House was situated by the river and was used regularly by visitors to the estate. The housekeeper and cook from the Big House were delighted when asked to cater for the guests. It would not be a lavish affair but Jack couldn't wait for the day to arrive.

The harvest had been gathered and, as the leaves began to turn crisp and golden, the sunshine continued to cast its bright light across the landscape. Old John said the omens were good and the weather should be pleasant right up to Thursday the 25th of September, which was the day of the wedding.

On the eve of the wedding, Eliza met Jack's family when they arrived for a meal at the farm. The Turners took an immediate liking to Jack's Granny Sheila and his mother Molly.

"I'm so pleased to meet you all at last," said Granny Sheila, beaming, as all they sat at the table to eat. "I get nothing else in his letters but news about the Turner family, so I feel that I already know you all!"

Meg sat by her side with Molly on her other side and Meg was delighted with their praise for her culinary skills.

"You're cooking is up to hotel standard," Molly said while enjoying the succulent roast beef.

Meg's face flushed red with both pride and embarrassment as Robert agreed that Meg was the best cook in the county.

The three women soon looked like old friends as they

talked garden produce and recipes that had been passed down the generations.

Julia whispered to Jarad, "Aren't the two sisters beautiful?"

All the younger folk were enjoying getting to know each other. Once Lily started to talk fashion and wedding dresses, Jack thought how lucky he was to have his two families so comfortable with each other.

As the wine flowed, Robert stood up and gave a small speech.

"I want to propose a toast to Eliza and Jack, but I also want us to remember those who are no longer with us, in particular my wife, Kathleen. I also wish you to raise a glass to a wonderful substitute mother for my two beloved girls." As he turned to Meg his smile was enough. "To you, Meg, for the wonderful care you have given to Eliza and Lily. Finally, I wish to welcome the Ryan family into our home and hope we continue to have you all in our lives in the future."

As everyone stood up to leave for the inn, Eliza squeezed Jack's hand and they both sighed with relief that the family meal had been a success.

When the Ryan family returned to the Haven Inn, hats and shoes and some dresses that had been bought in Cork by Granny Sheila for all her family had been delivered by the shops. This was necessary as they could not buy a lot of new things all together without arousing Septimius's suspicions. For the same reason they could carry little luggage. They had left a note stating that Sheila's sister needed them urgently and ample money for him to spend while they were gone.

Before Jack returned to Rose Cottage, he had a word in Granny Sheila's ear but she informed him that she knew about Septimius and his lady friend. They both agreed that something needed to be done to save Molly from hurt in the future.

The following morning a very nervous Jack was supported by his family and friends as he waited at the top of the church for his Eliza to arrive. The organ played as a very proud Robert walked his eldest daughter up towards her husband to-be. Her dress had layers of muslin and an overdress of cream satin. A choker around her neck was beaded with small pearls. Her hair was lifted and a pearl wreath sat on her head, making her look, in Jack's eyes, like a goddess. Her veil flowed over her sleek hair towards the ground and was held up by Lily and Helena.

Jarad was at Jack's side as the organ played and the bride and her smiling father walked up the aisle. Jack turned and with a shaking voice whispered, "I love you."

Later Jack would maintain that he could remember little of the service until he heard Eliza say, "I do."

After the vows were taken Jack and Eliza looked at each other and both had tears of joy in their eyes as they sealed their marriage with a kiss.

The food provided by Isaac and Deborah, as their gift to the happy couple, was as wonderfully presented as if they were members of the Beconsford family. After the meal Jack gave a speech of thanks to everyone in the room and asked his bride if she would sing for him. Eliza knew this was coming and, as she sang with Lily at the piano, everyone listened in admiration as the words of love brought joy to everyone.

"When your heart lets you know that it's time to let go
Of some people, places and things,
Hold your head up high and reach for the sky
As the dawn of a new day begins."

As the last song came to an end there were tears in many eyes and Granny Sheila was shaking her head in wonder at the talented and admirable wife her grandson had married. She felt she could deal with anything in the future now that all the family, except her daughter Molly, were secure. But she had plans in her head to deal with Molly's future.

Then Isaac asked for quiet as he made an announcement.

"I want to congratulate my dear friend Eliza for finding a husband who is not only my friend now, but has been a wonderful addition to the staff of the estate. I just have one important announcement to make. Eliza, you might not be spending too much time living in your new cottage, because, as some of you know, our longstanding estate manager Maurice Howard will be retiring soon and is moving with his wife Edith, because their son has got a fine position in West Cork. Maurice and Edith want to move closer to their grandchildren. Therefore, with Maurice's agreement," Isaac smiled as he nodded towards his estate manager, "we are offering Jack Ryan the position of Estate Manager from the start of next year. This means that if Jack accepts, he and Eliza will be moving into what I know is a delightful house, on the estate."

There was cheering from everyone, as Jack made his way to Isaac's side and hugged him as if he was his brother. He called Eliza to join him and they both embraced Deborah. Then Isaac took Eliza's hand and thanked her for being such a good friend to his wife since she had first arrived in Ireland.

Jack and Eliza had been generously offered and had accepted the senior guest bedroom in the Big House for the first night of their wedding, before leaving to join their friends Gerry and Rose Harris the following night in Tipperary, prior to travelling with them on to Dublin.

Jack had a quick word in Eliza's ear and, as she smiled and nodded, he took himself in the direction of his granny, who thanked him for giving her such effusive thanks in his speech. They both smiled and Jack asked her if she would come to the garden for a few quiet moments.

As they sat in the summerhouse, within the Secret Garden, Jack took her hand and thanked her for everything she had made possible for him.

"I have another reason for asking you out here, Granny Sheila. I had a word with Eliza after Isaac's speech and we both agreed to invite yourself and my mother to live in Rose Cottage, when we move to the estate manager's house in the New Year. Of course, it is you who paid for it anyway and I'm just returning it!"

"Nonsense, young Jack!" Sheila smiled. "Of course it belongs to you, but I believe that it fits into my future plan for your mother very nicely."

Jack lifted his eyebrows and waited.

"I had been planning to sell off the market garden as I got a good offer from Fergus Murphy who farms up on the Bandon Road. He'd like to buy it for his son, who is getting married. He thinks it makes sense to have market garden produce for sale close to the city centre. I had agreed with your mother that I would give Septimius a good sum to leave. Then me and Molly would buy a house at the other side of town near where Hannah is living. Your offer now sounds almost too good to be true." She lifted his hand and held it to her cheek. "You were always a good grandson and to end up living near you would be heaven on earth and I know your mother will feel the same."

Jack and Eliza left the party and went to their elegant room overlooking the secret garden. As Jack stood, holding Eliza tightly, they watched the moon shining brightly on the gardens below. As they turned to face each other with shining eyes filled with love, they both knew that tonight would seal a love that would never die.

The following morning, after Rose and Gerry had departed, Eliza and Jack smiled and waved at all their family and friends as they left in the estate carriage that was taking them to an inn in County Tipperary that Gerry had recommended and had been booked for both couples, way back in the spring.

Eliza and Jack had plenty of time to enjoy each other's company on the journey.

They sat in the cosy carriage and, as Jack gazed at Eliza, she laughed.

"I think you have lost your tongue, husband," she said with a laugh.

"I don't have to speak to show you my love," he retorted as he reached to hold her in his arms and sealed his love with an urgent kiss.

He then looked at her solemnly.

"I want to promise that you will be loved and cherished all my life."

Eliza answered with a smile and promised him anything if he would just seal it with another long kiss!

The inn had pulled out all the stops for the newly married couple. Eliza's father had sent money ahead for a bottle of the best wine and an expensive dinner. Having enjoyed the company of Rose and Gerry early in the evening, the newly married couple adjourned to their splendid large bedroom, complete with a dining table by the window, overlooking a garden rich with flowers. The table was covered with a fresh Irish linen cloth and two candles threw light onto the Waterford crystal glasses and wine goblets. The cutlery was the best silver and Isaac and

Deborah had sent flowers from the Beconsford Estate that were rich with colour and scent. They were in a crystal vase, with a card wishing them well from the staff of the estate. In the centre of the wall, a log fire burned brightly.

They both laughed at the grandeur of it all and agreed that they wouldn't want to get too used to their luxurious surroundings! Dinner was served by the owner of the inn and, as Jack and Eliza relaxed with the delicious drinks, they stood at the window together and watched the moon and stars in the distant sky.

No words were needed while the silence of their deep love filled the room and consumed them both, as they set out on the first stage to their journey towards a future that was yet to unfold.

Part 2

Chapter 24

1829, Midleton

Eliza sat on a large comfortable garden chair, designed by her husband Jack and built of the finest oak. She smiled indulgently at the three delightful children playing on the lawn of her home, known as the estate manager's house. It was the first day of summer and it was also her daughter Margarita's 9th birthday.

Margarita at nine years was tall for her age with dark hair just like that of her parents. It was tied back with an elaborate red-silk bow, as she raced around the grounds with her Aunt Alice who was less than a year older than her. They were chasing their older friend, Victor Beconsford, who would someday be lord of the Big House. Margarita was much more outgoing than her wonderful parents, much to their delight. She had a ready smile and had inherited her mother's large alluring eyes. She had also inherited her musical ability plus the diligent work ethic of her parents. She brought an enthusiasm to everything she did, whether it was her schoolwork or her singing. Eliza thought her only blind spot was her hero worship of Victor Beconsford.

Shortly after her own marriage to Jack twelve years ago, Eliza had happily prepared for the marriage of her father Robert to Meg, his wonderful housekeeper. Eliza fondly remembered her time preparing for their wedding in the summer of 1818 and the excitement when Robert and Meg announced that they wanted Jack, Eliza and Lily to join them on a trip to Paris and Florence to celebrate with them. Robert had announced that he had enough money to indulge his new wife and his daughters in a dream trip and that Jack would now see the gardens, statues and fountains that he longed so much to see.

Meg announced shyly before they agreed: "I want you all to know that it would seal my love for my family to have you all join us."

Lily, as ever, was the first to agree. "I'd be very happy to accept a free holiday with all my family," she joked, as she hugged Meg and almost lifted her off the ground.

Paris was awe-inspiring but Florence, in particular, held enduring memories for Eliza that were still as vivid as if it were only yesterday. At bedtime she always kept those memories alive by telling her young daughter about the wonders of Europe. When they had arrived back from Italy, Jack was full of things he had seen, especially the richness of art and the beauty of the buildings and palazzi, from Gothic to Renaissance. When they stayed in Florence Eliza found as much delight at her husband's enthusiasm as being enthralled when listening to extraordinary Italian singers. After a wonderful month away, they returned home with memories that would stay with them forever.

On their arrival back in Ireland, Isaac and Deborah had by then produced an heir to the Beconsford line. As she watched Victor Beconsford, who was now nearly twelve years old, chasing the two girls around the garden, she felt some sadness as he would be going to England to school in the autumn, to prepare him for his future role as the heir to the manor. She knew the two girls would be devastated when he left. Eliza had been a tutor to all three since they started their education.

Looking at young Alice Turner running around the garden, Eliza was reminded of when Meg and Robert had sprung their big surprise when they announced all those years ago that they were to marry, but it was even a more wonderful surprise when soon after Meg fell pregnant. Alice was born during the summer that followed. Alice was much loved by everyone. She was easy-going and could adapt to almost every situation. She was less interested in school learning than Margarita but she loved sewing, stitching and knitting warm scarves for herself and her family. You could always rely on young Alice to produce warm and bright knitwear as a Christmas or birthday gift. Meg said that she could see her with a shop making stylish gowns for the rich when she was older.

Eliza smiled as her little half-sister now ran around the garden with Margarita, racing after Victor. Although Alice was Margarita's aunt, they were best friends and were more like sisters. Both Meg and Eliza were delighted by the closeness of their children as neither had siblings.

The year that Alice was born had also seen Lily getting engaged in London to Helena Beconsford's good friend Robb Chamberlain. Everyone was shocked but delighted with the news. Eliza, in particular, would miss her little sister who was now destined to live her life out in Hertfordshire, close to Helena's estate, where she and her husband Neville lived. Helena had got her wish to live her life away from her difficult parents. The two couples were very close friends and loved their lives near London.

Sadly, at that time when everyone seemed to be having babies, Eliza had not yet shown any signs of getting pregnant. When Alice Turner was born the excitement that possessed the family was unprecedented. Everyone was happy for them and Robert had an added spring to his step that Eliza had rarely seen before. It was during this time that Eliza shared the news with Jack that she was pregnant. They did not spread the news for months, as Jack seemed extra nervous that something might go wrong. At times, Eliza felt he worried too much, but she understood why. Life could be so fragile and he wanted this baby so much. Margarita Ryan was born in 1820 on the 1st of May. They called her after an opera singer that Eliza had heard and loved when they were in Rome. Margarita had a head of black hair and the same arresting blue eyes as her mother. Jack believed that she was the most precious child that had ever been born and Eliza laughingly agreed.

Everything was ready for a birthday tea for Margarita later in the day. As she sat on the chair, Eliza reflected over her life so far with Jack. Her thoughts brought back nothing but joy to her. She recalled her marriage and how things had changed since then.

Jack's Granny Sheila and his mother Molly had arrived to live in Rose Cottage in the spring of 1818. The sale of the market garden in Friarsland had gone through and the sum given to Septimius was large enough for him to disappear with his younger woman and nobody ever heard from him again. Since arriving in Midleton, Granny Sheila had started to help Old John with his healing herbs and plants by growing some in the gardens of Rose Cottage. Jack's mother Molly turned out to be the best pastry chef in Midleton and she worked happily in Mrs. Sexton's bakery. Molly had also become great friends with Laura Jennings of the Haven Inn and, if she wasn't with her, she was at home helping her mother with the herbs. Eliza often wondered, when Old John called to the cottage so often, if it was for an update on herb growing or to be with Molly! Eliza believed that Old John had a soft spot for Molly but maybe he was too set in his ways to do anything about it.

As Margarita ran around the garden on her ninth birthday, her permanently happy smile was that of someone who was not only beautiful but who knew she was much loved. As Eliza continued to enjoy the sight of the three friends, she reflected on the fact that she and Deborah would have loved more children, but it never happened for either of them. Meg and Robert were more than content with their Alice. Deborah and Eliza had often consoled each other by agreeing that were lucky to have such great children.

Eliza's contented life had changed little since she married. On afternoons when Margarita spent time with her Aunt Alice, up at the farm with Meg and Robert, Eliza continued to give lessons to children in the estate and also to a group of children in the town who had little chance of education. Jack had also given of his time and expertise to the town by creating a small garden where adults could sit and children could play in safety. It was built with Isaac's financial help and situated in the poorest area of the town. Jack's future vision for the town was to see an improvement in water supply for the poor and he sometimes shook his head in despair at the poverty some people were forced to live in.

As Eliza reflected on these issues, she knew that neither of them could change the world but needed to be content to make a little difference, where possible. Her thoughts were interrupted when Victor raced up to her, ahead of the girls.

"*We're all starving and want something to eat, please!*" he shouted as he ran.

Eliza smiled as she told him to slow down. Victor was impulsive and always spoke before thinking. Perhaps it was just as well he was off to school in England as he needed to learn to stop and think more often, Eliza thought. The two girls adored him and it seemed likely that as they got older, if he stayed around, Victor was likely to make them into daredevils!

She smiled as all three clamoured around her.

"The party won't happen until all the guests arrive," said Eliza. "But you can go and get apple juice and a biscuit each from Ann Marie in the kitchen – just don't get in her way!"

They ran off towards the house. Ann Marie was the eldest from a poor family in the town, but her mother wanted her to learn to read and write and when she was thirteen Jack and Eliza had given her a job. That was three years ago and she now had a high level of reading and writing skills and she still hadn't left their employ. Eliza knew that Ann Marie wanted her younger brothers to be ready for work before she thought of her own future. The money that Eliza and Jack paid her and the food she brought home daily was more than a blessing for her family. Ann Marie had ambition and Eliza continued to educate her. Eliza had already begun to use Ann Marie's skills to help at her school in the village.

When the children reappeared, Eliza suggested, "Come and sit in the garden. You can greet the guests." She could hear people arriving by the sound of the gravel on the estate driveway. But she knew the children would do anything but sit still while waiting for the party to begin.

The garden had trellis tables set up. Chairs were brought out for all the guests and Meg and Robert had sent extra chairs in the cart. Nelly had taken over from Snugs who had been retired, and Robert had also bought a small elegant carriage. Sam still worked as hard as ever on the farm and was a very proficient carriage driver.

Soon all of the adults were seated. The children's parents were joined by Molly, Granny Sheila and Old John. Ann Marie was heaped with praise for the meat sandwiches and fruit bowls, placed close to a big jug filled with whipped cream made to go with the apple and rhubarb pies. Molly had made the perfect birthday cake, with Margarita's name written on it. There was a lot of cheering when she was allowed cut her own cake and each of the visitors gave her a little gift as she walked around giving each a slice.

She finally came to Eliza and Jack and she smiled, waiting for her gift. They asked first if she would sing for her guests as they all loved to hear her sweet voice. She stood at the head of the table and, without any fear, she sang a song about a robin who sat on her windowsill. Everyone knew that Margarita had an exceptional voice and Eliza encouraged her by getting the church organist to help bring her voice to fruition. Everyone clapped and all agreed that she should be on the stage, yet Margarita seemed to have no understanding of the effect her voice had on those who heard her sing.

The only people who were not interested in her singing were Victor and Alice who were hopping up and down behind her to see what present she was getting. Her parents had a small box on the table and they told her to open it. Inside was a delicate silver locket in the shape of a heart. They told her to open it and when she did so she found inside the locket a tiny sketch of her face at one side and another of her mama and dada at the other side. Eliza explained that her dada had sketched them for her. As she stared in wonder at her gift, Alice and Victor were bouncing around her to try and see what she was looking at.

When Eliza put it around her neck, Margarita said, "I am never going to take it off."

Everybody laughed as Eliza explained that she'd have to keep it in the box at night.

"Well," said Margarita, "I'll keep the box under my pillow every night!"

"I think we get the message that you like your present," said Jack, as she put her arms around him to give him a big hug.

As the children ran off to open the other presents, Eliza and Jack looked at each other, remembering the day he had given her a similar gift, before they married.

Having enjoyed the tea and cakes, all the adults relaxed in the sun. The early summer evening brought great delight to Eliza as she watched all the people she loved sitting under the shade of apple blossom amid a garden still full of daffodils plus early summer blooms. As the shadows began slowly to cover the lawn, everyone agreed that it had been a grand day.

When her guests departed, Eliza wondered if future birthdays would be different, when Victor was away in England. She thought that perhaps they should hold next year's party later when Victor returned from his school. She also thought that perhaps Victor would not be as interested in the girls when he next returned to Ireland and that made her sad. When she mentioned this to Jack later, he told her that she could be right, but that children have to make their own way in life.

"Much as we'd like to, we can't keep them young and innocent forever," he added.

Reluctantly, Eliza had to agree with him.

It seemed that Jack was right about children growing up and taking different paths.

During the following years, Victor Beconsford grew tall and just as handsome as his father. Each time he returned from England he seemed to have grown another couple of inches. While the two girls still longingly craved his attention, he spent less and less time with them. Alice didn't seem to mind too much as she had made friends with some of the grandchildren of Robert's friends but Eliza could see that Margarita missed the fun she had when they had all been in school together. Eliza knew that Margarita had got some letters from Victor during the years he was at school in England. She was somewhat concerned that her young daughter was going to grow up hankering after a boy who would be likely to marry into the gentry. Jack told her not to worry, that it was a childish affection for her friend.

When Victor was sixteen, he moved from his school in England to live with his Aunt Helena's family in Hertfordshire, before going to the University of Oxford. That was the first summer that Victor did not come home to Ireland. He was learning estate management in Hertfordshire. Instead, Deborah and Isaac went to England to visit him.

Eliza could see that Margarita was heartbroken at his decision to stay in England. But, she thought, perhaps it was for the best.

Chapter 25

1836

Eliza was sitting alone in the Secret Garden, which Deborah had always urged her to enjoy, whenever she needed some peace. She was embroidering a handkerchief as a birthday gift for Alice.

Then she heard the cheerful voice of Deborah.

"Eliza!"

"Oh!" Eliza exclaimed in delight. "I thought you were not returning from England until tomorrow! This is a lovely surprise!"

She stood up and held her friend in a hug. Then, as she released her, she noticed that she was not looking as happy as usual. "Are you feeling well, Deborah?"

"Not really," said Deborah. "I'm so glad I've caught you alone, Eliza. I may have a problem and I'd like your advice."

"Of course, I will help if I can," she assured her. "Come and sit here."

"It's Victor I'm worried about. He has made a decision that he's not going back to Oxford in September. He says he just wants to start his work on the estate. His father and I told him that the estate would always be there for him in the future and that he's too young to make such a major decision."

"But would you not be happy to see him return to Ireland?" asked Eliza.

"Of course, I would," said Deborah. "But that is only half of the problem. I know he looks much older than his years, as he is so strong and tall, but I know also that while I love him dearly, he has an impulsive side to him and that is why I'm worried. On our last trip, he kept talking about Fleur Montgomery, the daughter of a family friend from Cambridgeshire. She sounded like a very lovely young woman but he announced to us last week that he wants to marry her! And not just in the future! He'd like to marry her before the year ends and bring his bride back to live here! There's no changing his mind but I want to know what to do!"

Eliza said nothing for a few moments as she tried to control her racing heart. She had known that at some stage Victor would marry into his own class, but she thought it would be later rather than sooner. She knew also that her sensitive young daughter Margarita would be heartbroken because she had always hero-worshipped him. Both girls did when they were young, but Alice was more like her Aunt Lily, exuberant and enthusiastic over invites to various houses where she loved to meet lots of boys who were present. Margarita was more serious and set more store on lasting friendships. Up to now her singing was her passion and Eliza just hoped that it would see her through the loss of her best friend to his new wife.

"What does your family in Hertfordshire think?" asked Eliza.

"They are somewhat concerned about how young he is – however, they think that if he is to marry, he has picked a good girl in Fleur. She has two younger sisters and an older brother. Fleur's siblings have known sorrow, because their mother, who had always been delicate, passed away eight years ago. A weakened heart. Her determined spirit wasn't enough to keep her alive. Just like your family, Eliza, when your mother Kathleen died and Meg stepped in, they too have a brilliant nursemaid who took over the role and has managed to keep the family on an even keel ever since."

"Well, I agree with you, Deborah, that he always went into everything with enthusiasm, but marriage is for a lifetime and he needs to understand that he's given himself no time to travel, as his Aunt Helena and our Lily did, nor to live the bachelor life at university for a few years. I think you need to tell him all of this and then just let him make up his own mind. However, you need to emphasise that yourself and Isaac will always support him, whatever the future brings. One can do no more than that."

They talked a little about other matters, watching the shadows lengthen and listening to the birdsong competing with the soothing sound of the waterfall nearby.

When they left the garden, they hugged and, as Deborah returned to the Big House, still thinking of her beloved son, Eliza walked through the estate towards her home, wondering how she would tell her daughter that Victor might marry sooner rather than later. Margarita was sensitive but deep, and Eliza did not always know what was going on in her head. She had an ability to hide her feelings and appear stoic even though she was still so young.

Chapter 26

Margarita Ryan was humming happily as she picked a selection of pretty flowers from their garden. She was smiling to herself because she was shortly going to be teaching, alongside her mother, on a fulltime basis. She had so many ideas in her head as to how she would teach the estate children and what work she would be preparing for the poorer children of the town, whom her mother, assisted by Ann Marie, had been teaching for some years. She knew that she was going to put singing up near the top of her list and planned to teach them to sing as a choir, even if many didn't have perfect singing voices. How happy music made her! She hummed as she clipped the stems of the flowers. She believed that singing might be a way of bringing children together to work as a group. Then perhaps they would help each other when they had difficulties with their reading and writing. She was glad that her mama agreed with the idea. Margarita's forward-thinking view was that if you could make learning fun, then the children would be more likely to keep coming.

Isaac was funding the classes in Midleton, where they now had the use of a parish hall. This meant that they could afford to buy milk and bread to give to the children when they arrived each morning, as many would have had nothing to eat since their supper. Indeed, Eliza said that many came because of the food!

She waved at her mother, who was coming through the trees. Then she noticed that she had a very thoughtful look on her face.

"Are you all right, Mama?" she asked.

"I'm fine, my love," replied Eliza. "What lovely flowers you have picked!" She smiled at her adored daughter. "Put them in water and place them on the table. We can enjoy looking at them while we eat." She knew how artistic her daughter was and how she arranged the flowers so perfectly. She usually added small branches from trees and that made them a delight to behold.

"I might teach the estate children how to arrange flowers, when the school reopens," Margarita said, as her mother laughed.

"You will have all these children so spoiled that I'll never get them to learn their adding and subtracting."

Margarita smiled at her mother. "You know they love you but some of them need a bit of fun in their lives."

"Of course, you are right, love, and I can't wait for you

to join me each day, but you must not forget your own music and singing. Remember your father and I want you to fulfil your dreams regarding your singing."

Margarita nodded her head enthusiastically. "You know how much I love my singing, Mama, and since I've been working on my breathing exercises Master Johnson is very impressed with the improvement in my voice. But I'm also very much enjoying writing my poems."

Eliza knew that Margarita hoped that someday she could turn those poems into songs. "You must let me see your latest ones."

As Eliza looked at her happy daughter, she wondered how she'd tell her of Victor's future plans. She looks so happy just now, she thought. I hope she can get past this without too much heartache. She decided she'd talk to Jack first.

"Let's go in and help Ann Marie with the evening meal as your father will be starved when he gets in from work," she said.

Eliza had a word with Jack before supper and they agreed that she should tell Margarita about Victor before she heard it from elsewhere.

"After you have spoken to her tell her to come in to me in the music room and I will take it from there," said Jack. "Margarita is going to be devastated, but it was always coming down the track, unfortunately. She's had a wonderful life up to now, with a supportive mother and so many relatives and friends who love her also. She'll deal with it. She has a lot of strength in her. She's a watcher of people, unlike sociable Alice, but she'll cope."

"I hope you're right," said Eliza as she offered up a silent prayer.

Later Eliza asked Margarita if she would like a walk to the summerhouse to watch the sun go down over the river. Margarita was happy to do so, as she wanted to talk about a few more of her ideas on teaching, in the hope that her mama would approve.

They walked along the pathway that led through the forest.

"There's something I need to talk to you about, my love," Eliza said as they approached the summerhouse.

Margarita wondered if it was about her Great-granny Sheila because she had noticed how thin and frail she had become lately. The whole family loved Granny Sheila so much that they would be devastated if anything happened to her.

"Is it about Granny Sheila?" she asked, as they reached the door.

"No, no, although I'm a bit concerned about her too. It's another matter," Eliza said. "Let's sit down and watch the sun go down over the valley. I've brought a couple of sweets for us to munch while we sit!"

Margarita was always ready for a sweet. Eliza always had a treat for her in the past if she grazed her knees when out playing with Victor and Alice. As she munched, she wondered what this was all about.

Eliza hesitated then forced herself to start. "You know that Victor has been at university in Oxford."

Margarita nodded.

"Well, he's made a decision to leave and learn land management instead."

"Oh, he never mentioned that to me when he wrote. I thought he was very happy in the university," said a puzzled Margarita.

"That's not all, love," said Eliza as she took her daughter's hand and gave it a squeeze.

"What's wrong, Mama? Is he not well? You have me worried now!"

"No, his health is fine," said Eliza sadly, as she squeezed more firmly on Margarita's hand. "He says that he wants to get married to a girl he met in England."

Margarita stared with a shocked expression at her mother.

"Is he not coming back to Ireland ever again to live?" she asked, as tears began to well up in her eyes.

"He is," continued Eliza, "but he wants to bring his new wife to live here in the estate, where he'll learn everything about running an estate from Isaac and your father."

Eliza was about to put her arm around Margarita's shoulder but her daughter jumped up abruptly and asked, in a cold voice, "When is this happening?"

"Well, Deborah and Isaac are trying to slow things down but we all know how impulsive Victor is and when he makes up his mind, he is hard to shift."

Margarita started to walk away from the summerhouse.

"I'm going back to my room. I have a lot of work to get ready for school, so don't disturb me."

Eliza hurried after her. She saw that Margarita was very close to bursting into tears.

"Please, Margarita, just do one thing for me before you go to your room. Your father wants to talk to you in the music room. He wanted to be with me because we both know how fond you are of Victor. So, please give him a few minutes and let him at least give you a hug."

Jack heard them returning and he walked into the hall in time to see Margarita in front, looking mutinous, in a way he'd never seen her before.

"Eliza, will you ask Ann Marie to make some tea for myself and Margarita?"

Apprehensive, Eliza silently left.

Jack put his arm around his daughter and led her into the music room. He sat her in the soft chair opposite to where he was sitting.

"What are you thinking, love?" he asked quietly.

"Why could he not have told me himself, in his letters?" she asked angrily. "We've been best friends for life and he couldn't even tell me! Does everyone know? Am I the last to be told?"

"No, lass, it's only your mother, Deborah and Isaac that know."

Ann Marie came in and fussed over Margarita, giving her a hot bun that had come straight off the baking tray.

Jack turned to his daughter when Anne Marie left.

"I know you have a soft spot for Victor, but you're very young and you have years ahead of you to meet many suitors. You're charming, talented and loved by everyone who knows you."

As Jack talked, the tears slowly began to flow from his daughter's eyes.

"But I love him and I don't want to meet anyone else."

Jack rose and went to sit beside her. Putting his arm around her, he promised, "It won't always hurt, my love, but cry for him now. I can promise you that you are too strong and talented to let this moment define your life. You're like your mother and Granny Sheila. You will survive."

They sat for a long time talking, with their tea untouched. Margarita was hard to console and something inside Jack broke again as he thought back to his own dark night of the soul from which he did eventually emerge with the love of so many people. Maybe he did worry about everyone too much and wanted to keep everyone safe but he felt that finally maybe tonight was the night he should tell someone other than Eliza about that fateful night in January 1816.

As Margarita at last took some comfort, by laying her head on her father's shoulder, he asked her if he could tell her something about his own life.

"Something only your mother knows," he added. "It may allow you understand how we've both cosseted you and stopped anything bad happening in your life. You're now reaching adulthood, what with starting your teaching job and your music going so well. Life, Margarita, is full of twists and turns and sometimes along that road you come to a brick wall and need to choose which way to travel. You might make wise choices or you might make mistakes but try not to regret the past, because it happens and you can't go back and change it. In 1816 I met that wall and I spent a long time trying to go back in my mind and have it changed. I wanted the past to be better. But I couldn't, of course, because it was the past and just like your friendship with Victor, while it might always be there, it is not possible for you to control what Victor does with his life. You on the other hand can control how you react to it. It can either define your future or with the support of all your family it can strengthen you going forward when it is only you who make the choices and decisions. Do you understand me, lass, because I'm not sure I understand what I'm saying myself?" He saw the hint of a smile on her lips and asked her if she wanted to hear his story.

She nodded.

"It's a very sad story, love, but I think I need to tell it and I think it's time you knew."

Jack began to tell the story, slowly. He started by telling her why he went to sea, although she always knew that her father was missing and hadn't been heard of for many years. He told her of the beating he sustained on his 18th birthday and told her of his time at sea. He hesitated before continuing his story regarding the horrific memories of the sinking of the *Seahorse*.

"I was homesick for my country. I had recurring dreams

of seeing myself standing in the middle of four green fields while looking up at the stars and I knew it was the call of Ireland pushing me to return to the land. I was full of joy as I made the journey home with all the soldiers and their families returning after the Napoleonic wars. They too were all joyful on that fateful day."

He paused to hold his daughter closer to his heart in the hope that she wouldn't see his tears flow.

"When we reached the coast of Ireland the weather changed and a storm blew up the likes of which I had never seen before. Panic set in as the ships' anchors were dropped." Jack hesitated again before continuing. "I stood on deck with a family and I prayed with them as the ship fought the relentless battle against the winds. It lost the battle and the boat heaved for the last time and everyone ended up fighting for their lives in the ocean near the town of Tramore. I was one of the small number of people saved on that day, thanks to the part played by Ellen and Cornelius Murray's son Henry who found me unconscious at the edge of the sea. Every single night Henry would sit with me until I fell asleep. Then, when I woke with nightmares, either Ellen, Cornelius or Henry would sit on my bed until I fell yet again into a fitful sleep. That's the reason, my love, that you always called them 'Auntie' and 'Uncle' and Henry your cousin. They saved my life that night and later they helped me to stop feeling guilty because I lived while so many others died. That has always been the hard part. The guilt."

As darkness fell and the only light was a flickering candle on the table, they both cried over the loss of so many people off the Irish coast on that fateful day. Margarita had in the past heard around the village about the losses that occurred during that storm, but in recent years very little was said about it.

As Jack held his daughter close to his heart, he stayed quiet and still. The only sound in the room was that of the timber crackling in the hot embers of the fire as they felt the dampness of tears rolling down both their cheeks. He then decided that the time had finally come to lay every ghost from the past that had cast a shadow on his younger self.

"Before we finish, Margarita, I need to tell you a story about a little girl with blonde curls and a sweet smile. Her name was Angel and you are the first person to whom I've ever spoken her name."

Jack recounted his first meeting with Angel and her family and his final promise to help them, as the children clung to their parents before being swept overboard.

"Angel, her brother and their parents all perished on that terrible day."

He finished the story by wiping Margarita's tears from her face with his handkerchief and telling her that was why every year he tried to make one trip to Tramore to offer a prayer of thanks for his life and to kneel by the sea and remember those who died, especially Angel. Margarita felt numbed by her father's revelation. She listened to her heart racing as she put her arms around him. She now shed tears for her father whose terrifying experience she couldn't even imagine. They held each other tight until Jack moved and touched her cheek with his fingers, wiping her tears away.

"Go and give your mama a hug. She is the one who saved me from despair all these years ago."

After Margarita had gone to bed, Jack and Eliza sat by the fire, holding each other's hands while each stayed silent, lost in their own thoughts of things long past. Later that night as Jack lay next to Eliza in the darkness, he allowed his tears to flow, as he finally told his beloved Eliza the full story of his memory of Angel, the little girl whose life ended at seven years of age, off the coast of southern Ireland. Eliza listened to him, feeling deep sadness and gratitude that maybe he had finally laid the ghosts of the shipwreck to rest. She then held him close as she knew, yet again, that no more words were needed.

Chapter 27

Margarita lay on her bed, covered with a cool soft sheet and a patchwork quilt lovingly created by her Granny Molly. Yet its softness did not dispel the hurt she felt as her tears continued to flow and sleep refused to claim her. She was glad her father had told her of his near-death experience, because it gave her something to think about other than Victor. She knew that but for that fateful night, her mama would never have met her dear father. She also gave thanks for the Murray family, especially Henry who saved him from certain death. She tucked the thought into her heart that she would talk to the Murray family in the future to understand more about her father during that frightening time in his life.

Victor kept returning to her thoughts, as the small cracks of light heralded the dawn. Yet this brought her no nearer to sleeping. Having got over the furious anger that she felt when her mother told her, she now clung to her father's reasoning that it was something over which she had no control. But how was she going to take his advice to stop feeling overwhelmed by the fact that Victor was lost to her? Her Granny Molly was always using the saying, "Ah sure, time heals everything!" but Margarita needed to know how and when this happens. She also kept telling herself that her father told her to stay strong.

As the rising sun finally broke through the darkness, she closed her eyes and kept repeating to herself "I must stay strong," as she finally cried herself to sleep.

When Margarita woke later that morning, she had a sick feeling in her stomach and struggled for a moment to remember why. As she sat up with the full brightness of the sun flooding her room, she quickly remembered.

There was a quiet tap on the door and her mother slowly opened it. She was carrying a cup of tea, with some hot bread that had been toasted by the kitchen fire. She sat on the side of the bed and held her daughter's hand.

"Your father told me that you know about the *Seahorse*. I'm glad he told you," she said. "I shouldn't even ask how you are feeling, but you can rest for the morning and you and I can go for a walk, if you like, in the afternoon. We can talk some more and the air might help to clear your head."

"I'd like that," Margarita said. "I'd like to talk some more about Father's tragedy but I don't want to talk about Victor."

"That's fine by me, pet. You know that your father is a very wise man. Why I say that is because he is so sensitive. He understands better than a lot of people how others feel. That is a very good gift to have. It's lucky we have no work for another week. So, feel whatever way you want to feel and we'll both be here for you. We'll keep all of yesterday's discussions within our own family and maybe it's no harm if you have to put on a brave face when we visit your Grandad Robert and Granny Meg at the farm. Also, we'll have to call during the week to Rose Cottage. As you know we're all a bit worried about Granny Sheila. She seems to have slowed up a lot lately. I'm not saying this to add more worries to you but perhaps you could go over and read a book to her, now that her eyes aren't as good as they used to be."

When Margarita had finished eating, she got out of the bed and put her arms around her mother.

"Thank you both for being the best parents in the world. I'm going to spend tomorrow practising my singing and my breathing exercises and I'll get my lessons ready for the start of my teaching career." She smiled at her mother, though inside she was feeling anything but happy, but she did know that no matter what the circumstances life must go on.

Chapter 28

On a warm late autumn day, Margarita arrived home, satisfied at having taught twenty village children how to do minus sums. Yet it was the improvement in just a few weeks of the school choir that pleased her most. At first the boys were reluctant to join in, saying it was sissy stuff, but after a visit from her music teacher, who was known in the village and in Cork as Master Johnson, they agreed to give it a chance. He had explained the value of learning to sing in a choir where you could sound good even without any great talent. He gave them a free lesson and guided the boys through a funny song which seemed to capture their imaginations. He also promised that if they stuck with it for a year, he would look for funding so that he could buy some musical instruments and they could learn to play them. Margarita got the children to clap Master Johnson when he finished and to thank him for his time.

She was smiling as she opened the front door of her home.

"Is that you, Margarita?" called Eliza.

"Yes, who else were you expecting?" Margarita answered with a laugh.

"Come on into the kitchen, I have something to tell you," said Eliza excitedly.

Margarita could see her mother waving an envelope in the air.

"It must be a love letter, Mama, for you to get this excited!"

"It's better than that. Sit down, pet, and I'll read it to you."

Margarita smiled and did as she was told. Her mother sat opposite her and, with a flourish, took out the letter and told Margarita that it was from Gerry Harris up in Dublin.

"Your father received it, just after you had left this morning. He said I was to read it to you the moment you came in."

"Well, don't keep me in suspense, Mama. Read it!"

Smiling, Eliza began to read.

"*Dear Jack and Eliza, Firstly, I hope your talented daughter is well because it is regarding her that I write. As you know, the Dublin Society always looks to the future and has great plans for the gardens here in Glasnevin. This year, in order to raise funds for our next project, we are inviting all the rich people (and even the not so rich!) to put their hands in their pockets and help fund the future of the Society. In this regard, we are arranging for a banquet to be held in the prestigious Shelbourne House on the second Saturday in October. We are going to have musicians playing during the dinner and after the dinner we will have a guest singer. As you know Theresa and I were astonished at the beauty of Margarita's voice when we visited you in Midleton. I am therefore sending an invitation for your daughter to sing at the banquet. I am hoping that many of the people from the music and arts world will be there to appreciate her charming voice. The hotel owner, Mr. Martin Burke, who hails from down south in County Tipperary, would like to sponsor the trip by inviting your good selves and Margarita to enjoy two rooms for two nights in his hotel, by way of payment. In addition, he will supply a carriage to bring you to Dublin and to take you back after the weekend. As Margarita's godfather, I have always had a special place for her in my heart, as I watched her grow into the admirable young woman she has become. I hope you all accept this invitation and Theresa said to assure you that you will be seated with us at the banquet. She sends her love and I await your speedy reply. I remain, as always, Your friend, Gerry.'"*

Eliza put the letter down and beamed at her daughter.

"So, Margarita, what do you think of that?"

Margarita had sat, with her jaw dropping further and further, as her mother read the letter. Now she was lost for words.

"Well, love?" Eliza asked, raising her eyebrows expectantly.

Margarita at last managed to say, "Mama, it would be incredible but it would take a long time to go up to Dublin and return. How can we be away that long?"

"Don't worry, love, your father has a lot of time owing as he spends so much time on estate work and I have lots of people I can ask to help with the school while we're away. Ann Marie is now highly qualified and she will act as a substitute teacher. Actually, I believe that she's going to be offered a proper teaching job by the council shortly and it's about time that one of their own from the village teaches the children."

Margarita sighed with delight for Ann Marie and relief that she could perhaps spend more time singing in the future. She was now grateful for all the hard work practising her singing, as her heart went into overdrive with excitement! Master Johnson, whom Margarita believed was way ahead of his time in his thinking, had spent the whole summer teaching her breathing exercises, to enhance the quality of her voice. He said, also, that she could use this breathing method to control any nervousness she might feel when singing in public. He even taught her to sing to her bedroom mirror and imagine that she was looking at an audience, advising her to pick out one person in the audience and sing only to them! It worked so far in her bedroom and she felt excited and ready to test it on an audience. After all, she had been singing in the church, in the Big House and for her extended family for as long as she could remember.

She stepped towards her mother and hugged her. "I would be honoured to do it and I think it's come at just the right time for me."

Eliza squeezed her tight, with tears in her eyes. She was really grateful for Gerry Harris's letter because Margarita needed this happy distraction right now.

When Jack returned from work, he witnessed the first

real smile on his daughter's face that he'd seen in a while.

They sat down to dinner and the chatter of the women, including Ann Marie, as she served the meal, made Jack laugh.

"I suppose I can write to Gerry tonight and say yes?" he said. "The only other question I need to ask is how much money it's going to cost to make you into two princesses!"

Margarita asked her mother if she could walk back with Ann Marie to the town and call on Master Johnson to give him the good news.

"Yes, love, go down and your father and I will walk to the town later and collect you at Master Johnson's house after we've had a catch-up with the Jennings in the Haven Inn. Why don't yourself and Ann Marie go by Rose Cottage and the farm on the way and tell them the news? You can take an apple tart as a treat. If Old John is there, it will make him happy." Eliza smiled tenderly at her daughter.

Within the hour, Margarita had imparted the good news to a delighted group at Rose Cottage, where she and Anne Marie were invited to join them for the apple pie with clotted cream.

Soon after they made their way to the farm where her granny and grandad and her young Aunt Alice, were thrilled with the news. Alice was especially excited. She insisted that Jack should sketch the room in the hotel where Margarita would be singing, so they could all visualise the scene. Alice's very indulgent father, Robert, told her that if it was that glamorous, they would visit it sometime and Margarita could come along as their guide! Margarita thought that was a brilliant idea.

As she and Ann Marie took their leave, Meg slipped a bag of food and vegetables into Ann Marie's basket, for her to take back to her hardworking mother.

The two girls were very happy. Margarita, thinking of her singing, felt like skipping the whole way into Midleton!

They parted company at the Johnsons' house.

Timothy Johnson's wife Esther opened the door to Margarita and invited her in. The Johnsons had no children and they loved when Margarita came for lessons. She was by far the best singer Timothy had ever taught, and she had a lovely nature. He often reminded Margarita that her mother Eliza also had a wonderful voice but she had loved her teaching too much to do the hard work necessary to become a great singer. When Margarita told them about her Dublin concert, Esther instructed them to go to the music room immediately and get to work on her repertoire.

Margarita had some favourites that she usually sang in church and she thought she could add a funny song as people were out to enjoy themselves.

Timothy agreed and then added, "I have a young friend in Cork called Denny Lane, who recently gave me what I think is a powerful song. Denny wrote the poem, called 'The Lament of the Irish Maiden', which has been put to music. Dónal, the young man in the poem, was one of the so-called Wild Geese forced into exile in Europe after their

211

leader Patrick Sarsfield was defeated in 1691. The maiden is lamenting their lost love."

He took music sheets from a drawer and went to the piano. After a short piano introduction, he began to sing:

"On Carrigdhoun the heath is brown,
The clouds are dark o'er Ard-na-Lee
And many a stream comes rushing down
To swell the angry Ownabwee.
The moaning blast is sweeping past
Through many a leafless tree
And I'm alone, for he is gone
My hawk has flown, ochón mo chroí!

The heath was green on Carrigdhoun,
Bright shone the sun on Ardnalee,
The dark green trees bent trembling down
To kiss the slumbering Ownabwee.
That happy day, 'twas but last May,
'Tis like a dream to me,
When Dónal swore, aye, o'er and o'er,
We'd part no more, a stór mo chroí!

Soft April showers and bright May flowers
Will bring the summer back again,
But will they bring me back the hours
I spent with my brave Dónal then?
'Tis but a chance, for he's gone to France,
To wear the fleur-de-lys,
But I'll follow you, my Dónal Dhu,
For still I'm true to you, mo chroí."

Margarita was moved to tears by the words and music. After Timothy played the last note, she looked up and said in a strong voice, "It's wonderful. I would love to learn it and I think it would be a good song on which to finish the concert." She knew she could put great feeling into such a song, understanding so well the anguish of lost love.

"Yes, indeed it would," said Timothy. "It mentions the Owenabue River here in County Cork and it will be a good song for you to sing as you are from Cork. Denny will be delighted when I tell him, as his family think he's too young to be putting his work out. Sure, we'll tell them that only you will sing it for now, until Denny is older."

"I won't tell my family about this song until I sing it in Dublin," she said.

"I'm sure they'll love the surprise," Timothy said with a twinkle in his eyes. "Now, back to the hard graft and we'll work on a two-week plan and then a week of dress rehearsals."

By the time Margarita's parents called at the house for her, she was consumed by the thought of the concert. Her parents were glad to see that. They knew she had a rare talent at singing but she also had the patience to focus on something and get it right. Not just at her music but in the school setting also.

Chapter 29

The weeks flew by and Margarita had her songs ready.

Alice begged Margarita to wear a magnificent dress that Lily had sent home from London earlier in the year. Lily had been sending clothes to Margarita and Alice since she had her third child and her waist had expanded. Meg and Alice were both brilliant at making them fit the girls.

"Meg and I tucked it in to fit me and it will really suit your colouring," said Alice. "I have nowhere to wear it until we go somewhere special at Christmas."

It fitted Margarita to perfection, as the girls were of much the same build and height. The dress was red in colour with white puffed sleeves. It was trimmed with shimmering diamantes woven into the material. The bodice was pinched at the waist and the skirt wide at the hem. The satin overskirt swished as Margarita moved. She was delighted to take Alice up on the offer, as buying gowns was never high on Margarita's wish list. Eliza had bought some hair decorations for her and she intended wearing the silver locket that she cherished so much.

Molly and Alice had also agreed to help Ann Marie do some work with the school children while they were away. Molly said she might teach them to cook!

Old John had promised Margarita that the weather would be good on the week of their departure. He was not wrong. The sun glowed through the trees, casting its light on the russet leaves covering the ground surrounding their home.

On the day of departure, the carriage arrived soon after breakfast. It had four horses and two liveried drivers out front.

Margarita and her parents were waiting. They smiled at the unexpected luxury of a carriage with soft seats and curtains that could be opened to watch the passing scenery.

A large sheet covered Margarita's dress which wasn't packed for fear it might get crushed. Everyone made sure that it was handled with care. They all laughed as they gave a seat in the carriage to the dress.

"I've never been in carriage before with a table for food," Margarita exclaimed in awe. Eliza agreed, while Jack just asked, "What am I going to get to eat?"

They were supplied with a food hamper filled with sandwiches, plus dainty cakes and drinks, all to be eaten before stopping for late lunch at an inn in Tipperary. They were to stop twice each day. Once for lunch and then to stay overnight at an inn. Everyone agreed that the journey was to be enjoyed as much as the destination. Margarita spent an hour each evening working on her voice before they ate supper and retired to bed.

On Friday afternoon they arrived in Dublin, tired but exhilarated by the luxury they had enjoyed during the journey, and full of excitement at the thought of a long weekend in Shelbourne House.

Chapter 30

Margarita rested for a while in the luxury of her bedroom. It had a view of the park opposite the hotel. She hoped to enjoy a walk there during the weekend. She also wanted to see the room where she would be singing, where she would later practise with the pianist. He was a senior organist in St. Patrick's Cathedral.

The hotel manager came to her room with a maid holding a large tray.

"I'm Desmond McMahon and Mr. Burke the hotel owner asked me to take special care of your family while you are here."

Margarita looked at the tray with its silver teapot and some delicately made sandwiches and tiny fairy cakes.

"Thank you so much and please thank Mr. Burke for his hospitality. My family and I are honoured to stay at your hotel, Mr. McMahon."

He thanked her and informed her that she would have the service of a dresser, plus he was available for anything else she required before her performance.

She felt close to tears at the graciousness of her hosts as she closed her bedroom door. The excitement was already building for her and she couldn't wait for the following day to arrive.

While Margarita practised, Jack and Eliza requested the carriage driver to take them to the Dublin Gardens. Eliza always wanted to re-experience the place that made her heart beat whenever Jack's letters arrived during his training and whenever they visited Gerry and Theresa Harris in their home.

Later, when they returned to the hotel with Gerry and Theresa, they joined a very excited Margarita for dinner in the dining room. She told them about meeting the hotel manager and that she had also met her pianist, Kenneth Kirwan.

"Slow down, child," her mother said, laughing.

"Well, I'm not going to tell you about the beauty of the banqueting hall, because I would spoil the surprise of it, but the piano is huge and the sound in the room with its high ceilings is wonderful."

Her mother laughed and said that she was like a child who was given a bag of sweets!

The evening flew by, as Jack and Gerry talked of gardens whilst the ladies talked fashion, with Theresa promising to take them to the top shops on Monday, before they left on their return journey home.

***

The next morning, from her window, Margarita watched in fascination the splendid carriages that drove past the hotel. The sun was shining and its light glinted on the tops of their ornate roofs. Many stopped close by as ladies and gentlemen alighted from them. The women were dressed in high-necked coats with hats that were adorned with jewels. They carried parasols and were mostly accompanied by equally well-dressed males. Margarita had never seen so many superbly dressed people in her life. Most seemed to be making their way through a gate to walk in the park, but some were entering the hotel. Margarita was glad that she was eating in her room with her parents. She didn't want to join those people as she could never compete with their grand clothes. She rarely in the past considered herself different even to Deborah, Isaac and Victor but she now knew that if she wanted to make her dream of singing come true, she would have to take more of an interest in fine clothes. But their lifestyles of dressing up to go walking in the park and to have leisurely meals in hotels did not in any way make her envious. Her mother and father always worked hard and she wanted to do the same. Yet she thought that it was a good education to see how the rich city people spent their time.

After lunch, the family walked across to the park. While Jack absorbed himself in the different flower displays,

Margarita and Eliza sat on a bench and watched the people strolling past. They joked that the ladies only wanted to be seen by others.

"Those shoes were certainly not made for walking," Eliza said, nodding her head in wonder. "They are so dainty that they are guaranteed to give sore feet by evening!"

They were both giggling as they returned to the hotel, where Margarita met her dresser, Adele, who would be with her for the whole evening, to be available for anything she required. Adele explained that top singers from England and Wales stayed regularly in the hotel when they did recitals in Dublin. She told Margarita funny stories about some of the more difficult singers, and that included men as well as women!

They enjoyed each other's company during the early meal that Margarita needed, as she didn't want to eat too close to her performance.

"I'm not very fashion conscious," Margarita apologised. "However, I'd love to know more about dresses needed for performances."

"When you go home, I'll write and send some sketches of what some of the London singers wear," said Adele generously. "I love the dress that you'll be wearing, but I will add some little sequined pieces to create more sparkle when the candlelight falls on them." She then lifted Margarita's fine silky black hair into a chignon at the back of her head, a more grown-up style. Then, with dexterity, she fitted a silver tiara which was the property of the hotel.

It complemented the locket that Margarita always wore whenever she sang. She felt the love of her parents whenever she touched that.

Adele walked her over to the long-bevelled mirror and let her see the transformation.

"You look quite exotic and so grown-up." Adele smiled as Margarita looked at herself in the long mirror.

Margarita smiled back and asked if she could take her back to Midleton to dress her every day! They gave each other a hug and Adele offered to listen if Margarita wanted to practise. She agreed to sing her funny song about Johnny, the donkey and the cart and, as soon as she was finished and Adele had applauded her, the call came requesting her presence in the Banqueting Hall.

As Margarita entered the room, to say she was overwhelmed would be an understatement. She was completely taken aback by the flickering candles, with different colours of lampshades surrounding them. The room had been transformed since she had done her rehearsal. Yet, she felt also a sense of privilege to be performing in such opulence. Her training from Master Johnson had paid dividends. She breathed calmly and slowly as she listened to the audience, before she stepped onto the stage.

There was a very warm round of applause as Margarita moved to the centre, while Kenneth stood by the piano. He bowed as she walked past and she gave him a big smile as Master Johnson had told her to do. As she turned to the audience, she sought out her parents and nodded in their direction.

Be yourself, Master Johnson had advised. She commenced by introducing herself. You are young, he had said and audiences are usually kind to newcomers. She hoped this was true. She let them know what a major night this was for her, before she announced her first song. As she did so, she turned to Kenneth, and informed the audience that Kenneth had insisted that, because she was in Dublin, she had to sing a composition by Mr. Handel. She could feel the audience warming to her as she nodded to Kenneth to begin. She was ready to sing. Kenneth began by playing an introduction to the beautiful aria "Lascia ch'io pianga" from Handel's opera *Rinaldo*.

Then Margarita began to sing. To the amazement of the audience, her voice soared up and down with grace and breath control and a maturity beyond her years.

Eliza and Jack were enthralled listening to her. Jack squeezed his wife's hand and they looked at each other, smiling with pride.

As Margarita gazed at her parents, she knew at that moment that she wanted singing to be a big part of her future.

Margarita continued her repertoire and had everyone laughing when she told them that her mother had taught her about Johnny and the donkey and cart and that she always thought they had lived on their farm until her mother confessed when she was ten that it was a made-up song! She encouraged everyone to clap when she sang the chorus and everyone was laughing by the time the song came to an end.

As Margarita came to her last song, her parents wondered what she had up her sleeve – she had kept it a secret. She announced that she was singing a song called "Carrighdoun" or "The Lament of the Irish Maiden", written by a young man called Denny Lane in Cork. She laughed as she told them it was set near the Owenabue River and she had wondered if Denny could change it to the Owenacurra river that ran through her home town of Midleton. Denny had laughed and said it wouldn't rhyme with the rest of the verse if he changed it! However, the Owenabue also flowed through her county of Cork.

"I know I might be too young to talk of love and loss but many people here will remember perhaps the first person they loved and it will bring back memories. I hope you enjoy it."

Eliza and Jack listened with sadness and pride at the emotion in Margarita's voice as she put her heart and soul into the song about lost love. A maturity beyond her years was there for all to hear.

> *"The moaning blast is sweeping past*
> *Through many a leafless tree*
> *And I'm alone, for he is gone*
> *My hawk has flown, ochón mo chroí!"*

The guests were hushed, listening to the haunting air beautifully delivered. Even more moving was the note of hope at the end:

"'Tis but a chance, for he's gone to France,
To wear the fleur-de-lys,
But I'll follow you, my Dónal Dhu,
For still I'm true to you, mo chroí!"

As Margarita finished the lament, there was total silence. She looked at the pianist who was smiling broadly. Suddenly the guests rose as one and they clapped and cheered for at least five minutes. Mr. Burke came onto the stage with a bunch of roses and as Margarita let out her breath with relief, she saw her parents and Adele standing with them, all smiling proudly at her. Her first thought was for her teacher back in Cork and she almost couldn't wait to get back to tell him all about her night. She also thought of Victor and again reminded herself of the words often quoted by Meg: "What doesn't kill you, my love, will just make you stronger." She had found that helped reduce her pain.

Margarita ended her evening sipping tea at the table with her parents, Gerry, Theresa and Adele. People kept coming to the table to tell her she had a bright future ahead. By the time she finally got to her room she truly believed that she would never sleep, but when her body sank into the soft feather bed, she remembered nothing more until the sound of birdsong woke her.

The carriage was waiting to take them to see the beauty of Trinity College, once they had enjoyed a hearty breakfast that Eliza said would feed a family for a week! They met Theresa and Gerry at the famous Dick's Coffee House.

Theresa was highly animated. "The concert you gave, Margarita, has been a huge success financially. Many of the rich merchants said their wives had enjoyed a wonderful night and suggested that, if it happened again, they would continue their support of the Dublin Society!"

"Margarita, dearest goddaughter, you more than worked your magic for the Society," Gerry said.

It was a lovely meeting and, eventually, while the ladies continued to chat, Gerry and Jack went to view some exotic plants that had recently been planted in the Dublin Gardens.

By the time they all went to bed that night in the Shelbourne, the Ryan family knew they were happy to start the journey back to Cork, with great memories they could hold on to forever.

Chapter 31

Life returned to normal for Margarita when their trip ended. She was congratulated by everyone in Midleton, as word had got around about her Dublin debut. Jack and Eliza were very happy that they had raised a lovely daughter who had no airs and graces about her, as she happily returned to teaching the children each day. She was looking forward to getting the choir ready to perform at Christmas and Master Johnson had surprised her with the news that the town councillors in Cork City had invited the children's choir from the school in Midleton to perform some Christmas songs at a location in the city, provided Margarita sang also. She was delighted, and very excited for the children.

"If you all work hard at your school work, you will have a great day out in Cork to look forward to," Margarita promised them.

It seemed to work as the offer of a day out in Cork with

treats generously promised by Isaac's fund was something that few of them had ever experienced. Most of their families worked, if they were lucky to have a job, just to put food on the table and pay the rent.

It was early in December when Deborah invited Eliza for tea in the Big House. Eliza had her suspicions, which were confirmed when they sat down in the comfort of the drawing room. They were served dainty sandwiches and hot rhubarb pie by Jessy, the assistant to the cook. When she left the room, Eliza lifted her eyebrows and nodded at Deborah, hoping she would confide in her.

Deborah shook her head as she began to speak.

"Victor is announcing his engagement when he returns to Ireland, and he is bringing Fleur with him to introduce her to everyone on the estate and to show her around. Isaac is actually delighted to have him coming home but I'm still in shock as I think he's too young and immature to marry. You know him as well as I do, Eliza, and you could never get him to sit for a moment and think things through."

Eliza nodded, knowing that this would be tough on Margarita, but she needed to be there for her friend also.

"I think if he's made up his mind, you should support him all the way and welcome Fleur into the family with open arms. It's what he wants and you have always been a loving mother and you need to show that love to them both. You will just have to get used to sharing him in the future."

Deborah smiled at her friend.

"You always were so sensible and wise. I'm glad you're around to keep me from interfering in their lives too much! Now let's drink a toast to the future – to ours and theirs!" she said, with a smile brighter than Eliza had seen in a while. "To my son and of course your daughter, who is going to be a star of the future!"

When Eliza left the house, she decided to go to Rose Cottage and have a word with Granny Sheila before she made her way home to break the news to Margarita. Sheila is a rock of sense, she thought, and will hopefully have some advice to hand out. Although she left the house less often these days due to what she described as her aching bones, Eliza knew that her mind was as keen as ever and she always seemed to know how to deal with a crisis.

Later, after her trip to Rose Cottage, she returned home to help with the preparation of their evening meal.

"Your father and I are going over later to the farm for the evening and I know that Granny Sheila would like a visit from you in Rose Cottage," Eliza said to Margarita as they sat down to eat.

"I'd love to have a chat with her." Margarita nodded and smiled. "I was just going to practise a few songs as I'm going to Master Johnson's tomorrow to finalise the Christmas concert programme. I can do that in Rose Cottage."

"Great, we'll collect you afterwards at the cottage and maybe Molly will give us a few cakes to eat over the weekend," said Jack, as ever loving the thought of his mother's baking.

Granny Sheila was sitting in her bed, propped up by soft pillows. A fire glowed in the cosy room. When more turf was added it began to hiss as the smoke chased its way up the chimney. She always seemed to be cold lately. She had her hands around a hot cup of tea and had a big smile on her face when Margarita entered the downstairs bedroom where Sheila now slept. Margarita hugged her slight frame and sat by her bedside.

Molly arrived with a cup of tea for Margarita.

"I'm just going to take a batch of cakes from the oven as I know your father will want some when he collects you."

"You're not wrong there," Margarita laughed. "He is always teasing Mama about how good his mother's baking is!"

Granny Sheila and Margarita chatted after Molly left, mainly about Margarita's singing and the school work in the estate and down in the village. Sheila adored Margarita and thankfully saw her as being strong like Eliza. As she smiled at Margarita, she pondered on how to open the conversation about Victor.

At last, she said, "I want to say something to you, love, but would you promise me that when I finish you will sing me a couple of songs so that I'll go to sleep with a smile on my face?"

Margarita patted her hand and assured her that she

loved singing for even an audience of one! Then she settled back and wondered what was afoot.

"You know how much I adore you and of course all the other great-grandchildren. But you're very special, because your father always felt to me like he was the son I never had, instead of being my grandson. Years ago, as soon as his low-life of a father turned out to be such a nightmare, I always felt that your granny, Molly, was too soft to make the family function properly, without some help from me. So, I took over the reins and made sure that my grandchildren saw a lot of nurturing in their home, even without a loving father. But your father Jack seemed to rile Septimius, mainly because the boy was bright and a quick learner. On a certain night when his father hurt him on his birthday, I made it my mission that Jack would never be hurt by him again. I practically packed his bag and put some money in it to keep him going. I knew he was happy travelling the world but I knew also that he'd eventually want to come home. He was a strong utterly dependable man and when he returned from his travels with cuts and bruises, I had my own view of what might have happened to him – but he never would say and I never did ask."

Margarita nodded, knowing what had happened.

"Why I'm saying that is because you know how your father met your mother. It was when he was at his lowest ebb and many things had gone wrong for him. Yet he knew when he met Eliza that there was a light at the end of the tunnel and he had the strength of mind to stay tough during bad times and you see what good came out of that strength. You are the product of that strength and I see the same strength in you. You are like your father – though your mother has that spirit also." As Sheila paused to draw breath, she took Margarita's hand in hers. "There's no easy way to say this but you will need that strength of mind now because your great childhood friend Victor will be returning to the estate with his bride-to-be. I want to tell you that you need to stay strong right now. Don't turn your heart into a stone but keep the love you have for him in a part of you. The problem is that we have no control over the way other people behave, as you know. We can only choose how we respond to it." As she saw Margarita's eyes fill with tears, she continued. "Let your tears flow but don't let this difficult time define you. Explore your singing and continue your teaching. Be the friend to the village that you have become and continue to be the kind and generous-hearted person you have always been. When Fleur becomes Victor's wife, be kind to them both. Victor has not stopped being your friend and I understand you well enough to know that you haven't a nasty bone in your body. Be kind to Fleur and you will find that goodness will follow. I'm long enough in the world to know that many things are neither right or wrong, they are just different. The same goes for people, my love. Now, before you send me to sleep, I'll finish by saying that only you can choose how you view Victor with Fleur. I just hope you make a good choice."

As Sheila lay back on the pillows and closed her eyes, Margarita had to dry her tears.

She then sang a lullaby, which usually brought a relaxed smile to Sheila's face. Before she finished singing Sheila was asleep and Margarita sang "Carraigdhoun" into the still of the night, allowing herself time to cry into the quietness that surrounded her.

She left the room and, as she quietly closed the door, Molly approached her and put an arm around her.

"That was wonderful singing and I know it was from the heart. You will make an awful lot of people happy by sharing that voice. Now sit down and have a bite of my new fruit cake with a cup of tea before Eliza and Jack arrive and eat it all!"

Later that evening Margarita told her mother about her time with Granny Sheila and that night, when Eliza retired to the bedroom and put her arms around Jack, she told him that she loved him very much.

"You have given me so much more than yourself and Margarita. You have also given us an exceptional granny."

As he held her close, he knew that he would never have had the confidence to ask Eliza to marry him without the help of that granny.

They slept soundly that night knowing that Sheila's words seemed to have brought some balm to their hurting daughter's soul.

Chapter 32

Margarita was kept busy over the next few weeks. The whole town had offered support when asked to lend a hand and make sure the choir looked smart for the event. They had been informed that they would sing in the magnificent limestone Blackrock Castle, which was situated downriver from the centre of the city. The children were even more excited than before when they heard that.

Mrs. Sheridan, the best seamstress for miles around, got the mothers and Alice, with her great talent as a seamstress, into her workroom each day and they sewed white dresses with lace trimmings on the collars for the girls, from cotton supplied by Isaac's fund. Money was also found to buy shirts for the boys. Trousers were bought from the second-hand market in Cork so the boys would look smart. Coats and shoes were borrowed and bought from the market from the donations given to Laura Jennings at the Haven

Inn, who was given the task of asking local merchants to donate even a few pennies for the children.

Margarita was also kept busy in the evenings with several trips to sit with Granny Sheila at bedtime. When she arrived at Rose Cottage, Old John was always hovering, having made a potion to help Sheila feel less pain from her thinning bones. They knew that her time with them was getting shorter but Sheila insisted that she be brought to the Estate Chapel, where the children's choir was doing a dress rehearsal before their trip to Cork.

The day before the concert in Cork, all the mothers and fathers of the children and other family members arrived there to hear the children sing. Their pride as they walked into the church dressed in their best clothes brought tears to Margarita's eyes.

Eliza and Deborah were in charge of laying out the cakes, biscuits and orange drinks for everyone to enjoy after the concert. Granny Sheila had a place of honour in the front row where she sat with a warm wool blanket covering her knees. Margarita introduced the children as they filed in perfect order onto the altar. They each bowed to the crowd as they took their places. After the children were clapped by the audience there was a respectful silence as Master Johnson opened the concert with a flourish on the small organ in the church.

Margarita sang the first verse of a well-known Christmas hymn and, when the choir joined in, their sweet voices rose to the church roof in perfect harmony. Eliza and Jack breathed a sigh of relief and like the rest of the townsfolk were immersed in the music for over an hour. They finished with a sublime rendition of the hymn called "Silent Night" which was first sung in Austria in 1818. As the concert came to an end, everyone including Granny Sheila stood up and clapped so loudly that the echo from the church ceiling seemed to bounce the claps and cheers off the walls.

The children all smiled with delight. They returned to their parents, where the tables with food and drinks were now set out. For the next hour the children and their excited families enjoyed the food and drink supplied by the Beconsford family, before they left to return to their homes.

Margarita joined her family and they all went back to Rose Cottage to finish the night by continuing singing by the fireside. Sheila retired to bed, announcing that it was one of the best concerts she had ever attended.

The trip to Cork was arranged. Two of the estate carriages were used and the Trust paid for extra carriages to be hired for the trip to Cork and back. A parent from each household joined the singers to look after them while they were in Cork. The children were given a couple of pence each to spend when they reached the city.

As the carriages approached Cork city from the east, Blackrock Castle was pointed out to the children. They could see its turrets from across the river on the far bank. Their excitement grew when they actually saw the castle where they were going to sing.

One of the parents summed up the excitement to Alice Turner.

"This is like a dream come true for us. When did we ever think we would see such a day?"

Alice only then realised how all the hard work getting ready for this trip was having a profound effect on a lot of family members, not just the children who would sing.

When the carriages arrived into the city, the mothers took the children to the shops, while Margarita and Master Johnson continued in their carriage to check the venue in Blackrock, which was situated at the water's edge close to the river, where it flowed gently down past the castle towards the sea. The piano in the castle was first class and the excitement was mounting even for Master Johnson.

Later, the children arrived and were given their places where they practised their opening hymn.

Master Johnson smiled when they had finished and said, "Children, that was excellent and I'm very proud of you and later I want you all to enjoy your time on the stage." He knew that one song was enough to give them a feel for the place.

Shortly afterwards the host families arrived and each child and parent were introduced to the people they would stay with overnight. The mothers from Midleton were very nervous, especially those of little means who had to borrow nightwear in order to feel as respectable as possible. The host families seemed to understand and were very friendly and warm, as they happily greeted everyone.

Margarita and Eliza were staying with friends of Deborah's in a house close to the castle.

At seven o'clock the audience had arrived and the Mayor of the Cork stood with his chain of office around his neck to welcome the children. He was a kindly, rotund man with receding hair.

"I want to thank the children from Midleton for making the journey to sing for us this evening. I know this would not have been possible without the work of their singing teacher Margarita Ryan and her mother Eliza. I also want to congratulate the parents on the wonderful way the children looked when I saw them at rehearsal earlier and I will finish by welcoming my friend Timothy Johnson who will accompany the singers. These children are a credit to you all and a model for us in the city, showing us ways of improving how we see education, as it may not just be teaching children to read and write."

As he turned to invite the choir onto the raised stage, everyone in the audience clapped.

As the music started, Margarita stood with her back to the audience. She smiled at the children and as she raised her hand, they started to sing. The children, as they had been taught, lifted their heads proudly and let their voices soar. The atmosphere in the room seemed very positive and Margarita was delighted when after their first hymn they were loudly applauded. Margarita then sang two songs alone and she smiled as even the children clapped when she finished!

As they came towards the end of the programme,

Margarita announced she would now sing the song written by the Cork lad Denny Lane whom she introduced to the audience where he sat, looking embarrassed, with his mother by his side.

When Margarita finished singing of Donal Dhu leaving Ireland's shores, the audience stood as one to cheer and she invited Denny to take a bow also.

Finally, Margarita and the children ended the recital by singing the haunting "Silent Night". You could hear a pin drop as the hymn unfolded and there was a long silence as it ended before everyone rose to their feet, clapping and cheering.

Margarita felt a more deepened sense of satisfaction on this occasion than she had ever felt before, as she looked at the smiling happy faces of the children who had made that night possible. As they all stood with Master Johnson, Margarita knew it would take a lot to beat the feelings that touched her tonight.

On the week before Christmas, Eliza voiced her concerns to Jack about the impending arrival of Victor and Fleur and its effect on Margarita.

"She'll be fine, hopefully," Jack said. "With her Aunt Lily and her husband and children arriving at the farm, she'll be kept occupied over the Christmas break. She'll also enjoy her time with Sheila in the evenings, although my granny appears to be shrinking in front of my eyes. Thank goodness for Old John's dedication to keeping her pain-free. I've never seen so many potions that seem to work. We'll have to make sure this Christmas will be everything she will enjoy. She's overjoyed that Hannah and Julia will bring their families here this Christmas. What would we do without our friends at the Haven Inn? The children are so excited to be staying there. You know it will be one of the few Christmases ever that all my family and yours will be together. I'm hopeful that even Margarita will have fun with everyone about."

Eliza had her doubts but decided that there was nothing she could do except support her daughter, whatever happened in the future.

Chapter 33

Deborah had overseen the placing of a large fir tree from the estate in the hall of Beconsford House. Queen Charlotte had started the trend in early 1800's, learning from her German family. Deborah heard about this when she was young. Her father had spent time with some noble relatives living in Stuttgart, and had told her that he had also seen decorated trees on his visits to Germany. As a young child her imagination pictured the decorated tree and she had promised herself that when she had a child, she would decorate a fir tree each Christmas. When Victor was young, she tied carved figures and paper chains on a little fir tree with his gifts underneath, in the round hallway near the great fireplace each Christmas Eve. She and Isaac would watch excitedly each Christmas morning as Victor came down the staircase and saw his presents under the tree. Now, every year, she watched as Isaac helped Jack manoeuvre a bigger tree into the same place. Since Victor got older, oil lamps were lit and placed carefully beside the tree. The spectacle was delightful, even for the adults.

She was apprehensive at the imminent arrival of Victor and Fleur, but promised herself that she would welcome Fleur with open arms. She was even more excited that Helena and her family were arriving, along with Lily and her family. Thankfully they rarely had to tolerate the aging Lord and Lady Beconsford who now spent most winters in the heat of the Mediterranean sun and their summers in London. It was a blessing for all the family and the reason why Helena was happy to bring her children to the estate. But they would not arrive for another day and Deborah was glad of this time for herself and Isaac to talk to Victor and Fleur and enjoy dinner with them both.

At five o'clock, the carriage drew up at the front door and Isaac squeezed Deborah's hand as they waited at the open door for Victor and Fleur. As Victor gently helped his wife-to-be from the carriage, Deborah and Isaac got a glimpse of a very pretty petite young woman whose smile would light up any room.

As she approached them, Deborah noticed how pale her skin was, like porcelain. It was surrounded by beautiful soft black curls. As Fleur looked up at Victor, Deborah saw that true love for Victor shone from her eyes.

As they greeted everyone with hugs and kisses, the carriage driver was bringing in what looked like a mountain of baggage. Mrs. Hudson, the housekeeper, fussed around and asked if Fleur needed to go to her room. Fleur answered immediately, suggesting that she would love to have some tea and refreshments before going upstairs. As the family retired to the drawing-room Mrs. Hudson sent Jenny scurrying to the kitchen to prepare a tray.

Victor was, as ever, his happy and cheerful self, and Fleur was put at her ease by the genuine welcome she received. She experienced the loving nature of the family she was about to marry into. She had admired the enormous size of the Christmas tree and told them she had brought some delightful baubles and trinkets to hang on it, Victor having told her of the German tradition. She said that she herself loved the idea and had made some embroidered heart-shaped decorations to tie with ribbons on the tree. Deborah laughed and told the men that she might finally have found another Christmas enthusiast!

As tea was brought in, Mrs. Hudson was very happy to see that they were all relaxed with each other. As she nodded her approval, Deborah was pleased that she seemed happy with the demeanour of the lady who would marry the Honourable Mr. Isaac.

On the week before Christmas the school closed early, so that the children could help with preparations at home with their families. Ann Marie had let Eliza know which children's families were in most need and Margarita helped her mother put parcels together to ensure that everyone had some good food on the table on Christmas Day. This meant that some could only be delivered late on Christmas Eve, otherwise a few of the greedier fathers would sell the stuff at the market, just to get money for drink, and indeed a small number of the more desperate mothers would sell it too. For all families, Isaac's fund contributed money to pay for small gifts for the children. Eliza knew that they couldn't feed everyone and it sometimes felt like a balancing act to try and give help to those who could not, for whatever reason, help themselves.

They were busy at their task when a smiling Deborah arrived in the kitchen.

"Victor and his Fleur have arrived and she is lovely. A bit delicate and pale but she has a lovely nature and she can't take her eyes off Victor!"

Eliza glanced at Margarita, whose head was bent over a wooden box where she was packing some of the parcels. Then Margarita lifted her eyes, turned to Deborah and smiled.

"I'm delighted that they are happy. I'm looking forward to meeting her," she said.

Eliza breathed a sigh of relief and yet again said a prayer of thanks that she had raised such a gracious daughter.

"That's why I called," said Deborah. "We would love you both to join myself and Fleur for tea tomorrow afternoon before Helena and Lily's brood arrive! Fleur says she has heard so much from Victor about Margarita and, of course, you, Eliza! She can't wait to meet you both."

"We'll be delighted to go and we're both so pleased for

Victor. I'm also glad that you're very happy!" Eliza laughed as she sat herself down beside her friend.

Margarita said she'd go and make some tea.

When she reached the kitchen, she put her hands on the kitchen table, watching the flames in the hearth heating the suspended kettle. Almost a calmness or was it just relief came over her? She had been expecting it for a while and the finality of Deborah's words didn't overwhelm her, as she had expected them to do.

As she made the tea, she lifted her head and put a big smile on her face, to stop any unshed tears from falling. As she walked back into the parlour, she knew that the first chapter of her adult life was over and she must concentrate on the future, whatever it would bring.

The meeting with Fleur was also much easier than Margarita had expected. Victor was with her to make the introductions and she really was a delightful young girl. Margarita felt that she was much older than Fleur even though they were both quite close in age. Perhaps it is because I have already experienced lost love, thought Margarita. She hoped the maturity it brought would stand to her as she knew she would have to live with seeing Victor and Fleur when they married and were living close to her. Victor, of course, was as always effervescent, as he hugged and kissed herself and Eliza. He then left to go and talk to Jack about the estate and left the women to their tea.

Later, as Margarita walked home with her mother, she

opened the conversation they never had had in the past.

"I'm going to be fine with Victor and Fleur. I've come to accept what Granny Sheila and Father said to me. I have no control over the feelings of other people. I must just deal with my own thoughts. I'm actually very happy that he has found someone who seems to adore him as I would have hated him to fall for someone who just wanted his money or his title. He was always so impetuous when we were young."

Margarita remembered the many times had she had to save him from getting into trouble. She once had to resort to tears when he decided he wished to see the whole of Cork County from the top of the tallest tree in the forest. He was three-quarters way up before her screams made him change his mind. Knowing Victor as she did, he probably wouldn't even remember that day. Even though she was only eight years of age at the time, she still remembered her heart nearly bursting with worry until he laughingly jumped down and said a very unapologetic "Sorry" to her. *She* would never forget that day.

Eliza patted her hand and they walked in silence towards home.

"I'm very proud of you, love," she said as they stepped into the warmth of the house where Jack was waiting expectantly.

Eliza nodded at him reassuringly as he stood up and reached out to embrace the two women he loved so dearly.

Chapter 34

Christmas was upon them and everyone was very busy. Margarita sang at three church services and had little time to concern herself about Victor and his lovely bride-to-be. Lily and her family were ensconced at the farm.

Preparations in Rose Cottage were going ahead full steam as Molly had invited Jack, Eliza and Margarita, plus John, Meg and Alice, to spend Christmas Day with her and Granny Sheila. Jack's sisters Hannah and Julia and their husbands and children would also be crammed into the cottage. Thankfully, Lily and her family had been invited to have dinner with Deborah and Isaac's family as Helena's children wanted to enjoy Christmas with their young friends from Hertfordshire.

Old John and Sam were also looking forward to their trip to Rose Cottage, even if multiple chairs had to be brought from the farm to seat them all with the entire downstairs rooms needed, in order to sit down to eat.

Molly believed that it mightn't be too long before her mother would be unable to sit at the dinner table. Old John had worked miracles with his lavender and St. John's Oil which he cultivated in a small closed area of his garden. He gave Sheila many other potions, to see which worked best. He used them only to keep her comfortable and alert, while not suffering too much pain. But she was visibly shrinking before her daughter's eyes and Molly kept reminding herself of how lucky she was. After all, her mother was now going into her late eighties and very few people lived for so long in Ireland. Yet she prayed for one last good Christmas for her family and she knew that Sheila was in a happy frame of mind, having spent so many years living without the presence of Septimius and had seen all her family with secure futures. Yet Sheila's greatest gift had been helping Old John with his work, especially with poor people in the town where she could pass money over when doctors or food were necessary for their survival. Molly had tears in her eyes as she remembered that her mother was at her happiest when she helped anyone who passed her way.

Everyone was kept busy with final preparations. In most of the houses of the village, parents spent time in the evenings making the best paper chains. They trimmed small pegs and twigs to make stick figures for the boys and they stuffed material with straw and made them into dolls for the girls. Pieces of timber were used to make carts and some of the village men had carved horses and donkeys which the excited children would tie to their small wooden carts. Everyone worked to make sure that all the children would enjoy the holiday. At home, whether they were rich or poor, logs were decorated and placed around fireplaces. Little stockings were filled with apples and nuts and Granny Sheila had donated a coin to be put into each given to the poorest children in the town.

Up at Rose Cottage holly and ivy were put on the top of picture frames and into any jars that could show off the red berries which grew in abundance in the estate forest.

Christmas Day dawned with the sun forcing its way from the east to melt the sparkling shards of ice that lay on the fields and roads.

"It's a nice crisp day," Eliza announced, as the family got ready to go to the estate church for a Christmas service. "I don't think we'll have any trouble walking up to Rose Cottage later." She hoped that Margarita's good spirits would see her through the trip to the Big House for mulled wine and pies to which they had been invited after the church service.

Margarita appeared at the kitchen door, smiling and displaying her cherry-red bonnet, given to her by Jack and Eliza as one of her Christmas gifts.

"You look wonderful, love. It's a pity you can't wear it while eating later," Eliza said with a laugh.

Margarita looked lovingly at her mother and took her

arm. "Father is waiting at the door. We can't be late for anything today."

"Doesn't he look smart in his new shirt that I bought in the best shop in Dublin!" said Eliza.

The church service was enhanced by the light of the sun beaming through the stained-glass windows, drawing coloured shadows on the candlelit altar. The fulsome sounds of the church bells called everyone to prayer and as the service began Margarita sang the entrance hymn, encouraging the congregation to join in the chorus. They all sang with enthusiastic voices, entering into the wonder of Christmas Day.

Victor sat with Fleur and listened with awe and astonishment to the richness of Margarita's voice. She did not look like the little girl who had been his best friend when he was young and had followed him around when he was older.

Fleur tapped him on the arm and whispered that the singing was marvellous.

He whispered back, "Just like you, my love."

A feast of mulled wine, nuts, sticks of bread and rich dips were placed on the table alongside sparkling cut-crystal glasses in the ballroom of the Big House. Dainty sandwiches with fillings of chicken, beef and salmon were placed beside the small cups and saucers for those who enjoyed tea and coffee.

Everyone was in a happy mood as Isaac Beconsford

welcomed his ever-growing family, his friends and the senior estate workers to his home. He made his usual promise to continue his work in supporting a prosperous community and helping where possible those in most need.

He then called Victor to his side and they introduced his bride-to-be to the group. Fleur smiled sweetly and blushed as Victor placed a protective arm around her shoulders.

Victor then spoke and said how much he was looking forward to helping to run the estate in the future, allowing his father and mother to take more holidays and some well-earned rest.

"Now go and enjoy the food, drink and the company! Happy Christmas to you all!"

When Eliza, Jack and Margarita were sitting on some of the soft-cushioned chairs placed around the ballroom, enjoying the delicacies on offer, Margarita announced, "She's a beautiful young lady and I can see that Victor loves her very much. I'm really happy for them both, and I'm looking forward to getting to know her."

Eliza breathed an almost audible sigh of relief and beamed at her daughter.

"They are two lovely people and they were so effusive about your singing after church. I think you will get on very well with Fleur."

After joking that they'd all be too stuffed to eat dinner later, they mingled and chatted to everyone for the most relaxed hour that Eliza had enjoyed for a long while.

***

The Christmas dinner, present-giving and joyous mood around the table at Rose Cottage made Eliza so happy. The only people she missed were her sister Lily and her family who were enjoying Christmas dinner with the Beconsfords. But she had promised to come to Rose Cottage the following day with her husband Rob and twin boys, Josh and Bernard, and their little sister Elizabeth. Everyone was pleased that Granny Sheila sat at the dinner table, in a chair made comfortable with cushions. She insisted she wanted to hear every one of her family singing to her before she would retire to bed that night!

At eight o'clock that evening, having enjoyed food prepared with great pride by Molly, Old John took out a banjo and began to play. Sam then started playing the spoons, which made them all laugh. Finally, Eliza was coaxed to play the piano. She was joined by Margarita and the sing-song requested by Sheila began!

They all had a great time entertaining Granny Sheila, who sang along with all the songs she knew. Finally, when Meg started to dance with Robert, Sheila decided to retire to her bedroom and the tables were pulled back so that everyone could dance. They spun around the room as if they hadn't a care in the world.

It was midnight before Sam left to get Nelly and the carriage to take the Ryan family home. Before they left,

251

Margarita crept into Granny Sheila's room and found her still awake with a smile on her face and a hint of tears on her cheeks.

"It was wonderful tonight, love. Listening to you singing and the sound of all the dancing in the parlour made it one of the best Christmases of my whole life. That voice of yours will bring you and others great joy. I'm lucky to have lived to hear it at its best."

She took Margarita's hand and asked her to sing a Christmas song. Margarita sang "Silent Night".

And, as Margarita's voice soared through the air, Sheila closed her eyes while still smiling.

Margarita's thoughts turned to how happy she too was on this day and she wanted to hold on to it as long as possible.

The clapping from downstairs when she finished brought her back to her senses as she gently laid Sheila's hand inside the covers.

Chapter 35

In early January, Lily and Helena had returned to Hertfordshire, with Victor and Fleur. The New Year brought its usual variable Irish weather with some cold, frost, rain and sun. Snow fell softly on to the green fields and turned them into a delightful fairyland, but it lasted only two days before disappearing along with the hurriedly made snowmen.

Margarita had enjoyed playing snow fights with the school children but was glad to see it end as the very cold weather made it difficult for the poorer families.

Granny Sheila had not left her bed since Christmas and Old John and Molly were giving her every easing herb they could grind into drinks. Herbs also filled her room with soothing smells. Lavender was her favourite.

On the second week in January Old John agreed with Doctor Lynch that a small dose of laudanum was necessary to allow her have some pain relief. On that day the family knew that Granny Sheila's days were numbered.

On a cold frosty night on the 19th of January 1837 Granny Sheila passed away in her sleep, surrounded by her daughter, her three grandchildren, Eliza, Margarita and Old John. At two in the morning, she slipped away gently. It was a peaceful death but tears still fell fast and furious on the faces of her family as they watched her leave them. Margarita was the first to go to her side and kiss her goodbye. She begged everyone to spend a while reminiscing on joyful things that had happened in Sheila's life while she still seemed to be asleep in the room. In the next hour they laughed and they cried and Margarita sang a lullaby as everyone took their turns to say goodbye to a wonderful woman.

Granny Sheila was so well thought of around Midleton and the Beconsford estate that she was brought to the estate chapel for a church service to celebrate her life. Eliza and Margarita sang as the coffin, made of good solid oak and crafted in the town, lay on a stand at the steps of the altar. Eliza and Margarita together sang hymns of joy as Granny Sheila would have wanted.

From the altar steps her grandson Jack spoke words of thanks in praise of Sheila who lived her life always with hope for the future. He finished with the recent words of the Danish philosopher Soren Kierkegaard: "'*Life can only be understood backwards; but it must be lived forwards.*' My beloved granny would want us all to live our lives as fully in the future as she has done in the past. May she rest in peace."

As the procession left the church, only Margarita knew what was planned in the town. Everyone walked behind the carriage and four horses, who were bedecked with elegant white plumes. As they entered the main street it was lined with men, women and children with heads bowed, praying for her soul. When they arrived at the town square they were met with even more people. On the steps of the Haven Inn stood every child from the choir, with many of their parents. Margarita stepped from her carriage and joined the choir and, as Master Johnson stepped forward and stood in front of the group, the procession stopped and silence descended on the village. After a few quiet moments the soaring sounds of the young choir singing John Newton's "Amazing Grace" into the cold air, giving goose bumps even to those dressed in warm clothing. Eliza and Molly were in tears, listening to the voices rise into the cold January sky.

As the cortege began its final short journey, the choir voices again rose and sang the beloved "Silent Night", its sound still echoing as the funeral party entered the graveyard by the town church where Sheila Ryan was finally laid to rest.

The entire funeral party returned to the Haven Inn where again only Margarita had known that Sheila had given money to Laura Jennings, so that everyone in the town could have a meal and a drink on the day of her funeral. Jack smiled as he said, "That woman thought of everything, even a way to have fun at her funeral!"

255

The children were fed in the square and Isaac and Deborah joined all the family and adults who crammed into the inn on the day. Jack was so proud of the send-off the town had given his granny that his tears moved from sorrow to joy as the day ended. Sheila Ryan had died as she had lived, a thoroughly decent human being who brought light to the eyes of so many people.

Chapter 36

Spring came early that year, when daffodils, crocuses and snow flowers peeped from the ground in late February. News from Victor and Fleur from Hertfordshire indicated that preparations for the wedding in May were going well. As Fleur was a godchild of Lord Salisbury of Hatfield House, they were going to be married in St. Etheldreda's Church, inside the grounds of the Hatfield estate. Lily wrote to say how excited everyone was with this news and to tell them how proud they were that her eldest son had been asked to be a groomsman on the day alongside Helena's boy. They would all attend the banquet later in Fleur's home after a reception in Hatfield House. Lily had heard that two members of the Royal family would attend the wedding and reception.

Eliza was delighted for her but could not herself travel because she would be too busy with her teaching and Jack had to take on the full management of the estate, with the family abroad. Eliza knew also that Margarita wanted to stay in Ireland, as Victor marrying would be too painful for her to witness. The entire Beconsford family would be staying on in England for the entire month of June. Eliza had been drafted in by Deborah to help out with all the charities supported by the estate and Jack would be up to his eyes with the farm and forest. Margarita and Eliza would continue to teach estate children each morning and join Ann Marie to teach the town children after lunch.

As summer came, Margarita was invited to sing in Cork on numerous occasions and particularly enjoyed two recitals in St. Ann's Church in Shandon. She had to refuse invitations from any Dublin events as she couldn't spend time too much time away from home. She was particularly disappointed to miss an invitation to sing for the La Touche Huguenot family who requested she sing at their home Luggala Lodge set in the heart of the garden of Ireland in County Wicklow. Travelling to Wicklow would be too time-consuming for her parents. She knew also that she still had progress to make on her voice, so she spent many evenings just practising the breathing exercises recommended by Master Johnson. She knew her singing was getting better, when she found she could hold a high note for so much longer on one breath. She knew also that Master Johnson was very pleased, both with her voice and her work ethic. He was also delighted with her grounded common sense.

"I could never imagine you as a singer who would be highly temperamental!" he joked on many occasions.

It was early July when Eliza came back from her teaching with Margarita, knowing they could both enjoy some months of rest, as the school closed to allow the children help in the farms and home chores plus the harvest in early autumn.

Jack was excited that his newest play park and nature walk for the town dwellers was to open that weekend and the newlyweds were returning from their honeymoon in Italy.

"Are you going up to the house when Victor and Fleur return tomorrow?" Eliza asked, as she turned to her daughter.

"I'll wait until after the weekend as I want to explore Dad's gardens with a few of the children on Sunday," Margarita replied.

Eliza smiled in amusement. "Knowing you, you will be seeing those kids all summer and you will get no rest the way you're going!"

At twelve noon on Saturday, Jack stood proudly beside Isaac as the local town councillor, Mr. Dillon, gave a speech and unveiled a plaque thanking the Beconsford Estate for providing the funds required to create a place of play and sanctuary for the people of the town. Gravel paths and many benches allowed the adults to walk and rest, while the children played on swings and small wooden roundabouts that even the little ones could sit on. A special area was set aside for children to kick balls to each other and little mazes were designed by Jack for both small and bigger children. Trees and flowers were planted along pathways and carved wooden stakes had the names of all the plants and flowers. A large area was also set aside for children to bring seeds and plants to put into the ground and hopefully see them grow.

The townsfolk came in their droves and the women with small children were grateful for a seat to sit on away from their humble homes and allow their children to play in safety and freedom.

Everyone clapped when the park was officially opened by the town officials who were fulsome in their praise for Jack and Isaac.

The head of the town council got everyone to stay quiet as he thanked the benefactors. "We owe a great debt of gratitude to Jack Ryan for his vision and hard work in putting together a place of fun and relaxation for the children and adults of the town. I want also to thank Isaac Beconsford for financially supporting the project. I now promise that the town guardians will continue with works that will make the town of Midleton a place of excellence in the future."

After the ceremony, orange and lemon drinks and biscuits were provided for all the people in the park. Eliza was very proud of her husband's work and the estate for their financial support. As she chatted to Meg and Deborah, she felt so happy when people from all walks of life came over to Jack and Isaac and thanked them with a genuineness that brought Eliza close to shedding a tear. Deborah and Isaac had to leave early to be at home for the arrival of Victor and Fleur.

A very satisfied Jack Ryan returned to his home knowing that some of his hopes had come to fruition on that day. He dared to believe that his granny would have been proud of him.

On Sunday, Margarita arrived at The Park, as it was now called, armed with a basket full of small plants and seeds for the children to begin to plant their own flower garden. The girls were more interested while the boys ran around the play area, kicking rolled-up cloth balls to each other and chasing each other through the mazes. Margarita was delighted that the weather held up as so many families came out, some eating as they sat on rugs thrown down on the grass. She had brought some small cakes baked by Molly. When the planting was finished, she distributed them amongst the children and left them to enjoy the rest of the afternoon.

One of her youngest pupils came up to her with a little posy in her hand. As she gave it to Margarita she shyly said, "Thank you, miss, for giving us the cakes and the park to play in."

Margarita laughed as she took the posy and ruffled the curly head.

"Thank you, Kitty, I will put these in water and place them on my desk when I get home."

As Kitty skipped away, Margarita turned for home, smiling, but with a few tears in her eyes also. It had been a school year full of many joys mingled with the sadness of the passing of Granny Sheila.

Victor and Fleur's arrival sent great waves of excitement around the county set. A new future Lady Beconsford was great news around the upper classes who all wanted an opportunity to meet with her. But Victor seemed very protective of his wife from the day they arrived. Margarita and Eliza had joined Fleur and Deborah for tea on Monday and the three women had created a very warm atmosphere into which the quiet and gentle Fleur could enter. They spent time also in the Secret Garden where the perfume of summer roses scented the warm air.

Margarita and Fleur went for a walk together and arranged to go to see The Park the next day and eat cake in the Regency Room at the Haven Inn, still provided by Mrs. Sexton.

Margarita told Fleur about the singing engagements she had coming up and Fleur begged to join her. Margarita laughed as she said, "I can sing for your family at any time!"

Fleur smiled but was adamant that she wanted to watch Margarita in public. A friendship that had grown since Fleur first arrived the previous Christmas was cemented, as the two girls linked arms and returned to Eliza and Deborah.

Eliza had watched with delight the generous way her daughter had offered her genuine friendship to Victor's wife.

In late autumn, Victor and Fleur announced with pride

that Fleur was expecting a baby to be born the following April. Everyone at the big house was excited. The Ryan family were also joyful, as Lily had come for a vacation with her children. Meg and Alice thought the two boys in particular were wild, as they involved themselves in everything on the farm. Robert laughed at their antics, delighted to spend some time with his sweet grandchildren. The fact that Lily had enjoyed life around Europe having fun before having children had him worried that she'd never settle down to family life so he would not have a word said against her exuberant family!

As all the Ryan and Turner families sat around for Sunday lunch, cooked as always by Meg, they discussed the good news about the baby and Lily regaled them all with an account of the opulence of the wedding which was held in the tall graceful St. Etheldreda's church in the grounds of the home of the Lord Salisbury. The Cecil family were close friends of Fleur's family and the after-church reception was held in their large mansion, built in grounds that stretched for acres and acres in the middle of Hertfordshire. The house was constantly visited by members of the Royal household including Princess Victoria who would often be seen painting and sketching in the grounds. The gardens with their year-round display of flowers and plants from all over the world were a wonder to behold, according to Lily.

"You and Eliza will have to come over some time, Jack," said Lily, turning to her brother-in-law. "I could arrange for you to visit if you get time."

Eliza smiled. "Jack says every year that we'll travel abroad! I would be delighted at the thought of such a trip but I won't hold my breath!"

Jack patted her hand and agreed that perhaps they could take a trip there the following summer. Margarita said she'd love to go as well and John laughed and said that perhaps the whole family could go before next year's harvest time. Alice, who loved her older sister Lily, said she would definitely join them on any trip the family made. She had a great interest in designing clothes and wanted to see the shops in London.

Later, as they all sat in the back garden drinking tea and eating rich fruit cake, Eliza sat on the same rug that she had sat on the day she had first fallen in love with Jack Ryan.

Life has been very good to me since then, she thought, as she looked around at her father's happiness at having all his children and grandchildren around him.

The late autumn sun was throwing its blanket of warmth over the Secret Garden where Deborah and Eliza were sitting in their favourite sun trap, with warm blankets on their knees, enjoying each other's company and keeping up with the gossip from both the town and estates in the surrounding county.

Deborah admitted to Eliza that she was worried about Fleur's health.

"She's been sick for the last few months and is eating only very lightly. I'm worried about her general health also.

Victor has said before that she had always been frail and I can see he is worried too. Doctor Kearney, the baby doctor from Cork, has asked Victor to get a report of her early childhood health if that is possible. You see, because her mother died when she was young, nobody ever discussed anything about health with her. I believe he is concerned with her heart rate and says that it might only be because of her natural pregnancy sickness, but he needs to keep an eye on it."

"Well, she's in good hands with Doctor Kearney," nodded Eliza. "He is one of the best physicians in the county. He'll take good care of her. Also, I think she's enjoying Margarita's company. Perhaps Margarita could take some time off from the estate school if Fleur wants her around more?"

Deborah thought that was a great idea.

As the Ryan family sat around the table after their evening meal, Eliza turned to Margarita and said she had something to ask her.

Margarita smiled. "That's sounds ominous! Have I broken your best china, or hidden your silver spoon?" As her mother continued to look serious Margarita grew more concerned. "You or Dad aren't sick, are you?"

"No, no, nothing like that. It's about Fleur."

Margarita breathed a bit easier. "Go on, Mama."

"Deborah is worried about Fleur's health and the doctor is trying to get her childhood health records from England.

Deborah was wondering if you could spend some time with her, because they want someone her own age around her. I offered to do all the teaching at the estate school for now if you were prepared to spend the mornings with Fleur?"

Margarita was taken aback at this turn of events, realising it must be serious.

"Of course, I'll go to her. We've become great friends. Victor asked me to take her to Midleton and let her meet people. I knew he had a worried look about him but I just thought it was because of concern for the baby. I didn't realise he was worried about her also. I know she has a slight frame but I didn't worry about her." She paused. "I have grown so fond of her this year and I'll do anything it takes to help her."

Eliza gave a sigh of relief, not for the first time.

She and Jack smiled at each other as he shook his head and said, "I don't know what I did to deserve such a wonderful daughter as you, Margarita."

Margarita swished her table napkin at him and laughed as she left the room, saying, "Be careful that I don't run off with the silver one day!"

Jack just laughed and blew her a kiss as she closed the door.

Chapter 37

Margarita opened her bedroom door and entered. Warmth radiated from cheerful flames, casting light in the darkening room. She lit a candle and placed it on a table beside her comfortable armchair, close to the fire. She sat down, facing the window where the setting sun and rising moon were competing for space. She liked this time of day in late autumn, especially the glowing embers of the fire wrapping itself around her. She needed time to think and organise her thoughts around the task she was now asked to fulfil with her new friend.

She recalled Victor when he spoke to her last week, saying that she had always been around in his life when he needed her. He was being his own cheeky self when he said it but she could see that his concern was hidden, as always, behind his funny words. She had laughed at the time and said that he couldn't expect her to save him from his mad antics now that he was all grown up!

Her singing was going well and she knew that her methods of teaching at the school were being accepted as innovative, having found ways of teaching the children and making it fun. Some of the crustier upper classes in the county even felt that perhaps she was making them too literate and they'd be less respectful towards their betters! Margarita just laughed at that type of thinking. She had learned from her mother that education was the key to living a richer life.

Now her only problem was living through the next six months in close proximity to Victor. She recalled Granny Sheila once saying to her that we can all have a private life inside our head and our hearts, yet still live life to the full while being forced to be stoic about our innermost feelings. Margarita wasn't convinced that it was right but knew that the pain she felt inside when she thought of Victor could not be allowed to fester.

When his baby was safely born, Margarita knew she could make a career of singing on the stages abroad, far away from the Beconsfords. Only then would she be able to feel whatever she wanted and maybe, just maybe, there was someone out there in the wider world who would bring her joy in the future and the children she would love to have because of the joy that would bring to her parents.

Margarita was delighted to find that by the end of November Fleur had stopped feeling sick and was looking much better, with her rounder figure making her even pettier. They had a routine whereby Margarita joined her in the house after breakfast and they would take a walk to the edge of the water or just around the Secret Garden. On two mornings each week they would get the carriage to the village and have tea at the Regency Room and make any small purchases they both needed in the haberdashery and clothes shops. They met many people known to Margarita who loved to meet Fleur and wish her well. Late each morning they returned to the big house for lunch in the cosy side parlour overlooking the gardens. When Fleur went to rest, she usually asked Margarita to sing a couple of songs to her. This made Fleur look so serene and relaxed that most days Victor would come in and sit and listen and then stay with his wife when Margarita left.

As Christmas approached, the girls had great fun buying small gifts at the market and in the small shops in the town. They had just one trip to Cork because Victor was being so protective of Fleur. Deborah and Eliza had joined them on that trip and the women loved buying more exotic gifts in the larger shops in Cork. Margarita bought a pretty heart-shaped jewellery box with coloured seashells for her mother and once she had got the charcoal, pens and drawing paper for her father, she knew she could relax and enjoy helping Fleur buy gifts for her new family. They met some of the ladies of the county when they went for afternoon tea to the home of the Perrott family in Hayfield Manor, where they enjoyed a most relaxed afternoon with the many Perrott children popping in and delighting the guests with their singing and dancing. Deborah was a good friend of Veronica Perrott and they had been invited to spend the night as guests to make the trip less tiring for Fleur. Victor joined them in the evening and Margarita and Eliza sang and played the piano, when dinner was over. A joyous evening of Christmas songs and Irish ballads delighted Fleur who kept begging Margarita to sing just one more! As Margarita was enjoying her trip so much, she was happy to entertain the families until late into the evening.

Eliza and Margarita shared the delightful bedroom with its four-poster bed standing tall in the centre of the room. The women laughed at how grand it all was and touched the richly embroidered tapestries that hung on the walls. They both agreed that Fleur was looking very well and they slept soundly, happy in the knowledge that everyone had enjoyed an outing that they would cherish.

Over the Christmas period Victor and Fleur entertained friends in their home but decided to refuse all invitations, to ensure that Fleur got enough rest. She had begun to have some swelling in her ankles and Margarita, with the approval of Doctor Kearney would gently massage Fleur's arms and neck as she rested with her feet propped on a footstool. The girls began to have fun with card games and would get Deborah and Isaac to join in to increase the fun. There were many cries of cheating if anyone broke the rules! Deborah was so pleased to see the sparkle return to

Fleur's eyes as her pregnancy continued. The girls also spent hours making jigsaw puzzles and Lily had brought over a huge one of Hatfield House which took them weeks to complete, it was so large and intricate. They both enjoyed picking out their favourite parts of the house and agreed that they preferred to have smaller homes! They also loved sketching. Jack joined them on occasional mornings and showed Fleur how to improve her already almost professional sketching skills. He taught her how to sketch small faces and Margarita suggested that Fleur should work on a sketch of Victor and herself and perhaps put it in a pocket watch, to surprise him when the baby was born. That gave Jack an idea to suggest to Victor that Fleur might like a locket as a birthing gift. He would draw the intricate pictures, just like he did for Margarita's birthday many years before. He knew how ladies loved lockets. Jack decided to suggest this to Victor the next time he met him in the house.

The idea of the pocket watch excited Fleur and she happily spent many hours creating a gift expressing her love for Victor, although she had to keep it all secret from him. Victor always came to join them for a while each day but Fleur would joke with Margarita that he was always too anxious about her. Margarita usually smiled and said it was only because he cared so much.

Christmas Day arrived but for everyone in the estate it was a quieter one than last year when Fleur had just arrived.

Jack and his family were going to miss Granny Sheila and this year everyone was going to be fed by Meg at the farm. Jack joked that in all the years of marriage his wife had never cooked him a Christmas meal – it was always his mother or mother-in-law! Eliza reminded him that when she did offer to do it one year, he appeared so shocked that she never offered again! Margarita always added that she had enough of her mother's cooking all year and loved going out at Christmas!

Chapter 38

1838

The New Year brought joy to the Beconsfords with the hope of the new baby due to arrive in the spring. There were a few cold and crisp days in the early months, but rain fell depressingly often, making work on the estate and the farms difficult for everyone. People were stuck indoors, with life in the town hard for many, as works for the town council were regularly cancelled. Deborah and Eliza worked tirelessly to ensure that poverty was alleviated, in particular for the families who continued to send their children to school. Margarita was brought by carriage from Fleur's home each afternoon, to teach the children in the village. They were working on their singing, as they had been invited to sing at a church, in Cork, before Easter. The singing class each day seemed to lift everyone's spirits and on the days that Master Johnson came in to check their progress he would always bring apple pies and a bag of biscuits baked by his wife and the day would end with a party. Margarita knew how much joy was generated by teaching the children to sing and she always told them to go home and teach their own little brothers and sisters the songs they were learning. She also knew that the weekly treat of a party, where the kids were also given some treats to bring home to their families, brought a joy to the people that surpassed any money spent on the gifts.

As February ended, the first sign that spring might bring some brightness to the landscape came in the shape of rows of early daffodils that sprang up around the estate. Margarita and Fleur spent most mornings in a large room close to her bedroom which was now fitted out as a parlour to allow Fleur and Margarita to spend time sketching and painting. The view of the Secret Garden brought pleasure to them both, as Fleur was now confined mainly to the upper floor of the house. Victor was afraid to let her come down the winding staircase when he wasn't around, for fear she slipped, as the baby seemed to be getting so much heavier. They had dinner each evening in the new upstairs parlour, content in each other's company and on many occasions joined by Victor's parents. The doctor was a constant caller to the house and everyone was warned to be on full alert for fear the baby showed signs of arriving early.

As Easter arrived, those around Fleur were glad to know that she had carried the baby to full term. Margarita was also kept very busy, in the afternoons and evenings. The children's choir sang in Cork on Easter week. At Fleur's request, Margarita and the school choir sang in the estate church at the service on the 31st of March. They sang of joy and hope and of renewal. Margarita noticed that Victor was not in the church and wondered if Fleur was well.

After the service ended Margarita and Eliza spoke to Deborah and Isaac and they said that Fleur seemed unwell and, with her being so close to her time, Deborah asked if the ladies would come up to the house in the afternoon.

"I know that Fleur wants you at her side, Margarita, when her time comes. I don't expect it to be today but Doctor Kearney is calling later and will give us more information."

"Of course we'll come up, Deborah, and this time I'll bring an overnight bag," said Margarita.

Deborah and Eliza had a conversation in the drawing room while Margarita went to sit with Fleur.

"I just wish this was over," said Deborah. "I know how concerned Dr Kearney is, but all I have done in the last month is try to remain cheerful for Victor's sake."

"That's all you can do, Deborah. We can but hope for the best in any situation." Eliza knew there was a troubled look on her own face and tried to smile. "Everyone in the estate and even the town is thinking of you all," she added, putting a comforting arm around Deborah and holding her in a hug.

Margarita met Dr Kearney as he went towards the dining room for lunch.

"She's asleep for the moment," he said, but then whispered anxiously in her ear that Fleur's heart was very weak and it would take a miracle to ensure that she and the baby would both live.

Margarita had begun to feel increasingly worried about Fleur's constant tiredness over the past few weeks, but now, standing on the first step of the stairs, she felt rigid with shock at the enormity of this announcement.

Doctor Kearney put a hand on her shoulder and said, "Go up to her now – she needs you beside her to reassure her."

At that moment Margarita knew she had to put her own feelings aside and just do whatever Fleur and the doctor needed.

Margarita entered the bedroom and saw an anxious and exhausted Victor sitting at Fleur's bedside. Margarita made a movement to tell him stay sitting, as she made her way across the soft and soundless carpet.

"Let her sleep for now. Dr Kearney is gone to have a meal downstairs. Why don't you join the family for a little while and I will call you if Fleur wakens?"

With reluctance he left the room and Margarita took his place by Fleur's bedside.

As she sat down, she felt that she had grown older in the past day and had to realise that life can be tough even for the young. She held and stroked the pale hand that Victor had kept warm, as she watched Fleur sleep fitfully. She looked exhausted and Margarita could see from the creases in her brow that Fleur was feeling pain.

As soon as Fleur stirred and opened her eyes, Margarita summoned Jenny, to fetch Victor and Dr Kearney. Margarita knew that a nurse was also due to arrive and she felt that she needed the burden lifted from her shoulders. She was so concerned for Fleur's welfare. She had to shake herself when she found herself forgetting about the baby, such was her concern at the chalk-like pallor of Fleur's face.

As the doctor entered with Victor, Fleur smiled and asked them if it would be in order for Margarita to stay by her side until the baby had arrived. The doctor and Victor looked at each other and nodded.

"Of course you can stay," Victor said, looking at Margarita with beseeching eyes.

Margarita squeezed Fleur's hand and nodded that she would be with her until after the baby was born.

Margarita took a break while the doctor examined Fleur. She ate a light meal with Deborah and Eliza but few words were said, as each seemed to be lost in her own thoughts.

A long night followed and it was late morning on the first of April that Fleur finally showed signs that the baby wanted to be born. Margarita had been briefed by the nurse and the doctor that she could chat, soothe and even sing gently to Fleur.

While she could still talk, Fleur pointed to where she had hidden the gold fob pocket watch with the sketch of her and Victor inside.

"Will you get it for me when the baby is born? It's inside the jewellery box. I want it to be held by him close to his heart forever."

Margarita smiled and assured her that she would.

Many hours later as darkness fell on a cool and cloudless April night, the labour began in earnest. Fleur was given encouragement by the watchful Dr Kearney. He had known from early in her pregnancy that forceps would probably be needed but he hoped that nature would be kind to Fleur and allow her enough energy to fulfil her wish to produce a healthy baby. He had spoken on many occasions of his worries to Fleur but she had refused to allow him share his fears with Victor. He had been instructed to tell Victor that all his wife ever wanted for him was a healthy baby. That was her wish, whatever the consequences to herself.

They all toiled and sweated throughout the evening, especially the brave and courageous Fleur.

As the clock struck midnight to herald in the 2nd of April 1838, Dr Kearney used all his skills and, finally, with muted sounds from the dazed mother, a little girl was born. The doctor cut the umbilical cord and proceeded to deal with the afterbirth.

The nurse took the baby girl to wash her and eventually brought her back and laid her in Fleur's weak arms. Margarita asked Fleur to open her eyes to see the small perfect face of her daughter, who had the beauty of her mother and the soft golden hair of her father. Fleur looked, and smiled tenderly at her baby.

While Victor was being summoned from outside the door, Margarita took the gift from the jewellery box and handed it to Fleur. She then carefully picked up the baby and placed her in Victor's arms.

Victor was weeping as he sat by his wife's side with his new-born child in his arms. Fleur handed him the watch fob. He smiled and kissed her. Then he handed his precious daughter to the midwife. He took out the locket he had for Fleur and placed it around her neck. He showed her the faces inside and, with tears in her eyes, she looked at him and said, "I will hold this close to my heart forever."

Margarita left the room in an exhausted stupor with the horrendous knowledge that the doctor was unlikely to save the life of Fleur. She knew the family happiness would last just a little while. Margarita asked for a tray to be brought to her room, thankfully situated on the top floor of the house. She couldn't face them. She needed time to cry alone.

The sound of Victor Beconsford screaming, one hour after the birth of his child, felt like a knife through the heart of Margarita. It could be heard all over the house. She knew that Fleur had passed into a place of peace to leave behind her pain that Margarita knew would be beyond bearing by most of the family and was likely to break the boyish, cheerful optimistic Victor into so many pieces that she feared for his future sanity.

Yesterday, when the doctor had told her that Fleur's heart was much too weak for childbirth, she knew she had to stay strong. The miracle was that Fleur had carried the baby to full term. He had been preparing her for the battle ahead of making sure the baby arrived safely. Margarita had played her part for the rest of that long night, but knew that the war would not be won.

At last, she fell into an exhausted sleep, unwilling and unable to allow anyone to comfort her on that dark night. The only moment of joy had been to see the perfectly healthy baby girl being born – one who would never experience the deep love of her mother.

Eliza watched with horror as Deborah and Isaac clung to each other. They were both in a state of shock. Nobody knew why Victor had taken so long with Fleur but the sounds of his screams told its own story. Dr Kearney sent the nurse to the parlour to hand the tiny little girl to her grandmother and grandfather. All Eliza saw was the soft downy golden hair adorning a cherubic face.

She knew that Margarita had gone to sleep and she mouthed to Isaac that she was going to get Jack.

Eliza ran back home through the trees and gravel paths, blinded by the tears in her eyes. She banged at the door and in seconds Jack appeared and she fell into his arms and the floodgates opened. He held her close while she babbled the news of Fleur's death. Jack sat her by the warm range in the kitchen and made hot sweet tea and heated some bread. He came back and sat with her and listened with tears in his own eyes. He asked how the baby was and how was Margarita.

"The baby is with Deborah and Margarita is in her bedroom upstairs in the house and told the maid she wanted to be alone. Come up to the house with me and help me make sense of this."

Jack left her for a few moments to grab his clothes and returned to sit with her, insisting that she drink the tea and try to eat a piece of the hot bread that still sat on the plate. When she had finished, he held her close and tried to console her.

"There's a new life in the Big House and you have to take some comfort from that, and Margarita did all she could for Fleur to make her last months as restful as possible. Let us go up and we'll speak to Margarita as soon as she wakes and we can only let Deborah and Isaac know that we will help them share Victor's terrible loss."

They sat quietly by the fire until a certain calmness came over Eliza.

"We have to go back up now," she said, her voice echoing the distress she felt. "Whatever we can do, we will."

Jack held her hand and rubbed her wrists with gentle soothing strokes because he too could not talk while tears fell down his cheeks.

The residents and staff of the Big House were in deep shock. There was an eerie silence all around as Jack and Eliza entered the parlour.

Deborah was in a corner holding the sleeping baby and Isaac was sitting with his elbows on his knees and his hands covering his face. Deborah beckoned them in and said that Victor had been sedated by the doctor and was sleeping in his parents' room.

Eliza sat by Deborah and Jack put an arm around Isaac. Eliza whispered to Deborah that Ann Marie had a cousin in the town, Hilda Bowe, who had just given birth to a stillborn baby boy.

"If the doctor or nurse can't find someone, perhaps I could ask her. They are a lovely family and I could ask her if all else fails." She touched the soft downy hair of the little girl.

Seeing the grief and exhaustion on Deborah's face, she asked if she could hold the baby and give her a break to perhaps have a cup of tea. Deborah looked at her as if in another world as Eliza asked Jack to get tea brought to the room.

Dawn was breaking over the countryside and birds could be heard singing at the end of this dark night. Eliza returned the baby to Deborah when she saw a little bit of colour return to her face having drunk the cup of hot tea. She stood up and said that she was going to check on a few things and would be back in a few minutes.

She walked to the parlour where the doctor was having breakfast. He was in a state of exhaustion but Eliza had to ask him if they had someone who would feed the baby. He said that the nurse who was due to come to help with the baby would be there within an hour and he had given the baby some boiled water which was fine for the time being.

Eliza made the offer to talk to Hilda Bowe and the

doctor, who knew the family, immediately agreed it was a great idea.

"I'll go as soon as I've spoken to Margarita. She's asleep at present but I'm going to take her breakfast and talk to her. Afterwards I'll go to the town."

Eliza climbed the stairs to Margarita's room, Jack accompanying her carrying a tray.

She knocked several times before the door was finally opened by a tired Margarita, her face streaked with tears.

Jack placed the tray on the dressing table as Eliza took her daughter in her arms and led her back to sit on the bed.

Jack knelt down in front of them both and took his daughter's hands in his.

"I knew yesterday evening that she was not going to pull through and I couldn't do anything for her!" she wailed. "I had to pretend and pretend for hours that everything was fine. She wanted that baby so much and now it's cost Fleur her life!"

Margarita broke down again as great sobs racked her body. Eliza motioned to Jack to sit with Margarita.

"Listen, love, I have to go to the town and ask Hilda Bowe if she could find it in her heart to feed Fleur's baby. I'll be back in no time and you try to have breakfast with your dad while I'm gone."

Margarita looked up with sad eyes. "I never even thought of that and only the other day I told Fleur I'd help with the baby."

"Don't worry, love, we'll find someone to feed her, plus a nurse is due shortly to help out. Just you rest for today and tomorrow we might all be thinking a little clearer."

Hilda Bowe was in her thirties and was a cousin of Ann Marie's. She had three girls who were now six, eight and ten. Her new baby had been a surprise and her husband, who couldn't work manually because of a weak chest had hoped it would be a boy. It was a boy but he didn't reach full term and died within hours of his birth.

When Eliza explained the problem to her, the sadness left her eyes for a moment as she answered, "It would be an honour to be able to help a baby in need." She also confided in Eliza that funds were low as she couldn't earn money over the past few months. "I've been worried about this for the last few days and maybe something good will come out this tragic week for our family and the Beconsfords. I'll just tell my Alfie to see that the girls are fed and then I'll come up straight away with you to the Big House."

All through the next two days Victor was inconsolable and refused to see the baby. All he wanted was to drink brandy and neither Deborah or Isaac could get through his wall of hurt. His grandfather Lord Edward was due to arrive and they heard that he was looking for someone to blame for causing his grandson's wife to die. This was the last thing the family needed right now but they couldn't stop him from coming home for the funeral. Thankfully, Lady Ethel was too fragile to make the journey and with that news at least everyone breathed a sigh of relief.

When Lord Edward arrived, Isaac quickly had to tell him to keep his bad temper to himself and to act in a dignified way while he was at home.

'Nobody is at fault for Fleur's death – she had a very weak heart," he explained as calmly as he could to his belligerent father.

Isaac tried, while dealing with his own grief, to explain responsibility to Victor, telling him to at least try get through the funeral with some form of dignity. He was also the only one who had the courage to ask what name Victor would call the baby girl.

"Fleur wanted a girl to be called Rosita," he answered though anguished tears flowing down his face. "She always said that her own name was Fleur and she wanted to be a little rose."

His father patted his hand. "That will do for now. Rosita is a perfect name. Now take the medicine the doctor left and rest for now. You have a lot to face over the next couple of days."

On the morning of the funeral the driveway of the estate was lined with workers who were joined by throngs of people from the town who had all came to pay their respects to the family. Fleur's family were holding a simultaneous service in Hertfordshire, as some of her siblings were too young to travel. All manner of people, rich or poor, were invited to the church to join the family. Master Johnson played the organ and a choir from Cork joined the local children to sing during the service. Margarita felt unable to hold herself together to sing and sat with her family. Isaac and Deborah had to support Victor as he entered the church and he appeared to those who saw him to be heavily sedated.

The dignified silence during the service was broken as grown people wept openly while the coffin was carried from the church towards the burial ground a hundred yards away. The children in the choir began to sob and the family and staff were by then overcome by tears. Margarita and Eliza held on to each other as Jack was one of those carrying the coffin. The funeral walk took place through a shaft of sunshine and then went through a shadow of darkness underneath the overhanging trees. That darkness was felt by all the mourners. Everyone stayed respectfully back to allow this time of grief be a private one for the Beconsford family. As prayers were said at the graveside the grief was palpable and Jack and Isaac had to hold Victor as he dropped a dozen roses onto the coffin. This bleak day did not promise any hope. It matched the dark mood of the people who had travelled from far and wide. A pall of great sorrow hung darkly by a single thread threatening to break the spirits of the bereaved as much as it had broken their hearts. They saw no light in their tunnel even though a beautiful little girl lay in her cot close to the burial place of her mother. This hope for the future did not seem to break through the barrier of pain felt by Victor. Fleur was finally laid to rest with the locket given to her by her husband sitting close to her heart. Victor stood by the grave and, after he dropped the last rose, put his hand on his heart to feel the watch with their love locked into it that she had given to him moments before she passed into a place of peace.

Later, Eliza sat with Margarita as they ate in the great hall. She thought that the large but subdued crowd was so different to those at the burial of Granny Sheila, where everyone had celebrated her long life.

Margarita turned to her mother and said, "I'm not hungry. I'd love to go and see Rosita, if you could ask Deborah?"

"Of course I will, love – just sit there and I'll be back."

Margarita watched her mother go to Deborah's side. Victor had taken to his bedroom, as the rest of the family were thanking the mourners who had been invited.

Eliza returned and nodded. "Deborah said we should both go up. Rosita is being cared for by Nurse Jean Andrews, and it seems herself and Hilda Bowe are getting on very well."

As they climbed the stairway to the nursery, Margarita could hear the faint crying of the baby. They entered the airy lightness of the nursery. It was bathed in sunlight, overlooking the Secret Garden.

Margarita stood still for a moment, remembering the love that Fleur had given in creating this haven of peace. Hilda had gone home to check up on her girls and Nurse Andrews was by the window, cradling the little baby in her arms. Eliza had already met the nurse and she introduced Margarita.

"I've heard everything about you, Margarita, and I'm delighted you're here. I can't shake hands but please call me Jean. Rosita isn't settling too well today. She should be asleep by now."

"Could I hold her?" Margarita asked tentatively.

"Of course you can. Please sit on the chair by the window if you wish. I like to sit there with her just after she falls asleep. It's lovely looking out on such a delightful garden."

Margarita sat down and Jean placed the baby in her arms. She held her as if she was fragile glass and rocked her gently to ease her crying.

As Eliza and Jean watched, Margarita began to quietly sing a lullaby as she rocked the baby. Within a few moments, quietness descended on the nursery.

As Eliza stood watching her daughter with the baby, Deborah quietly opened the nursery door and slipped into the room. The two friends looked at each other, as they observed how gentle Margarita was with the new-born baby.

"You certainly have the magic, Margarita, if you can get her to sleep that quickly," said Jean, smiling.

"I sang to her every day before she was born, especially when Fleur said she was kicking. Maybe she could hear me?" Margarita mused. "Can I stay holding her for a while? I'd rather not go back downstairs just yet."

Deborah nodded her agreement and Margarita happily spent the next hour holding the baby to her heart, as Rosita slept peacefully in her arms.

Chapter 39

Deborah knocked quietly on the nursery door and then entered the room. It was full of light, with the quiet pale colours on the walls that Flora had chosen for her child. The nurse was standing by the window, gently rocking the grizzling little baby.

"Can I take her and give you a break?" asked Deborah.

"Please do," said Nurse Jean.

Deborah took the baby and held her carefully against her left shoulder as she patted her back.

"I want to ask you something," Nurse Jean said.

"Yes?"

"Myself and Hilda are very happy here and we both want to continue to be with the baby. I have a suggestion and it comes from my experience of being with children whose mother has died. They need some attention from somebody who was very close to them while they were in the womb and I know that at this time your son is grieving too deeply to take on this role. The baby is not getting to sleep in a contented way except on the days that Margarita Ryan holds her and sings to her. I know Margarita sang for Flora when she was pregnant and I also believe that little Rosita was comforted in the womb by her gentle singing. Do you think there is any way we could get her to come and help with Rosita, while we try to build up a better sleep pattern for her?"

Deborah handed the baby back to Jean and sat on the chair by the window.

"That sounds like a wonderful idea, if she would agree to it. You are quite correct about Victor. He's in no fit state to comfort his baby and he's even talking about going to England to spend time with his aunt in Hertfordshire. He's drinking too much and his father and I are at our wits' end. His grandfather believes it might be good for him to go away for a while but I'm not sure that's a solution."

As Deborah stood up and stroked the baby's soft blonde hair she came to a decision.

"Yes, yes, I'll go and speak to Eliza first and see what she thinks about approaching Margarita. Thanks, Jean, for the suggestion." She kissed the soft downy blonde curls that looked just like Victor's hair when he was a baby.

Deborah left the nursery and went to Isaac's office. He was alone in the room and she told him of the nurse's worries. He agreed that something needed to be done and he encouraged Deborah to go and talk to Eliza immediately.

***

Eliza was busy in the kitchen, helping Ann Marie prepare the food for dinner, when she heard a knock on the front door. Ann Marie went to open it and Eliza was cheered to hear Deborah's voice in the hallway.

Eliza took off her apron and walked smiling from the kitchen.

"I think I'm just ready for a cup of tea and I'm delighted to have it with you. Come into the parlour. It's lovely and warm."

Eliza was smiling until she noticed the worried look on Deborah's face.

"Is the baby all right?" she asked anxiously.

"Yes, yes, she's fine but, yes, I am here to talk about her."

"Let me tell Anne Marie to bring us some hot apple pie and tea."

When Eliza returned, Deborah told her everything the nurse had said.

Eliza nodded wisely and slowly. "I know Margarita has enjoyed her time with Rosita and I could get Ann Marie to take most of her classes in the village but it obviously has to be Margarita's decision." She nodded and continued, almost in thought. "I hope she has the strength to do it. In fact, maybe it will be a good thing. Her life at present seems to have been fractured."

Anne Marie came in carrying a tray with the requested tea and apple pie.

When Anne Marie had greeted Deborah, unloaded the tray and left, Eliza said, "Leave it with me, Deborah, and I'll be up to the house tonight to let you know. But, now let us enjoy Anne Marie's apple pie."

Later that evening at the dinner table, Eliza broached the subject with her daughter.

Margarita was quiet for only a few seconds before a happy smile crossed her face.

"I'd love to be involved with the baby. I love my teaching but some of the joy has gone out of it for the moment. I knew that Nurse Jean was having difficulties with Rosita but I felt it wasn't my place to offer advice."

Eliza and Jack looked at each other and both breathed a sigh of relief.

"Maybe when you are with her you could start to put some of those poems of yours to music, as you've always intended to do? You could always try them out on the baby," Eliza said with a smile.

"Well, coincidentally, I have been talking to Master Johnson and he is enthusiastic about me writing new songs because he knows I have not the heart to perform in concerts at the moment."

"Would you like to come with me up to the Big House after we've had a cup of tea? I told Deborah I'd let her know tonight."

Margarita agreed and Jack said he'd accompany them and have a chat with Isaac.

At the Big House, Jack was informed by Isaac that Victor was about to leave for England the next day and nobody knew if that was the right thing or not for such a young man in the height of his grief.

Meanwhile, Margarita was already in the nursery cuddling Rosita and helping Jean get her ready for her bed. She'd had her night feed and Hilda had left a feed for the middle of the night.

Margarita agreed to stay there that night and the Beconsfords were overjoyed to have her fully involved with the baby. It was one less problem for the family.

The following morning, after a night of broken sleep, Margarita was holding the newly washed baby in her arms when the door of the nursery quietly opened.

Victor stood there with his grandfather.

"Kiss your daughter goodbye and promise her you will be back to her as soon as you have healed. You can see that Rosita is in good hands with so many people surrounding her with love." Lord Edward guided Victor gently towards the baby.

Margarita watched and thought that it was the first time she had seen His Lordship looking so old, frail and sad. Maybe somewhere in his heart he has compassion, she thought, as she stood up and turned Rosita to face Victor.

He was a pitiful sight. Tears flowed down his face as he kissed the baby's cheek.

"I'll be back, I promise. I'll be back, but I don't know when." He turned swiftly and stumbled towards the door. As he stepped outside, he turned his head and implored, "Take care of her for me, Margarita."

He was gone and a shattered Margarita had a feeling that it would be a long time before she would see him again. She sat down with the baby and for the first time in months sang the song of her lost love as a lullaby.

Chapter 40

As the first signs of summer appeared the overwhelming sadness in the big house began to lift. Around the estate, vegetables were planted, forest trees were being cut and replaced and the Secret Garden began to glow with the colour of roses and the scent of Sweet William. The herb garden produced an abundance of soothing, sweet-smelling lavender, rosemary and basil.

Margarita was finally contented. Working side by side with Nurse Jean and Hilda, she was happy to see that Rosita had begun to thrive. Deborah and Isaac were delighted to see the change in the baby. Her weight was increasing almost by the day and they all vied happily with each other to say that she smiled for them first!

Eliza found that Jean and Hilda refused to leave the room while Margarita sang lullabies to the baby. They laughingly said they enjoyed their free concert each day and often even persuaded her daughter to sing an encore while Rosita slept!

Deborah and Isaac often joined them all in the nursery and Eliza would watch them as the signs of grief slowly lifted from their faces. She knew that Victor had now gone to Deborah's Mitfield relatives in Hertfordshire, and they wondered why he had left Helena's home. In the two months since he had departed, nobody had received a letter from him.

Margarita still went regularly to give music lessons to the village children, but her priority was to watch with pride as Rosita thrived, with all the love that surrounded her.

Nurse Jean made sure that Isaac was often holding and playing with Rosita.

"You can't have a child think that only women are around her," she said. "She needs a male presence until her dad returns."

She was right. Isaac got the first smile from Rosita, or so he said!

Isaac said he was spending more time with her than he had with Victor when he was a baby! It seemed to surprise him that she kicked and gurgled when he tickled her. Deborah said to Eliza that she didn't know who was having more fun, Isaac or the baby!

As summer turned into autumn, Margarita found time to write some songs while the baby slept. Towards the end of autumn, she returned each night to sleep in her own home again as Rosita was sleeping through most of the night.

By day, the baby, in her perambulator, was propped up with pillows and thriving on the attention she received from everyone.

"Look, look, that's one of the last roses of the summer," Margarita said as she sat with Rosita, looking out of the window facing the Secret Garden. She always talked to Rosita as if she could understand her. "I'll sing you a song today that I thought was too sad for your mama when she was expecting you. It's called 'The Last Rose of Summer' and you now know that you were the first Rose of this Summer and you will continue to be my precious Forever Rose of Summer. It was a poem by Mr. Moore, written in County Kilkenny, and Mr. Bunting wrote the lovely music."

As Margarita gently began to rock Rosita, she sang the bittersweet words of the song.

"Tis the last rose of summer, left blooming alone
All her lovely companions are faded and gone;
No flower of her kindred, no rose-bud is nigh,
To reflect back her blushes or give sigh for sigh …"

She continued to sing until Rosita's eyes closed, unaware that Jean, Hilda and Deborah were standing quietly by the door, transfixed by the sound of her voice. Then, as she laid the sleeping baby in her crib, the women walked into the room.

"Young lady, you are going to have to start using that voice of yours again in the concert halls," said Deborah, smiling. "You will have to start to put yourself first and I'll begin by telling you that the main carriage and horses are going to be at your disposal for trips you will take around the county. I know from your mother that you have had offers to sing from far and wide."

"But I love being with Rosita!" Margarita exclaimed.

"We all know that but we know also that you need to sing! I've even heard whispers from the Perrott family in Cork that an up-and-coming male singer from Bantry called Richard Staunton, who is getting great reviews, wants to sing with you."

"But he's already famous – why would he want me to sing with him?"

Deborah and Hilda looked at each other and shook their heads.

"Well, whether you want my opinion or not, and you're getting it anyway," said Hilda, "you are just as famous from what I hear and you have the most delightful voice I ever heard!"

"I agree," said Deborah.

"Just let Hilda take over and come to the lounge for some tea and we'll talk things over. Your father and Isaac will join us."

Before the evening was over, Margarita had been persuaded to spend a little less time in the nursery and to spend more time with her music teacher. She had told the family that she had written a song and agreed to sing it at her next recital.

298

As Margarita lay on her bed that night, she felt more contented than she been for many months. She realised that she had been hiding away from life by focusing only on Rosita. She was so happy to hear the praise heaped on her earlier in the day by Isaac and Deborah, regarding how much their grandchild had blossomed during her watch.

But I'm getting almost possessive about Rosita, she thought, and she's not mine.

Before closing her eyes, she resolved to dream or even daydream of reviving her hopes of going abroad to Europe to sing, now that she knew Rosita was thriving.

Richard Staunton was in touch with Master Johnson within a week and the singer expressed a wish for Margarita to join him in a concert over Christmas for the Mayor of the City and their guests in Cork. Within a week Richard arrived in Midleton to meet Margarita at Master Johnson's home.

Margarita's first impression of him was his genuine open smile and his broad shoulders. His presence and happy personality made him an instant success with the Johnsons. He was a happy, very handsome man of 24 years and as he shook Margarita's hand with his warm strong handshake, he told her he had heard her when she sang in Cork in the past and he particularly loved her singing of "The Lament of the Irish Maiden".

"The night that I heard you sing that, I wanted to be that man returning to you," Richard laughed, "and here I am now, hoping for the chance to sing on the same stage with you."

Margarita blushed with embarrassment at the compliment.

"I didn't know you were in the audience, but I am the one who is honoured to sing with you."

"Well, that's a good start," said Master Johnson. "You both think the other is marvellous! Now let us try and prove that with some practice."

The ice was broken, everyone laughed and Margarita knew instantly that she had met a good friend.

Chapter 41

The summer had been hot and dry and that weather had carried on into the autumn. Margarita had continued seeing Rosita through the warm autumn days and the baby was now showing her happy and noisy personality as she banged spoons on pots. She reminded Margarita of Victor who had always had a happy disposition as a boy. But everyone in the Big House was tight-lipped about him.

Deborah met with Eliza one day in November and explained what had happened to Victor. "He got involved with the Ton in London."

"What is that?" Eliza asked, never having heard the name before.

Deborah explained that it was a group of young aristocrats who wooed the young women debutantes. However, many of those young and not-so-young men were rakes, who spent their time drinking and gambling.

"Victor has always led a sheltered life in Ireland, and he is, I believe, spending his time drinking to blot out his heartache. I'm told he has now turned up at your sister Lily's home. Thankfully, I'm also told that since he arrived in Lily's house he has stopped drinking. How long that will last, I don't want to think about. I'm so worried about him but don't know what to do."

"I'll write to Lily," said Eliza, "and see if perhaps they could get medical help for him. Hopefully he'll eventually come to his senses." She patted Deborah's hand, not at all sure that what she was saying would come true.

Margarita's days were full. They still included many trips to Rosita. She was now teaching only music at the school, because the local council had employed a new teacher to help Eliza and Ann Marie. Much to the delight of the Ryans, Ann Marie was now making an excellent career for herself as a schoolteacher, but still helped out at Eliza's house when she had time. Eliza always felt that the girl had given up the chance of marriage to pursue her ambition to teach and earn money for her family. Ann Marie's younger sister Hetty was now helping at Eliza and Jack's home full time.

Margarita was spending at least two hours each day practising her singing and Richard was a regular visitor to Master Johnson's house. Margarita regularly enjoyed afternoon tea at the Regency Room with Richard after practice, and her Granny Molly always made sure that they sat at a table by the window and served them the hottest scones from Mrs. Sexton's oven!

Molly often looked at Richard and Margarita sitting by the window and thought they would make a lovely couple. She was not alone in this as people in the town were calling them the Golden Couple and wondered how long before Richard put the band of gold on her finger. It was obvious to all that he was besotted. Yet Molly knew that all they seemed to have to talk about was music and travel to foreign shores. However, Molly loved to see the sparkle shining again from Margarita's eyes. She just hoped that her granddaughter wouldn't let singing stop her from finding a good man to marry.

Margarita and Richard were now ready for their first major concert. They had been invited to take part in a big Christmas fundraising concert for the poor of Cork city.

Everyone in their families were excited for them on the night of concert in the Commercial Rooms in Cork. Jack and Eliza were honoured guests along with Richard's parents and his two younger sisters. Deborah and Isaac secured invitations for Old John and Meg. Alice, Molly and Old John got invites from Master Johnson.

Margarita went to Cork in the early morning to practise with the pianist and to get a feel for the venue. The rest of the families followed later. They had booked an early dinner in the impressive Imperial Hotel, close to the Commercial Rooms. The whole party would stay in the hotel as overnight guests of the Committee of Merchants of Cork.

***

Eliza and Jack entered their room in the hotel.

"Isn't it big!" Eliza exclaimed, as she plumped herself down on the soft four-poster bed. Lying there she could enjoy looking at the opulence of the embossed cream wallpaper and the ornate carved ceiling, adorned with smiling cherubs.

"I could get used to this, Mr. Ryan," she said, laughing.

Jack came over and kissed her tenderly. "We will spend more of our money on trips like this, maybe go abroad for a holiday again, now that Margarita is becoming more independent."

"I've been hearing that from you, Jack Ryan, for years. Some year I might insist you take me to Italy again," she said with a laugh.

"Well," Jack chuckled, as he put his arm tenderly around his wife, "maybe we can finally stop worrying about Margarita."

"I agree, and maybe I'll also teach less next year and make more time for you and I to enjoy ourselves."

"I'm all for that," agreed Jack.

"Now come and let's tidy up. I can't wait for that banquet they are going to serve, and hearing our lovely daughter sing."

The exclusive dining room delighted Eliza. Candlelit chandeliers adorned the walls and the glow of light shone brightly on the sparkling cut glasses and silver cutlery on the table.

Jack looked really happy, seeing the bright smiles of his own family.

Richard's parents, Grace and Jerome, were small farmers from Ballydehob, outside Bantry. They were lovely down-to-earth people, who seemed bemused that their son was blessed with a great voice. Molly was delighted to hear that Richard's grandparents had known both Granny Sheila's family and her husband Alex's family who also came from the Ballydehob area.

"The Cotters and the Kingstons are lovely families and they were delighted to hear that Richard was singing with one of their relatives," said Grace.

Deborah and Isaac were also pleased when the Perrott family came over to chat between courses.

Everyone was in good spirits when they finally moved, after coffee, to the elegance of the nearby Commercial Rooms.

Richard had seemed nervous when Margarita had arrived at rehearsals, but as the day progressed they had built up a great camaraderie with the other musicians and Joshua Thompson, the pianist. Master Johnson kept a watchful eye on the proceedings and added a few suggestions, including reminding them to smile and look as if they were enjoying themselves!

The curtain rose at eight o'clock and applause greeted the musicians as they opened the evening with some Christmas hymns and songs. The audience had singing sheets and were asked to join in and everyone seemed to love that. Richard sang in his wonderful tenor voice and he was followed by Margarita who sang a jolly Christmas tune. They had both agreed that they were not going to sing anything obscure, but only melodies that most of the concert goers already knew. It worked and, when they sang together, they indeed looked like the perfect couple.

As the evening drew to a close Richard announced that he wanted Margarita to sing a song that she had written for baby Rosita Beconsford and this would be the first time it was sung in public. The audience cheered once more and, with Richard still standing by her side, she began to sing.

"When I was a child, I'd dream all day,
I'd dream of the sky, so far away.
I'd fly up to Venus and then to Mars
And return again, on a shooting star.
Although I love my Irish home,
I'll always roam, I'll always roam
But because I love my island shore,
I will return for evermore."

As Margarita continued each verse and chorus, Deborah and Eliza shed tears. When the song ended, everyone stood and clapped, as Richard hugged her and kissed her on the cheek.

They finished the concert together with the much loved "Silent Night" and as everyone requested another song, they sang together a love song, looking at each other as if they were actually in love.

The night was a great success and the mayor of the city announced that the Commercial Merchants had donated all the ticket money to the poor of Cork to help with food and clothing for many needy families.

As the clapping continued, Richard and Margarita announced that they too would be giving their fees to the poor and needy, Richard to the people of Bantry and Margarita to the folks in Midleton. Jack and Isaac now cheered the loudest. Everyone felt that they had attended a unique and special night.

Christmas was even more special for many people that year as the Merchants of Cork also gave money to Midleton and the surrounding small villages. The Haven Inn and Mrs. Sexton were kept busy organising parcels for everyone in need. Little knitted dolls were again added for the girls and carved animals were included with skipping ropes for everyone. The food parcels this year included cooked beef and hams, plus rich plum puddings.

As the festivities approached, Deborah and Isaac's hopes were dashed that Victor might return home. They heard that he had gone abroad, to Paris and then to Florence. He asked about Rosita but would not let them know where he was staying. He said he would write again in the New Year.

As Deborah said to Eliza, "As long as he is safe, that's all I can hope for. I always felt he was too immature to marry but, with all its sadness, we have all been blessed with his much-treasured baby Rosita."

On Christmas Day, having attended church, all the Ryan and Turner families, plus Old John and Sam, were invited to have dinner in the Big House, as a thank-you to Margarita for caring so well for Rosita during the year. They were all dressed in their best finery. Margarita dressed in a long soft silk lavender dress with a simple bustle. Her sleek black hair was adorned with discreet diamanté clips and tendrils of soft curling wisps fell softly on her face accentuating her midnight-blue eyes. She was the picture of her mother at the same age, thought Jack. Eliza thought that Margarita looked perfect and so mature for her years. She'd learned love and loss so young and yet her strength allowed her to hide her deepest feelings.

Everybody enjoyed the mulled wine and when they sat down to the feast prepared for them by Cook, great praise was heaped on the kitchen staff. The spiced beef and fowl topped with succulent sauces, with trays of roast and fried potatoes and a myriad of freshly cooked vegetables, were enjoyed by everyone.

The baby sat on a high chair, designed by Jack and carved by Joe McCarthy who was the best wood carver in the town. She played her usual happy games with her spoons during dinner and everyone enjoyed a wonderful meal at the end of a difficult year.

They all played charades and cards after, while Rosita napped. Later in the evening everyone enjoyed a light tea before the singing started. It was the first festivity in the big house since the death of Fleur. It was a sobering moment as they had toasted absent friends but the joy of having Rosita in all their lives was also not forgotten. It was a calm end to a rough year in the Beconsfords' home.

Later, as the guests left, Deborah told them that she wanted to see them all return next Christmas as she thanked them for their wonderful support during their most difficult times.

Chapter 42

1839

As the New Year dawned, the weather stayed cold but crisp. The schools would not return for a few weeks so Margarita went up each day to play with Rosita and give the nurse a rest. Hilda Bowe still worked in the Big House and her happy countenance added to the other good staff employed by Deborah. It was a contented house to visit.

On Saturday the 5th of January Margarita rose to see the first glimpse of the thick snow that would soon turn the fields and forests of the estate into a winter wonderland.

Jack was already up and after breakfast he agreed to accompany Margarita up to the Big House, as Nurse Jean had the day off.

"I'll stay over with Rosita tonight and save anyone coming out in the snow," she told her father, as they crunched through the deepening snow on the driveway. "I can't wait to take Rosita out to the Secret Garden and build her first snowman. I don't know who'll be more excited, me or her!"

"That's fine for you, but it's no fun working outdoors in this weather."

"Don't be so sensible, Father," she rebuked him with a smile as she tucked her arm into his.

Margarita was true to her word. She and Rosita, who was tucked up warmly, had a great time with the snow. To Rosita's great delight, they made a snowman with a carrot for a nose and she laughed as Isaac and Deborah arrived to join in the fun by throwing snowballs at each other. When they all returned to the nursery, they changed their clothes and happily sat in the nursery, enjoying tea by a roasting log fire. They all agreed that the day had been wonderful.

Margarita slept peacefully that night in the room adjoining the nursery as Nurse Jean had been unable to return due to heavy snow.

At five o'clock on the morning, Old John woke. It was earlier than usual and he wondered what had caused him to wake. He stepped onto the ice-cold floor and walked to the window. He lifted the curtain and looked out at the black sky. The glistening snow shone like a light on the ground. But there was something else. He turned and quickly put on his clothes and then raddled the fire in the corner before putting the kettle on to heat. By then he knew what was wrong. No birds sang. He sat by the window and waited for the kettle to boil. The snow was shifting slightly, as if a warmth had appeared, as light appeared in the horizon.

Still, he waited, but no sound could be heard from any wildlife. There's something not right, thought John. He made his breakfast and began to make up some herb potions needed for later that day. Molly would be around to help out in the afternoon after working at Mrs. Sexton's bakery. He loved the warmth that Molly spread around his home when she called. He welcomed her each day and wished he was a few years younger because he would have asked her for her hand in marriage. But he had been content to meet with her each day and have her by his side, whenever family events occurred. He was always included as one of the family. That's down to Granny Sheila, he thought. She was a good woman who brought people together, while expecting little in return, but her legacy would live on in the town of Midleton.

As he continued to watch the melting snow outside the window, he laughed as he wondered why he was being so reflective on such a still and quiet day. He stood up and shook off a shiver as he went and raddled the fire again, staying there until its flames brightened the room and lifted his mood.

Jack Ryan walked into the kitchen where his wife and daughter were chatting together while drinking tea.

"You're back early, Margarita."

"Yes, Father, the snow began to melt early and I came

home. I might go back up later so Rosita sees the last of it before it turns to slush."

"I'm off later to Deasys to collect seeds for planting next month," he said. "With the snow melting, once I've had a quick chat with Isaac, I'll be off with the cart. I'll be home well before dark, so I'll see you both for supper." He sat down to his own breakfast, smiling with satisfaction at the sunny eggs and bacon on the plate.

"Grand," said Eliza. "I told Hetty to stay away in the snow so, as Margarita is up throwing snowballs in the Secret Garden, I'll be left here to cook." She laughed. "I'm actually looking forward to the school opening again next week!"

They sat in contented chatter until it was time for Jack to leave. He kissed his wife as he warned her, "You need to be careful and not slip on the snow while I'm gone."

Molly got ready for work and left Rose Cottage, and was surprised at the speed the snow was melting. It feels warm, she thought. I'm delighted. It's far safer even though the kids love a bit of snow. We could be busy to-day if the snow melts anymore, but I'll be finished cooking at one and can enjoy a couple of hours with Old John before catching a bit of fresh air.

Later in the morning as Margarita returned to the Big House, she smiled at the thought of the fun Rosita would have this morning. Deborah greeted her with a kiss and they both went to the nursery where Hilda Bowe was tidying up the room.

"Since that child started to crawl, I spend my time falling over toys," she laughed.

Rosita scurried towards Margarita and pointed to the window.

"'No, 'no," she kept saying, as they all laughed.

"I think you mean snow!" said Margarita. "Yes, we'll be out once we get you bundled up, young lady – we don't want anyone catching cold!"

Deborah joined Margarita in the garden and they returned to the nursery only when the snow seemed to disappear before their eyes.

After Rosita was settled for a sleep, Deborah and Margarita enjoyed a leisurely lunch and a chat in the parlour overlooking the secluded Secret Garden.

Deborah told Margarita that she had heard again through her sister in England that Victor was now in Italy.

"She said he's still trying to get his head together and will be in touch with me shortly."

Suddenly Isaac rushed in without knocking.

"Have you two not seen that the wind is rising out there? Your father is gone to Farmer Deasy's and I hope he returns quickly. Everything was too quiet this morning. I think a storm may be coming. I'll walk you home, Margarita, and don't leave your house once you're inside."

Deborah frowned. "You're alarming me now – are all the horses settled?"

"I'll check on my way back from Margarita's. Just stay indoors and tell that to all the staff. There are too many trees in this estate and I don't want any accidents happening."

He and Margarita hurriedly left the house.

Molly had arrived at Old John's, windblown and laughing.

"I just want a cup of tea and some kind of a sandwich. I think I'd better get home before this wind gets any worse."

"I have the lunch ready and I agree with you," said Old John. "You could always stay here for the night, or else we'll set off as soon as we've eaten."

Molly blushed. "I think perhaps we should go only as far as Eliza and Jack's house. I can stay with them for the night if the wind gets any worse."

"I agree. You need to be with family if there is a storm brewing."

Molly sat by the fire, enjoying the rest and food after a long morning in the busy tearooms. She looked around and smiled.

"I love this room. The smells of the herbs and plants are so calming and relaxing. In future, I'm going to fill Rose Cottage with all these smells. I'll have lavender in my bedroom and I'll check what scents work in the rest of the house."

Old John laughed, "I've finally converted my assistant to follow my dream of every house having relaxing scents all around them! Now, let us be on our way and you can take my book of knowledge to start you on your quest for understanding the value of the healing herbs and plants." He placed the book in the large pocket of her pinny and helped her put her coat back on as they left the warmth of the house.

The wind was howling as Molly clutched Old John's arm and bent her head into its driving force. It's not even cold or wet, she thought, but I never remember wind blowing this hard in all my years in the market garden at Friarsland.

After five minutes, Old John stopped and suggested they turn back, but they agreed that they were now at the estate gate and only a couple of hundred yards to Jack's house.

They opened the small side gate with the key that Isaac had given them years ago, and hurried through the last of the forest towards the gravelled path leading to the Ryans' home.

Margarita was safely back home but her mother was extremely worried by the fact that Jack had not yet arrived home. The sounds of rattling door knockers and the almighty wind sounds blowing soot down the chimney into the room was panicking both of the women.

"What can we do?" asked Margarita.

"Nothing, nothing at all! We can't go out in this. We just need to wait and pray that he's indoors somewhere."

Margarita began to cry and said she at least wanted to look out to see if there was any sign of him.

Suddenly they both froze. Higher than the growling of the wind and the groaning, creaking sounds of shifting timbers in their home, came the sound of a voice so shrill and frightening that they both rushed to the door which almost knocked them both down as they pulled it open.

The hysterical sound continued from the end of their short driveway. Before her mother could stop her, Margarita was running into the wind in the direction of the sound. Margarita thought her legs were glued to the ground, as she forced them to beat through the elements that she now saw had ripped a large gaping hole through the forest. At the edge of the forest, she looked and stared in horror at the scene before her. In the distance, trees had toppled one on top of the other, like dominoes falling to the ground. She froze with terror on the pathway as all she could see was the light of the fading day where the trees had once stood. She could hear no sound now as she cautiously walked forward, staying well away from the forest edge.

"Is there anybody there? Can you hear me? Shout if you can! I'm here to help!"

Margarita stood still. A low whimpering sound could be heard. Having a good ear for sound, Margarita knew it was the voice of a woman. Behind her she heard another running sound. Her mother arrived breathless and dishevelled with a large shawl over her arm.

"My God Almighty, what has happened here? I can see the village church where the trees should be."

Margarita threw her arm around her. "It's the storm that's doing it and I can hear the sounds of a woman's voice."

"Dear Sweet Divine, who is out on such a day? Let us

317

stay quiet for a moment and we'll move slowly on the path because it seemed to come from over there."

Within seconds they heard crying and they both started to run in its direction.

"*Shout if you can hear us!*" Margarita yelled.

A shrill voice came from the edge of the forest. "*It's me, it's me Molly! Come quickly, he's injured! It's Old John!*"

Margarita turned a slight bend on the pathway and there sitting, surrounded by fallen trees, was her grandmother.

Before her mother could follow her any further, Margarita turned to her and said, "Please, Mother, go back the path and see if Father has returned. We need help. I can't even see Old John. Don't you come any closer and I'll stay and see what I can do. Just keep safe and away from any area with trees."

"I'll try to get help," answered Eliza. "But you are not to go anywhere close to those fallen trees either. Just stay strong for her, love." She handed the shawl to Margarita. "If Jack is not back, I'll bang on the door of William Doyle and he'll round up some men."

Eliza ran back towards the cottages and the Big House, now even more anxious about her husband, but she had to just pray he was safe. It's like the end of the world, she thought, as the wind ripped at her clothes and did its utmost to knock her to the ground.

Margarita inched her way towards Molly.

"*We nearly made it, we nearly got to the path!*" Molly cried. "*He threw me in the direction of the gravel when he saw the trees falling! He's underneath there!'* She pointed in the direction of the enormous mountain of wood and branches just feet from where she sat. *"I've just hurt my arms and legs, but he's under there still!"* she sobbed.

Margarita gingerly walked as close as she could and threw the shawl to Molly.

"Put this around you and let me see if I can see him."

Margarita hid her horror as she spotted Old John's feet stretched out behind two huge tree trunks that must have fallen from behind him as he threw Molly forward. She could not see any part of his upper body.

Molly began to cry again. "He shouted, 'I love you, Molly, I love you, Molly!' before the tree came down and I have not heard a word since."

Margarita had always known Old John had feelings for Molly but nobody ever spoke of it. She realised that she couldn't help Old John, but she wanted to calm Molly down. She thought of the only thing she could do.

"Molly, will I sing to him and you, while we're waiting for help to come? He'll know then that help is on the way."

"He'd love that. Could you sing the new song you're learning from that opera, *Norma*? He told me he loved hearing you sing that when you were in Rose Cottage over Christmas."

Margarita smiled through her tears as she sat on the gravel path and began to sing. Her haunting voice soared up into the wind.

"Casta Diva che inargenti
Queste sacre antiche piante . . ."

319

***

Isaac had left the Big House when he had seen some of the destruction caused to the forest from the top floor of Beconsford House. He believed Jack's house could be in danger. Deborah begged him to stay put but he got the men who were calming the horses to join him. Before long they met with a tearful, incoherent Eliza who said Jack wasn't home and pointing towards the side pathway and saying Margarita was trying to help Molly and Old John. By now three of the farm tenants had run up to them and Isaac sent the saddle man back to the Big House with Eliza, warning her to stay indoors and assuring her everything would be done to help Molly and Old John.

The men continued at a slow speed, holding each other in an effort to stay upright as they battled the relentless winds. Suddenly, they stopped, as they heard the sound of Margarita's exquisite voice soar above the wind. They were by her side in less than a minute.

Isaac knelt and put his arm around her as her voice faded and her tears flowed faster. All she could do was point at Molly, but three strong farmers were already making their way towards her, through and over the mounds of forest trees and debris.

"Where's Old John?" Isaac asked.

Margarita pointed to a huge tree to the left of Molly.

"*He's under there!*" she cried and tried to rise to follow the men towards Molly.

"Stay there, please," Isaac begged. "Molly is going to be safe. We'll get her out and you go to our house with her. You will both be safe there."

"Did my father come home?"

Isaac answered in some trepidation. "He never came back from the seed farm. I'm sure he never left there, in this wind." He looked at her and said a prayer in his heart for the life of his best friend.

"He'll be fine. Your father understands weather changes very well. Let us just concentrate on Molly first and get her into the warmth."

Just then another farm worker arrived with a large wooden carrier.

"*We can carry her back on that, sir!*" he shouted.

"*Good thinking, lad — give it to the men and go back and find another one because we have two people here.*"

The boy quickly made his way towards the men who were near Molly and he was sprinting back in a few seconds with the wind at his back. The men worked quickly as they lifted Molly onto the wooden stretcher.

"*It's her leg and shoulder that are injured, both on her left side where she must have fallen, sir. We'll get her up to the Big House and one of us can support Margarita.*"

"*Well done, men!*" shouted Isaac. "*I'll stay here while you round up some more men to help get Old John out!*"

It took nearly fifteen minutes to carry Molly to safety.

321

Eliza and Deborah then took over and got the men to take her to the bedroom that Margarita used when she stayed in the Big House.

Mrs. Hudson, the housekeeper, fussed over Margarita and insisted she sit by the fire and drink a hot sweet cup of tea.

Jack had continued to chat with Farmer Deasy inside the farmhouse, after loading the seeds onto the cart. They both enjoyed a cup of tea, because the snow had fully melted. As he left the farmhouse, he realised that the wind was getting up and he needed to move swiftly. The horse was twitchy and edgy as they went down the mile to the main road and Jack was getting anxious with the increasing ferocity of the wind. He urged the horse on and was grateful when he reached the road going in the direction of Midleton. But without the shelter of the hedges along the laneway, the cart was nearly upended as they turned to go across the road. Jack used an expletive and slowed the horse down and stepped off the cart to think.

The cart hasn't enough weight to stay upright if this gets any worse, he thought.

He walked for a few minutes holding on to the horse and patting him, but as he looked into a field on his left, he saw a sight he had never seen before. A mature tree was breaking its roots. It lifted into the air and landed some forty feet further on. Jack's heart nearly stopped as he suddenly remembered Eliza and Margarita in the house in the middle of the forested estate. He suddenly decided to unhook the cart and upturn it off its wheels. He left it at the side of the road and didn't care whether it would be there whenever he returned for it. He patted the horse a few times and then took a jump onto him. With his arms almost holding the horse by its head, he urged it forward. Jack no longer feared for his own life but only for the lives of his family. The destruction he saw as the wind drove the horse on was tragic to witness. The tin roofs of houses lay in fields and he prayed for anyone who lived under those roofs.

After two miles the road was full of tree trunks, wicker gates, iron gates and he had to get down and walk. He held the reins and gently guided the horse slowly and carefully along the road which held evidence of the devastation the wind had brought. He was now joined by dozens of people who thankfully were alive but who were afraid to stay indoors.

As they neared the town, they were thankful to see the church steeple still standing tall and one of the women began to pray out loud. Jack promised some families that he'd help them as soon as he knew his family was safe. As he walked past the town towards the estate entrance, with the horse by his side, he prayed that everyone was safe. Nothing else matters, was his only thought. When he entered the estate and saw the destruction of parts of the forest right in front of his eyes, his brain went into overdrive and he raced in the direction of his home. He thought the worst had happened to his beloved family.

At ten o'clock that evening, Jack held his wife in his arms

inside the parlour of the Big House. His daughter had gone to bed and his mother Molly was asleep, having been given a sleeping draught by the doctor. Her injuries were not too serious and were caused only by falling heavily after Old John had thrown her forward to safety.

Sadly, Isaac and the farmers had just brought in the body of Old John. He was being prepared by Nurse Jean, and they waited for the doctor to certify his death. Everyone in the house was in shock. The wind had by now begun to die down, but Isaac felt that the destruction it brought to the countryside would take a long time to heal.

Jack held Eliza even tighter as he told her that the lads from the town had come to help and even though roofs were lifted in many houses, only one house was totally destroyed.

"That was Old John's house which took the full force of the wind and the falling trees completed the damage," the villagers told him.

"My mother was so lucky," said Jack, looking at Eliza as tears flowed freely down his cheeks. "I thought that tonight my whole world was coming crashing down around me, but instead you are all safe."

Old John died a hero, thought Jack. We will have to honour him for that.

Old John got a fitting send-off, one week after the Night of the Big Wind. He was allowed to have his funeral service in the estate chapel and Margarita was asked to say a few words about his death.

"Molly asked me to sing Mr. Bellini's *Casta Diva*. She said he loved it."

Margarita then sang the haunting aria and, when she finished, she bade a final farewell to Old John.

"*Take your goodness into the earth and into the sky and may you rest in peace.*"

It was a bitterly cold day as the funeral procession made its way from the estate church to the town. The road was lined with people, all wishing to pay their respects to one of their own. Before the first sod was put onto the coffin that held the body of Old John, Molly stood and scattered scented flower petals, in memory of a special man. He was laid to rest in the same grave as Granny Sheila, at the request of Molly, as she knew that someday she would join them both.

As a few snowflakes fell and sprinkled a white veil over the coffin, the minister read the wonderful words of John Donne:

"*No man is an island,*
Entire of itself;
Every man is a piece of the continent,
A part of the main.

If a clod be washed away by the sea,
Europe is the less,
As well as if a promontory were,
As well as if a manor of thy friend's
Or of thine own were.

Any man's death diminishes me,
Because I am involved in mankind.
And therefore never send to know
For whom the bell tolls;
It tolls for thee."

Chapter 43

Jack had already had a carved wooden plaque set up inside the Park in Midleton, to honour Old John's life. It was placed close to a plot of herb seeds, planted by the children of the town. Certainly, a man whose knowledge had helped so many people, and who had died saving the life of Molly, would not be forgotten.

Molly stayed in the house with Jack and Eliza for a week after the storm, but she was anxious to return to Rose Cottage.

Alice had suggested to her parents that she could move in and help Molly, as it was so close to her home.

"It would give me a bit of independence and I can help her with some of the potions. I know she wants to try and continue Old John's work. I'd also see more of Margarita because she practises a lot over in Rose Cottage. And I'm hoping she'll introduce me to Richard's brother!" She laughed. "Or at least someone who's as handsome as Richard. It's a pity he has eyes for no one but Margarita!" She pulled a face, as her mother busied herself in the farm kitchen.

"Everyone knows that you have a good flair with making clothes, love," said Meg, coming to sit by the kitchen fire. "Maybe you could help Margarita get a decent wardrobe for her singing this summer. I hear she might even be going to sing in Italy and France with Richard."

Alice agreed to talk to Margarita as she had started to design some clothes with charcoal pens. Maybe she could design something exciting for her.

During the weeks after the storm the estate was a hive of activity. Jack barely got home to eat and sleep. Isaac had informed everyone from the village that anyone who came to help the clear-up could take home enough wood to keep fires going for a year. The men arrived in swarms and Eliza, with help from the Big House, supplied hot tea and sandwiches throughout the weeks.

As the workers finished another hard day clearing up the forest, Eliza took a walk down to the summerhouse. As she passed through the last of the trees, she stopped in her tracks. Coming down the wide path from the direction of the barge that crossed the river she spotted a large cart filled to the brim with high-quality wood. She stepped behind a tree as the slow-moving horse, with a driver and a helper, moved past. The driver was beating the horse, trying to get it to move faster, and roaring at it. As they drove past, Eliza couldn't believe her eyes when she recognised the now balding head of Dermot O'Leary with his younger brother Brendan sitting beside him. They hadn't been seen in the town for nearly twenty years but Eliza would never forget the men who tried to murder her husband and ruin her good name.

As soon as they had passed, she lifted her skirts and raced in the direction of her house.

Luck was on her side. Jack and Isaac were chatting outside her home, having just finished a long day in the forest. She was breathless when she reached them but quickly told them her story. They knew the gate that the O'Learys would leave by and they quickly ran to block them off. They shouted at the first farm cottage and told the farmer's son to round up as many men as he could and bring them to the side gate as quickly as possible.

The two men reached the side gate of the estate and spotted the cart. They stayed out of sight, watching the slow progress of the O'Learys' horse. By the time it reached them more men had joined them.

As Isaac and Jack walked to block the cart, they saw two more estate men jumping onto the timber logs stacked at the back of the cart.

Dermot O'Leary gave a roar but he had nowhere to go. His brother Brendan wearily dropped his head into his hands.

As the horse and cart drew to a halt, Isaac was the first to speak.

329

"What the hell are you two doing stealing timber from the forest?"

"We heard you were giving it away," answered Dermot sullenly.

"And what have you to say for yourself, Brendan?" Jack asked.

Brendan lifted his head, looking as if he was already a condemned man.

"I'm sorry, Mr. Ryan, and I'm sorry for what happened to you all them years ago and I never meant for you to be hurt."

Before he could continue, his brother turned to him and with a blow nearly knocked him off the cart.

"*You fool! You were always stupid! Don't admit to anything, you idiot!*"

Isaac turned to Jack.

"What do you want to say to them before I haul them off to the police?"

Jack moved forward and asked Brendan to get off the cart. He looked painfully thin and undernourished, whereas his brother had a fat beer belly that spilled over his trousers. Jack knew that Eliza had taught the O'Learys in the town school. Although she had little sympathy for either of them, she had always said that Dermot led Brendan astray. She had seen some good in him. Brendan looked as if he was going to cry like a child as the men surrounded the cart.

"Do you want to stay with your brother?" Jack asked.

"*No!*" Brendan yelled. "*I want to go home! I'm only going to starve if I stay with him!*"

Jack could see from his face that he was petrified of his older brother and he came to a decision. The Night of the Big Wind had once again shaken Jack's faith in his own belief that he could guarantee to keep his family safe. Looking into the eyes of Brendan O'Leary, he saw the look of despair and defeat that was once in his own eyes.

Jack turned to Isaac.

"If you agree, I'd like to let Brendan go back to his family and we'll deal with Dermot then."

"What have you in mind, Jack?" asked Isaac.

"I'd like to give Brendan a second chance, and I won't press an attempted murder charge on either of them for now, for their attempt to burn down Rose Cottage with me inside. However, I want Dermot to be escorted from the village and if he ever returns, he'll face prison. Also, he can leave the cart behind and Brendan will get it when the timber has been returned."

Jack walked up to Dermot and looked directly into his eyes.

"You can keep your own horse, Dermot, but I never want to see your face again or to hear you spewing vileness about anyone in the future. I advise you to get as far away from Midleton as you possibly can and never again set foot in the town."

Within five minutes, the cart was left inside the estate walls, Brendan O'Leary was heading home and what looked like the entire village was marching Dermot and the horse out of town. As he mounted the horse, he shouted abuse at everyone. There was a collective sigh of relief as he left the town.

The following day, Jack went into the town and stopped outside the poor hovel of a cottage that was home to the O'Learys. Brendan might be able to make some kind of a living using the cart, thought Jack. The door was answered by Eileen O'Leary, who held Jack's two hands and thanked him for allowing Brendan to return home. Brendan joined her with his thanks and kept apologising. Jack said he'd accept the apology and told him that he might have a horse going cheaply that could set Brendan up in the haulage of goods business. He'd allow him pay for the horse over a couple of years.

The tears in the eyes of Eileen O'Leary were enough thanks for Jack. Much to his embarrassment, she hugged him before he left to return to the job of clearing the estate.

Later, when he told Eliza what he had done, she was very pleased at his act of kindness. "They didn't deserve it but that's why I love you, Jack Ryan," she said, putting her arms around him.

Isaac accepted his decision but was seen shaking his head on many occasions for days, saying that Dermot and Brendan O'Leary should be in jail.

***

With the clearing of the forest completed, Eliza realised that she was worried about Margarita who was again spending most of her free time with Rosita. She hadn't practised her singing since Old John had been buried and Eliza was so concerned that she sent a message to Richard explaining the situation. Being the gentleman he was, he arrived three days later and Eliza sent him straight to the Big House.

"You're wanted in the parlour, Margarita," Jenny said.

Margarita looked up from where she was reading in the nursery, while Rosita had her nap. "It's Mr. Richard, the singer, and Her Ladyship said I was to sit with Rosita until she comes up herself in a few minutes."

Margarita thanked her as she felt a sudden nervousness in her stomach. She couldn't work out if it was fear or excitement.

She descended the stairway and entered the parlour, where Deborah was sitting chatting with Richard. They both stood up when she arrived and Richard walked to the door and spontaneously hugged her.

Margarita was grateful for Deborah's presence as she sat down while struggling to keep tears from her eyes. She saw the kindness in both their eyes.

"I'm going to get tea for you," said Deborah. "I'll leave you to chat for a while."

"I was so happy you were safe after the storm, Margarita. Our family were lucky. We just lost a barn roof but all the animals were safe. I'm so sorry about Old John but I'm glad Molly is recovering. I hope you will be happy when you hear why I'm here."

Margarita clasped her hands together and hoped Richard didn't notice how nervous she was. She hadn't sung since the funeral but knew that she had to start again soon. She knew that hiding away with the excuse of minding Rosita wasn't right, yet she didn't seem to know how to start back.

"You might remember that at the end of last year there was speculation that we might be invited to sing in concert halls abroad? Well, I've had great news from my man in Dublin who arranges these concerts. He's now had concrete bookings for the two of us to sing in Paris, Milan and Florence, as well as London, during the summer!" Richard was unable to keep the excitement from his voice. "Word got to Dublin about your bravery on the Night of the Big Wind and some of the county people who heard you sing at Old John's church service have been so excited about your voice. Does that make you happy?" He finished with a big grin on his face.

Margarita, for the first time in weeks, smiled and lifted her head.

"I thought everyone would be consumed by thoughts of the storm."

"No, no," said Richard. "Everyone is shocked by what happened around the country where hundreds of people died. As people begin to rebuild homes and properties, they also need some hope and inspiration and to celebrate someone they are proud of. Our singing can give them the lift that they need in this terrible time."

Margarita nodded in understanding. She lifted her head and looked Richard in the eyes. "We'll do the concerts, but we'll also do some locally and allow those who have suffered most benefit from the proceeds. I think it's what I need at the present time."

Richard jumped up and was hugging and lifting Margarita off the ground when Deborah, followed by the maid with the tea tray, appeared.

"I hope I have not interrupted something," she said, laughing.

"No, you have not," Richard said, smiling, as he stepped back from Margarita. "She's agreed to do concerts in Paris, Milan and London with me in the summer! Everyone in the country loves her voice and now she can show it off to the rest of Europe!"

As the maid put down the tray, she smiled with the lovely bit of news she had for the other workers in the household. They all loved Margarita and how she had cared for both Rosita and Fleur. They all thought she needed a life away from the Big House.

Deborah walked over and kissed them both.

"You can only go on one condition, Margarita, and that is we all get a concert in the Big House, with your two families before you leave the country."

They both laughed and nodded their heads.

"We're going to do a few charity concerts also this year," Margarita said.

"Perfect. Now get on with discussing your repertoire and enjoy your tea," Deborah said, laughing as she left the room.

Chapter 44

Molly returned to Rose Cottage and Alice joined her. Her recovery was going well and she was looking forward to returning to Mrs. Sexton's for the morning trade in February.

"I'm going to dedicate my afternoons to continuing Old John's work in healing and supporting the poor around the village."

She had shown Alice the book of herbs that John had put in her pinny on the night he died. Alice was very excited and agreed to help her with the work. The knowledge in the book was endless and Alice wondered if he'd had a premonition about his death by giving it to Molly. If he hadn't done that it would now be buried in the rubble of his home.

Margarita arrived as they were talking. They greeted her and she turned to Alice.

"I know that you have offered to dress-make for me, but how would you like to get on board and make gowns for my proposed tour of Europe? I'd love you to be the one to make them. I'm told I'll need at least six for the tour. Adele, who dressed me in Dublin, said if you wanted any help just write to her and she'll give some ideas on materials that don't crush too much when travelling. Of course, Mr. Deacon, who is arranging the tour, said that all expenses for clothes will be covered, so you will get well paid for your work."

"*Yes!*" Alice jumped about with delight.

"There might be something else happening also," Margarita said, "but I can't tell you at the moment."

Alice's eyes opened wide.

"Has Richard asked you to marry him?"

Margarita laughed loudly.

"Of course he hasn't."

"Because, if he has a good-looking friend, you can send him around to me!" said Alice, with eyes twinkling. "Sadly, Richard has eyes for no one but you."

Margarita laughed again. "There's no need to worry on that score. I'm interested only in my singing career for the next few years," she said primly.

"Well, I'm going to make tea," Molly said, as she lifted the kettle to fill with water. "I'm too old to think about the love life of the most eligible bachelor in Ireland. I'll leave you two to sort that out. Margarita, you know that you have to sing for your supper here so how about a song while I make the tea?"

***

Richard stayed with Meg and John whenever he visited Margarita. They practised in Molly's house and Molly made supper for everyone there. Alice was working hard on creating gowns to suit Margarita's graceful figure. She was happy and contented, working on the gowns and helping Molly prepare her herbs and potions each evening.

She loved when Richard called and found it hard to understand that Margarita wasn't throwing herself at him. Alice thought he was the most divine man she had ever met but knew she couldn't compete with her gorgeous, talented niece. But I can have my daydreams, she thought, as she listened to the sounds of two perfectly blending voices while she returned to her delicate stitching.

Jack walked from the Big House with a smile on his face as he looked forward to eating lunch in the company of his wife. It was now late spring and daffodils grew in profusion, untroubled by the big wind in January. The forest was almost cleared of debris and his family were all well. He wasn't looking forward to Margarita leaving for Europe in the summer but knew she had to spread her wings.

Richard and Margarita had already held two charity concerts. The first was in the city of Cork, and they then performed in nearby Castlemartyr in the beautiful castle of the Earl of Cork, to help those in east Cork. All the generous people in the county had put their hands deep in their pockets to help. It seemed that everywhere in the country there were people who suffered during that fateful Night of the Big Wind. Jack was so proud of his daughter.

Eliza was putting some ham and bread on the table when he arrived.

"Before I forget to tell you, Deborah wants to know if you would call to her after lunch," said Jack, as he kissed his wife before sitting by her side. "You can walk back with me after lunch."

"Fine. Ann Marie is doing so well now with the village children with the help of the new monitor, that I don't need to go in each day anymore. I'd love a chat with Deborah. What with all the work in the forest over the past few months, we rarely get an afternoon for a catch-up."

When Eliza returned with Jack to the Big House, Deborah greeted her and suggested they make the most of the warm sun to take a walk in the Secret Garden.

Eliza suspected that she wanted to tell her something. Things seemed easier to discuss as they looked at the latest flowers blooming in the garden and breathed in the different scented herbs.

"I've heard from Victor," Deborah said, with anxiety in her voice.

"Well, that's a good thing, isn't it? How is he and where is he?"

"He's in Vienna," she replied, still sounding anxious. "I think that he heard about the Big Wind in Ireland and it shook him badly until he knew we were all safe. He said that he is attending a very good doctor who has told him that he's suffering a trauma since the death of Fleur. The doctor is helping him deal with it in a sensible way, whatever that means, and he might come home, if only for a while when he feels strong enough. He wants me to tell him everything about Rosita and has finally given us an address to write to. I'm worried that he will not get better, Eliza."

Eliza put an arm around Deborah and a smile on her own face.

"Deborah, that's wonderful news! He's right to see a doctor and it's very hard to get anyone in Ireland who would treat his mind. They would just tell him to get on with life. I believe this will be the turning of a corner and he'll be all the better for seeing someone who understands his painful experience. It's the best news I've heard in a while. Now let's go and have a cup of tea and take me up to see your darling granddaughter, Rosita."

Eliza decided not to tell Margarita about Victor, as she was so absorbed in her music practice.

Later that day Richard arrived for three days' practice. He was staying in Meg and John's home and he immediately went to Rose Cottage to seek out Margarita and Alice. He had exciting news that he knew would make the girls happy.

The door was opened by Alice who greeted him with a huge smile.

"Come in, we were expecting you later but its lovely to

341

see you. Molly is just cooking and Margarita has been practising diligently all morning."

Richard entered the large warm and welcoming kitchen where Margarita was helping to lay plates on the table. She smiled as he kissed her on the cheek.

"I hope my name is included in that pot – it smells delicious," Richard said with a laugh, as he sat at the table.

"It's only chicken stew with carrots plus my special herbs added to the stock. It should be ready in a few minutes."

"That's good," Richard said, smiling at the ladies and nodding his head at Margarita. "Now, Alice, Margarita and I have something to ask you. You know that we're off on our trip to Europe in May?"

Alice nodded and frowned, wondering what was coming next. I hope they are not displeased with the gowns, she thought with apprehension.

"The news is that the tour manager Mr. Deacon wants Margarita to have a chaperone and we wondered if you would like to join us on the continent during the summer."

Alice jumped up from her chair and nearly fell into Margarita's arms.

"Of course, of course, I can't believe this! Is it really true?"

Margarita laughed and assured her that they had wanted her all along but the manager might have had someone else in mind.

"Richard asked your father and mother before coming over today and they agreed."

Alice then went to hug Richard and felt embarrassed when he happily kissed her on each cheek.

"Now, could I have some food, please?" he said. "It's a long time since I had breakfast, and a starving man can't be expected to sing on an empty stomach!"

Molly laughed as she brought the whole pot to the table and said he shouldn't get fed now that he was taking her assistant away for the summer. As she served the meal, Molly was praying that Alice's infatuation with Richard would not in any way spoil the tour for the girls. Yet she felt confident that the girls loved each other so much that they would find a way around it.

"All I can say to all of you is that my mother Sheila would have been so proud of you both this day."

The months of April and May seemed to fly and Margarita spent her time between practising, helping with the choir in the school and spending time with Rosita who was now walking and talking and learning new words and places to search each day. Everyone agreed that she needed an army to keep an eye on her as she loved to explore the house and always wanted to end up in the kitchen with Cook, who would give her some fairy cakes. She was turning into a very pretty young child, with blonde curls surrounding her pert face and a healthy strength that she had inherited from her father Victor. She never seemed to cry when she fell and Deborah said that she reminded her of Victor when he was a toddler, always into mischief.

Chapter 45

The time arrived, in June, when preparations were finalised for the trip to Europe. The large trunks were packed and ready for the journey. Alice had never taken the smile off her face since being told she was accompanying Margarita.

On the weekend before they left, they held the promised concert in the ballroom of Beconsford House and it was attended by all their families and friends. Deborah and Isaac invited the Perrott family, who had given the Beconsford and Ryan family some wonderful evenings in their Cork home, including an open invitation to stay whenever they wished. They still resided in Hayfield Manor, the house much admired by Margarita and Eliza.

The longest table available was set out in the ballroom for the almost thirty invited guests. On the night, chandeliers gleamed overhead, candles lit up the table and the wine flowed. The room danced with colour as candlelight shone on the myriad of Waterford cut glass bowls as well as the necklaces worn by all the ladies.

When dinner had been eaten and coffee and tea served, Margarita and Richard began to sing. They sang opera specials and the sacred music loved by many and they turned the guests into a choir by singing many well-loved Irish and English songs.

With the cheers still ringing out, Margarita finished with her usual few words about what she called "her song". When she stood up, she told the same story she would tell at each concert. Denny Lane had allowed her alone to sing his song for its first ten years and only then would the song be published. He was still a young man and she acknowledged how precious the song was to her. As the last notes died away Margarita had to work hard to keep the tears from her eyes but she finished by telling everyone how much she would miss them all when she went abroad.

As they stood as one to cheer the singers, Nurse Jean appeared from behind Margarita with Rosita in her arms. The child was clapping and smiling, and she stretched out her arms to Margarita who embraced her and whispered to her how much she loved her. Rosita had begun to call her 'Mama'. Margarita knew it was because she couldn't pronounce her name, but the child calling her 'Mama' touched her heart with bittersweet pain.

The night had been a great success and Margarita knew that she would have no fear singing in the large concert arenas abroad, because she would bring with her the warm cloak of love that she now felt in the midst of all those whom she cherished.

Two fine carriages set off for Dublin on a warm sunny June day. The party was joined by Eliza and Jack who decided the time was right to take a week's holiday with Gerry Harris and find out what innovations were happening in Dublin. Eliza also wanted to visit the much talked-of Zoological Gardens. The trunks were divided between the two carriages and Margarita sat with Richard and Alice in the larger one as they wanted to go over some business during the journey.

Alice surprised Richard and Margarita by being excellent at managing more than the wardrobe. She had taken care of everything that came that the tour manager, Mr. Deacon, requested. She told the singers that whatever they needed during the trip she would be on hand to provide and that her reward would be to see their wonderful performances. Margarita and Richard had both begun to call her Mrs. Manager and all three laughed at the thought of what Mr. Deacon would have to say if he heard them! But they both felt that Alice Turner was going to be worth her weight in gold during their adventure in Europe.

Margarita, Richard and Alice arrived in Dublin and enjoyed a lovely few days of early summer sunshine staying in Shelbourne Hotel and, much to Alice's delight, they also visited the various shops and teahouses, with Eliza and Theresa Harris.

Eliza was joined by Margarita and Alice for her trip to the Zoological Gardens where they were amazed at the exotic animals, although caged and out of their natural surroundings. Margarita thought how wonderful it would be to show those animals to Rosita. It was an exciting experience and Jack and Richard were envious when the ladies returned, having enjoyed a great day out. They all agreed to visit again when they next had free time in the city.

Mr. Deacon joined the party on the day they were due to leave for Britain. They were sailing on the British and Irish Steam Packet company ship to Liverpool. He would stay with them until they reached London, just to make sure that everything was organised for the weeks they would spend abroad on mainland Europe.

Margarita went to rest for a while before going up on the deck of the ship to watch the eastern coast of Ireland fade into the distance. She noticed that Richard had joined Alice on the deck. She knew that Richard enjoyed Alice's company. She's so open and fresh with no inhibitions, thought Margarita. Yet she can negotiate with anyone and is a very intelligent young woman. Margarita hoped this trip abroad would show Alice that there could be more to her life than helping Molly in Midleton.

Margarita continued to observe them as they watched the sun dipping into the sea, and darkness began to fall.

As she turned to go inside, Richard saw her and he and Alice came to join her.

"We'd better go in for our meal," Richard suggested. "I

can feel the chill of the evening breeze."

He held onto Alice's arm as they descended the stairway and Margarita observed Alice smiling to herself and knew how happy she looked in Richard's company. Richard really is very charming, Margarita realised. He seemed to turn the heads of all the young women he met. Yet, when he sang with her and spent time in her company, it seemed like she was the only woman in his life. I'll spend this tour acting totally professionally and let time and Richard decide where his heart wants to go in the future. She noticed that the smile never left Alice's face during a delightful meal in the ship's ornate dining room.

As Margarita later lay in the comfortable soft bed, she was determined to enjoy every second of the journey to Europe. Nothing could spoil all the memories she would make.

It was a still and calm crossing and Margarita woke to the sound of a ship's employee asking her if she would like some tea before dressing.

The dream continues, she thought as she took the tray from the young lad.

"We will be arriving, madam, in two hours. Breakfast is being served in the dining room whenever you are ready."

They left the ship and then took a carriage to the centre of Liverpool, where they joined the train from Liverpool to Manchester. Everyone was excited at this chance to enjoy the luxury of a train that Alice and Margarita had only heard about but had never travelled on. It was just 30 miles but the girls wanted it to go on forever as they loved looking at the countryside passing by and the smoke from the steam engines billowing overhead.

"You know Mr. Robert Stephenson invented the engine called the Rocket that's in the locomotive for this train," said Margarita. "He won a competition and the Liverpool to Manchester line bought six of them."

The others laughed.

"How do you know that?" asked Alice.

"My father Jack, of course! He's a very knowledgeable man I'll have you know!"

"Well, that's great to know," Richard joked, as the train pulled into the platform in Manchester.

"At least it got us here safely," said Alice, laughing.

They stayed in Manchester for just one night and they were met after breakfast by a magnificent carriage with eight horses, to take them on the journey to London. There was a table inside the carriage so that they could eat the food supplied by the hotel.

Alice and Mr. Deacon pored over itineraries with maps spread all over the table. Alice took copious notes and fired questions at him about hotels, the weather and the transport arrangements. Mr. Deacon laughed and said he felt he had earned his money for the tour with all the work he had to do to make Alice happy! Yet he was satisfied that everything would work well and that Margarita had chosen a good chaperone.

On the day they arrived in London everything was set for their trip abroad. They sat in their hotel overlooking the River Thames while looking forward to the thought of a luxurious bed for the night. They weren't disappointed. Alice had promised the singers that everything was in order and that Mr. Deacon could go back to Dublin. He had appointed a young translator to meet them at each stop on the Continent as none of them was proficient in French or Italian, although Richard and Margarita each had a smattering of Italian because they sang so many of that country's songs.

As the magnificence of the white cliffs of the Dover coast receded, Margarita's spine tingled at the thought of her first glimpse of France. When they entered the port of Calais, in warm sunshine, her mood was buoyant. She had waited for this moment all her life.

As the party stepped onto the gangway, accompanied by porters carrying the trunks, they were greeted by a man holding a placard with their three names written in large letters. It was carried by a young Frenchman dressed in a long coat and high collared shirt, with a tall hat and knee-high leather boots.

The girls smiled at each other and Alice murmured, "He's very elegant, I hope he's not as starchy as his shirt."

He stepped forward and introduced himself by kissing the hands of the two ladies and shaking Richard's hand.

"Welcome to France. My name is Jacques du Blanc, but please call me Jacques. I learned to speak English in your University of Oxford."

"Oxford? Why did you study there?" Richard asked.

"My father was happy I was away and missed the student riots in Paris. Your carriage awaits and we can talk as we drive through the countryside."

Well, he's very efficient, thought Alice. I think we might get on fine together.

While Richard was impressed by his efficiency, he was a bit annoyed by what he perceived as a lecture on politics, as Jacques continued: "I'd like to explain. It would be good if you didn't discuss any political issues while here. Many people do not take kindly to hearing opinions from those who do not understand our culture."

The girls looked at each other with some amusement in their eyes as they nodded, but Richard interjected with a stubborn look on his face, "As we are Irish and have an interesting history, we too would prefer not to talk about politics."

Good for you, Richard, thought Margarita.

"I understand," Jacques replied, "and now I will let you know what is required of you while in Paris." He bowed at the travelling party. "As you know you will sing in Paris and then move to Versailles. These two concerts will include all peoples of our society. The first one in the church of Saint-Germain-des-Prés, has been organised to fund raise for the poorest people who live in the city, whereas the concert in

Versailles will fundraise for the restoration works at the Palace of Versailles. The city concert will consist mainly of clerks and guild members but in Versailles it will be attended by the French and European aristocracy. There is much flux in my country since the rebellion of 1799 and the uprising, mainly by students, in 1832. That, as I mentioned, is why my father sent me to college in England."

Richard was beginning to feel he was talked at rather than to.

"I just wish to say, Monsieur, that we are well informed in Ireland of your political situation. Indeed, we have our own particular issues about the English rule in our country. However, we are just bringing our music for you to enjoy and, although we speak English, we are truly Irish."

Margarita was beginning to get worried at the tone of the conversation and interrupted. "Jacques, we fully understand your point, but in life I have always found that most people are good at heart and we just bring our music to fill everyone's heart with joy, whatever views they may hold. Be assured we will be gracious to everyone we meet. Please remember that we are extremely grateful for the invitation to sing in your country."

While Alice was glad that Robert had a word with Jacques, she was delighted that Margarita was always such a good peacemaker.

Jacques smiled and assured them that everything would be done to make their stay memorable.

***

The next three days were spent in practice and sightseeing in Paris. They were overcome by the beauty of the paintings on display in the Muséum central des arts in the Grande Gallerie of the Louvre but Alice and Richard were far happier when they were brought down the River Seine in a brightly bedecked river barge, where they were served lunch as they watched the elegant buildings and houses of Paris pass by. When they entered the Canal-Saint-Martin, Alice said she felt as if she could almost touch the houses at each side.

"I love this way of travelling. I think we should have it in Cork," she said with a laugh.

"Well, Cork was like this not so long ago," said Margarita. "The main streets in the centre are actually built over canals!"

"Really?" said Alice. "Well, they should have left it like that!"

"I would love to own a barge like this," said Richard, "and come here on my holidays."

"Well, if you do, I'll be the first to ask for an invite," bantered Alice.

Margarita smiled, adding to the conversation.

"You're like two small children dreaming of spending your lives on holidays. You will soon be back in Ireland, in the rain, so just enjoy this moment and stop planning the impossible!"

Alice swished a scarf at her and called her a spoilsport! Yet they all knew they were living the dream, while knowing they had to return to the work of getting ready for the performances.

They would leave for Versailles the day after the Paris Church performance, where they would have a few days to enjoy their surroundings.

On the day of the first concert, they had dinner in the hotel before a carriage picked them up and drove them to the church of Saint-Germain-des-Prés.

Alice was really excited at the thought of relaxing for the evening while watching Richard and Margarita perform. As she left them, Alice reflected that Richard seemed to be paying her a lot of attention this week, but she wouldn't allow herself imagine anything other than he was grateful for her organisational abilities. Yet, she thought, I can always dream.

The concert was to begin at seven o'clock. As they went into the church for rehearsals, Margarita looked in awe at the stained-glass windows and the ceiling, which had paintings so spectacular that she wondered how the artists had completed them. A choir stood on the altar and the musicians sat to the side. The front of the altar had a dais close to the pews, where the singers would stand.

The sounds that filled the entire church as the choir began to sing augured well for the concert performance that would follow.

Well before seven o'clock, Alice was delighted to see that the church was full to capacity. When the concert began, she was transfixed by her surroundings and what music could sound like in such a sacred place. It must be the bouncing off the walls or ceilings, she thought. Richard and Margarita will be delighted to know that the sound of their voices was almost heavenly to hear.

With Jacques introducing each song, Alice could see that every member of the audience was captivated by the singing of Margarita and Richard. The applause they received after each song was a great tribute to them both.

As the finale arrived, Jacques explained to the audience that Margarita had written the song especially for them and it would be sung by her in French, with the musicians playing, and the choir chanting in the background. Alice knew that Huguenot friends of the Perrotts in Cork had translated the words into French for tonight's concert and that the song had been written by Margarita while Rosita slept.

There was a hush as the choir and musicians began. Richard joined with the choir as Margarita began what Alice would later describe as almost a spoken prayer. As she read the words in English, Alice sat with tears in her eyes at how lucky she was to be present on this night.

"Darkness comes and unfurls its cloak
Around this church and steeple
Deep shadows descend like a great black coat,
Around the factories sleeping.

When morning throws its shards of light,
The steeple again stands tall
And later when the church doors open,
Gives warmth and peace to all.
When the church bells make their morning call,
They chime out peace to all
The steeple bows its head once more
In homage to those on the factory floor.
Amen."

As the cheers and applause rang out, it took five minutes for Jacques to thank everyone for their support of the charity. Margarita asked Alice to join them and she added her congratulations to the extremely happy-looking pair.

It was a long time before anyone slept that night as they drank coffee and Richard sampled the French wine at a supper laid on by the concert organisers. Singing in French apparently won the audience's approval. The following morning the newspaper Le Presse described them as *"Le couple d'or"* – the Golden Couple.

As they sat in their carriage on their journey to Versailles, Richard was very impressed with the critic's report and Margarita just smiled happily and said she wasn't too bothered with anyone's opinion once she was happy with her performance. Jacques was all smiles and he assured them that they would be very impressed with their venue for the second concert.

That was an understatement. Nothing would have prepared them for the opulence surrounding them at

Versailles. However, Jacques seemed to be the most impressed by his surroundings which amused Margarita and Alice. They were brought to the chateau of a Count, where they would stay for the week. The Count was not in residence but his staff were put on notice to look after the needs of the guests.

Once they had made their way to their suites of rooms, Jacques was anxious to take them in the carriage to the concert venue. There, they were even more impressed. Jacques explained that it was the residence of Queen Marie Amelie, wife of Louis Phillippe I.

"It is called the Grand Trianon and today we will see it only from the grounds. The family are in the South of France for vacation but the main ballroom is being opened for the concert. All the proceeds on the night will go to help in the restoration of the main palace, which was somewhat destroyed during the Revolution. The Counts and Dukes of Europe will attend a dinner before the concert and all the artists will then perform. It is expected to raise many millions of francs as only the rich families have been invited."

Margarita said that her father would love to see the expansive gardens and the Baroque style buildings and Alice added that nobody would believe her back in Midleton if she tried to describe the palace buildings!

Jacques was delighted to see them impressed and told them that they would be brought for a tour of all the estate of Versailles during their stay.

They returned to their chateau and later, having enjoyed a substantial supper, they sat on the terrace and watched the sun go down. They sat quietly, each with their own thoughts, but all of them wondering how they had managed to be truly living the dream, if only for a week.

The night of the concert came. Margarita and Richard had a light supper, as always, before singing. Alice spent an hour getting Margarita prepared and the chateau housekeeper kindly offered a small tiara. This, she said, was with the agreement of the Countess. She explained to Alice that all of the women participating in the evening recital would be expensively dressed. Margarita was grateful for her thoughtfulness. The tiara looked perfect, as Alice wove some diamante clips at the back of Margarita's hair, which was lifted into an elegant chignon.

"You look like some princess," said Alice.

Margarita smiled as she put her silver locket around her neck.

The concert was a tremendous success but the size of the ballroom and the numbers of bejewelled women and men sitting around their fine dining tables made it a less personal experience for Margarita.

When it finished Alice couldn't be silenced, as Jacques had pointed out to her the various princes, dukes and counts accompanied by either their wives or lovers. She had spent her evening in the wings of the stage, mesmerised by her opulent surroundings.

Another night to remember, she thought, as she helped Margarita out of her gown back at the Chateau. She returned the tiara to the housekeeper, happy to know that it was once more in safe hands.

The following day again brought what seemed like never-ending sunshine in France. They left in the carriage at noon and as Margarita gave a final glance at the beauty of Versailles, she found that she was really looking forward to going to Italy. When she was young her parents told her stories every night about their trip to Florence and it was only many years later that she discovered that some of the stories of meeting artists and singers were somewhat embellished! They usually laughed when she mentioned it and told her that she needed to go there herself.

Jacques stayed with them for some days until they came close to Milan, where he left the carriage. They thanked him for his help but they all seemed to relax more as he joined a carriage going north.

"I found the French a bit sharp," said Alice.

"I agree with you," said Richard.

"While they are excitable, I also felt they were a bit on edge all the time."

"I agree," said Margarita, "but they have come through very turbulent years. They had the Revolution and the Napoleonic wars where they won and lost empires. They are a people in flux. I think that they are at present between worlds. Their aristocracy are wondering where their place is in the future. I hope everything works out peacefully for them."

"Well, Richard, that's the teacher Margarita putting us in our place and, of course, always the peacemaker," Alice laughed. "Anyway, Margarita, I hear there's nothing edgy about people with Italian blood!"

When their carriage drove into the centre of Milan they were driven to the spacious square where the Duomo stood majestically in the centre. They had been told that there were new stained-glass windows installed and they looked forward to viewing them. The carriage continued across the square and the driver pointed out the building they wanted most to see, the Teatro alla Scala. They thought it was a magnificent building but could hardly wait to see the inside of the theatre in which they would perform.

The carriage pulled up close to the left side of the theatre in front of their hotel. As the carriage door opened, they were helped out of the car by a smiling young woman who, like Jacques, spoke perfect English. As they stood on the pavement, she kissed all three of them and introduced herself as Carmella. She would be with them throughout their time in Italy. "I need to show you the beauty of our country, where you will be warmly received because you sing and singing is in our soul," she said.

Over the next few days Carmella was true to her word and for Margarita the highlight of her trip was being allowed view Leonardo da Vinci's painting of *The Last Supper* in the convent of Santa Maria delle Grazie.

Their trip to the Teatro alla Scala came with a warning from Carmella.

"It has many boxes that are owned by private families who helped pay for the reconstruction in the last century. Do not be surprised to find people playing cards in the pit or even bartering, but on the night if you sing well, it will be respected."

They found the interior of the theatre amazing with what seemed like hundreds of those private boxes. They had never expected to experience a theatre so full of grandeur, yet its architecture still managed to make it an intimate place. They couldn't wait to begin.

Carmella introduced the singers to the large audience and they began with Italian arias to embrace the audience. It worked. They sang for two hours and with just one break for water. The audience requested three encores which the pair were delighted to give.

After the performance they met some of the audience, including the author Mary Shelley, who told them they were well received, as there were no interruptions by the barterers during the performance. Margarita was delighted to chat with her, both of them enjoying meeting English-speaking people.

Miss Shelley invited Margarita to join her on the following day at a musical recital. Richard and Alice encouraged her to go, saying that they would prefer to enjoy the sights of Milan. On the following night, Margarita was overcome by the talent in the musical soiree she enjoyed in a small intimate salon. The pianist, the singers and the quality of the musicians made her even more aware of the fact that music was the beating heart of the people of Milan. She couldn't wait to tell her parents about her experiences.

Early the following morning the party left for Florence, taking with them great memories.

Margarita found that Florence was everything she had expected, and more. This was the city she knew about from the stories told to her by her parents. She loved walking by the River Arno and exploring the narrow streets that gave respite from the hot sunshine. The Cathedral of Santa Maria del Fiore, generally known as the Duomo and the Basilica di San Lorenzo, with their magnificent art works, were her favourites.

Whilst in Florence, Margarita loved the fact that they sang all their music in church settings. Just as it had been in Paris, the sacred church surroundings added to the atmosphere, especially when they were requested to continue singing long after the concerts were due to end. The enthusiasm of the audience was infectious and Margarita began to understand why her mother had fallen in love with the people of Florence.

As she sat in the carriage, after their final concert and crossed the *Ponte Vecchio*, she knew she had found a place to cherish in her heart forever.

The party began their return trip by enjoying the continued hospitality of the Italians and French. They stayed each night in palazzos and stately homes. As Alice told them, they had to "sing for their supper" each evening and entertain the owners and their guests, after dinner had been enjoyed. The weather happily cooled down to what Richard described as Irish summers. It was rare for their travel to be disrupted by rain and it was a happy trio that finally arrived at the harbour in Calais and stepped onto the ship for their return journey to England.

Chapter 46

Margarita stood on the deck of the ship, watching the magnificence of the white cliffs, standing like a sheet of snow, on the coast of Dover. I really loved that trip, she thought, but I can't wait to get back to Ireland. She missed her family and even the school choir, but most of all she missed seeing Rosita. She was comforted by letters her mother had sent of Rosita's progress in walking and talking. Yet it was not the same, she mused, as she heard her name being called from behind her.

"Are you, as usual, deep in thought, or are you looking at the beauty in front of you?" Alice asked, as she made her way towards Margarita, who stood serenely as ever in a quiet corner at the deck rails.

Margarita gave Alice a hug.

"Are you coming to enjoy the view, or as usual are you going to give me a list of instructions for our concert in

London?" She smiled indulgently at one of her favourite people. "You have done a brilliant job on this tour and I can't even begin to think how it would have been without you. We now have a week before the London concert and I believe it's time you enjoyed a holiday for a few days in London, before going home." As she smiled at Alice, she noticed her expression.

"Why are you looking so pensive, Alice? There's nothing wrong, is there?"

Alice hesitated as she placed her elbows on the rail.

"There is something I need to know and after the conversation I want us still to be friends, if I have got things wrong."

"You're worrying me now, Alice! I'd never fall out with you."

"Well," continued Alice slowly, "I was doing a lot of sightseeing while in Europe, with Richard, while you tended to spend time more quietly, especially on days close to each performance. Does that worry you?"

Margarita looked at her and raised her eyebrows.

"Do you love him?" Alice asked.

"Who? Richard?" Margarita had to think fast, as she prepared a suitable answer for Alice. "I love singing with him. I love his family. I love what he's done for my career, but we are not romantically involved." She hesitated and continued. "Richard is his own man, he has many admirers, as you know. Whoever he loves, he will let them know, I am sure of that."

She patted Alice on the shoulder and was amazed to see

tears began to roll down her face.

"Go for him, Alice, if you think he is interested. You have my full blessing."

"Well, he's been very attentive to me and I've held back because I had thought he loved you. Oh, by the way, I was actually sent out by Richard to ask you to join us for a meal."

"Go and eat with him alone, Alice. I wish you luck and, for what it's worth, he would be a very lucky man to find a wife and partner as special and talented as you."

Alice almost squeezed her niece to death before she ran towards the dining room as if she didn't want to waste another moment of her life.

Margarita stood on the deck and shed some tears. The conversation had unsettled her but she was again reminded of Granny Sheila's wise words: *You cannot control other people's feelings, you can only control your own.* Wise words indeed, she thought, as she made a decision to view it as a problem solved. She reasoned that she had only wondered about a romantic relationship with Richard and was never really ready to pursue it. She was now even more determined to enjoy every moment of her time in London.

The week in London was one of great enjoyment for the whole group. Mr. Deacon was back in London and took over the reins from Alice and congratulated her on her excellent organisational skills.

"You're in my book, lady, as a person I will call on whenever I have a crisis with temperamental singers," he said as he kissed her on both her blushing cheeks.

They were staying in the luxurious Browns Hotel in Albemarle Street in the heart of London. Margarita spent the first few days quietly browsing the shops and enjoying the sunny weather. She bought gifts for everyone in Midleton and had to purchase an extra trunk, which she hid from Alice in the hotel luggage room, because Alice would spend time worrying about how they would get it back to Ireland!

The three friends were delighted to get an invitation from Lily and Deborah's family to join the Cecil family in Hatfield House for a banquet in their honour. It was quite an occasion as many of the Hertfordshire County set and even some minor royals would attend. Richard and Margarita happily sang on the night and thanked the family for inviting them. It was, they said, a good dress rehearsal for their debut in the Opera House in Covent Garden. Everyone they met was gracious towards them, but Margarita was wondering if anyone would mention Victor's name. Nobody did.

She told Alice that she wanted to spend the two days before the concert quietly in her room, practising and preparing for what was the highlight of their tour.

Alice was having a great holiday and was continually smiling, much to Margarita's amusement.

Margarita woke in her opulent bedroom with its heavy rich red brocade curtains and lay relaxing, observing the cream-coloured drapes surrounding her four-poster bed. She smiled to herself. I have enjoyed this stylish living, she thought, but I'm not sure that I am cut out to spend a live travelling from venue to venue to sing. When tonight was over, she would return to Ireland and was incredibly happy at that thought. She knew that music would be part of her life forever but had a gnawing feeling that the life of a singer on the road was not going to be her pathway in life.

A knock on her door broke into her musings. The hotel maid entered, with a tray of silver covers over a luxury breakfast.

Margarita sat up in the bed. A tray with wooden legs was placed over her knees and as the maid removed the silver tops, the aroma of hot bacon wafted up to tantalise her taste buds. She always loved a good breakfast, as she recalled Granny Sheila telling her to start the day full of energy and she'd keep that energy throughout the day. As she luxuriated in her feather bed and ate hot warm bread rolls, there was a further knock on the door.

"Can I come in?" a voice called. "I have your second key!"

It was Alice and Margarita was delighted when she entered the room.

"You are looking so radiant! You must be really enjoying your holiday while I'm lazing about in my bed," she laughed.

Alice sat on the bed and took Margarita's hand.

"I have some news – some good news," she said hurriedly, knowing that Margarita was a worrier. "Richard got a letter this morning from my father. He had actually

368

written to him, so he told me, when we were in Milan. He was asking him if he would agree to his daughter marrying him. The news I have is about me! My father agreed and Richard asked me to marry him at the breakfast table this morning! I said yes, of course!"

The beaming smile that lit Alice's face transferred itself to Margarita as she scrambled from the bed, nearly upturning the teapot as she clasped Alice in a hug.

"I'm so happy for you both! Go straight back down to him and I'll dress myself immediately and then I'll join you. This is wonderful news and needs to be toasted. Get a bottle of Champagne and three glasses and I'll be with you in no time!"

And she shooed her aunt from the room.

Alice left the room in a sea of smiles and Margarita tried to compose herself before dressing. She truly was happy for Alice but a part of her felt sad that the "Golden Couple" era was now over. She found that she had to speak to herself and feel joy for them but acknowledged that in her heart she envied them their happiness. Will I ever feel the warmth of such a love for myself, she wondered as she finally made her way down to the comfortable hotel library.

The happy couple were sitting holding hands when Margarita entered the room.

"Now *I'm* going to have to be the chaperone until we get home to Ireland and I return her safely to her father," Margarita said, laughing, as she kissed Richard and again took Alice in her arms, confirming her full blessing on the union.

369

"We're off to the jeweller's in a few minutes," said Richard. "He already has a tray of rings waiting for Alice to choose one."

"I hope you get back in time for rehearsal," Margarita cautioned with a smile on her face. "What, miss rehearsals? My manager here, Miss Alice Turner, would leave me if I didn't prepare properly for tonight's performance! We are doing just one extra thing. I am also buying my bride-to-be a new gown and she will sit in the front row of the Opera House wearing it tonight, so that I can sing to her personally!"

They all laughed at the thought and, after a celebratory drink, Margarita waved to them as they stepped into their carriage. As they left, they promised to be at the Opera House soon after lunch.

Margarita returned to her room to practise and to write the news in her diary, which she had kept writing faithfully each day of the tour. She felt a pang of loss but she did not want to ever forget the wonder of this summer.

At rehearsal Richard sang with a new-found richness probably from the happiness he now felt and Margarita knew that tonight would be special.

Alice came to join them carrying a tray with hot ham sandwiches, plus tea for Margarita and coffee for Richard. He always said coffee revved him up for the performance whereas Margarita said tea calmed her down! Alice had already shown everyone who would look her delicate white diamond ring, that under the candlelight in the room shone with a myriad of colours.

Then she kissed them both and left to have some food before changing into her new gown and taking her place later in the front row of the theatre.

The atmosphere in the auditorium was heightened with anticipation as the orchestra played, prior to the arrival of Richard and Margarita on stage.

Nobody was disappointed over the next two hours. Richard sang favourite opera songs and sacred hymns and the much-loved "Silent Night". This was followed by Margarita's supreme voice that was best served with her singing of "*Casta Diva*" and her much-loved "*Lascia ch'io pianga*".

Thus ended a wonderful evening, with a standing ovation for the performers. They both acknowledged the applause of the audience and when Richard sang again, the crowd cheered even more. Richard quietened the audience only by telling them that Margarita would sing "The Lament of the Irish Maiden".

She stood in the centre of the stage and a pin could be heard drop as she told them the story of the song of lost love although she declined to tell them the political reason for why he left his native shore. Her voice soared; she sang the lament with such feeling that tears sprang to her eyes. As her pitch-perfect voice soared when she sang the final lines, she knew she had given a performance to remember.

At that moment, she raised her eyes over the heads of those in front, towards those at the back of the auditorium.

As she lifted her head to acknowledge the spectators seated there, her heart began to thump as she saw a certain face.

He was standing up. He looked so sad in the midst of the seated spectators. She thought he was saying something to her. Then he was gone. Had he ever been there? Margarita was by now almost visibly shaking when he opened the door and let the light in. As the door closed the light faded away. Was it a mirage? She thought it probably was.

Then reality intruded.

Nonetheless, she was shaking. At least she got a few moments to shake herself back to normality and, as she saw Alice standing and clapping in front of her, she lifted her hand and asked the crowd to quiet.

Then, she said: "Tonight, Richard and I have experienced the marvellous welcome of the people of London and, as we leave your special city and Opera House, I want to invite the wonderful Alice Turner – who has managed us in every way during our tour of Europe – and who today became betrothed to my wonderful singing partner, Richard – to join us onstage!"

As Alice made her way to the stage, Margarita thought she had never seen her look so lovely, in her shimmering silver gown. The cheers of the crowd grew until a blushing Alice kissed Richard. For Alice, it was the end of the best day of her life. As the audience continued to applaud, bouquets of flowers were handed to all three of them by the theatre manager.

As the satisfied audience began to leave the auditorium,

Margarita left the stage with Richard and Alice. She felt somewhat disturbed and unsettled, because of the thoughts that had gone through her head as she finished her final song.

The green room behind the stage was in uproar. Drink was flowing and everyone wanted to meet the artists. At some strange level Margarita felt it wasn't her night now. She wanted to leave the arena. She felt happy for the lovers but it seemed to emphasise her own aloneness. She had rarely felt lonely in that aloneness, but tonight was different. She needed space to think. She had a word in Alice's ear and told her she was tired and would get her carriage to take her back to the hotel and would see them both tomorrow morning at breakfast.

The carriage driver was waiting at the pavement when Margarita was escorted by the theatre manager to the stage door. He helped her in and she relaxed into the comfortable cushions as they made their way to Mayfair. Margarita asked the driver to let her off a distance from the hotel so that she could breathe fresh air before going into the hotel. He agreed but said he'd leave only when he saw her enter the hotel front door.

As she walked towards the hotel, she took many deep breaths and began to relax a little. She reflected on her performance and knew that she had won over the audience in London. Yet, the high level of excitement surrounding opera singers wherever they went never sat lightly with her. As she entered the hotel, she knew that although she had loved her summer in the sun she truly was relieved to be going home to Midleton.

The image that she thought she saw at the back of the theatre was of Victor. It disturbed her and made she realise that, although singing was a huge part of her life, she wanted more.

The hotel receptionist greeted her with congratulations as he informed her that many of their guests had returned from the Opera House and were delighted with their evening. Then, as he handed her the room key, he leaned forward and said: "A gentleman called and asked to speak to you, madam. I told him you weren't around and he asked if he could wait. I've put him in the library room. If you want me to send him away, I will be happy to oblige. He said that he knew you in Ireland. Or, would you like me to escort you to the room? You can then let me know if you wish to speak to the gentleman, or not."

Margarita looked in the direction of the library. It was a room she sat in for an hour each day, enjoying its quietness as she browsed through the magnificent books that stood on tall shelves of dark oak.

She asked the receptionist to escort her.

When they entered the room, she saw the outline of a young man standing still and gazing out the window. The bright moon threw its shadows into the room, lit only by a few candles. Margarita stood still and gestured to the receptionist to leave her.

She watched the figure for a moment, then he turned around.

He walked towards her.

"It's me, Victor."

Margarita knew who he was but all that registered with her was that he looked much older and sadder than the Victor she remembered.

"Will you talk to me, please, for a few minutes, Margarita? Could you sit down, and let me explain a few things?"

Margarita nodded and sat on the edge of a chair, afraid that her legs would collapse from under her.

"Victor, could I have a drink of water, please," she asked.

He quickly reached for a nearby carafe and poured water for her.

As she sipped the water, it gave her time to quieten her mind.

"I didn't know you were back in London, Victor. Nobody said anything. I thought you were still somewhere in Europe."

Victor sat on a seat opposite her.

"I didn't want you to know I was here," he said. "I went to watch you at the Opera House."

"So, it *was* you at the back of the theatre?" Margarita asked, with sadness in her voice. "I saw you. And you left before I finished. Why did you do that?"

"It was the song. I was crying. I wanted to say goodbye to you before I return to Europe. That's why I'm here."

"Why are you not coming home, Victor, to see your child and family?" she asked in an anguished voice.

Victor's head fell into his chest and Margarita could see the tears on his cheek.

"I was healing in Vienna and my doctor felt I needed to see you before I made further plans for the future."

"So, what had I to do with your further plans?" she asked plaintively.

"I knew tonight I was too late," Victor answered.

"What are you talking about Victor? Too late? Too late for what?"

"I told the doctor in Vienna that I loved you and he insisted I go back and tell you."

"*What?*" she said, stunned.

"I called here tonight to say goodbye and to wish you happiness. I had been told you were seeing a lot of Richard in Ireland and I could see how much he loved you, just by the way he was looking at you tonight. My doctor Mateo Bauer told me I needed to tell you how much I loved you, but now I'm just doing what my doctor asked. However, I can't go back to Ireland just yet and see you married to him. I'm returning to Vienna tomorrow and I'll come back to Ireland to take up my responsibilities when I feel ready to cope with a future without you."

Margarita, with tears in her eyes, leaned forward and took Victor's hand in both of hers. It was icy cold. She held on to it firmly and looked into his eyes.

"Who told you I was marrying Richard?" she asked, stroking his hand to put some life into it.

"I saw you together tonight," Victor answered, with his

head dropping.

"You left early, didn't you?"

"Yes, I'm sorry, that was rude of me. But I couldn't listen to any more of your song because I knew what it meant to have loved and lost. I now know that I left Ireland because I was a coward. I just ran away from my responsibilities. I'm so sorry. You also need to know that I was comforted, when I was at my lowest, by the fact that you were caring for Rosita. I need, at least, to thank you for that. I have been very selfish."

A smile appeared through the tears that flowed down Margarita's face.

"If you had waited until the end of the concert, you might have learned something important to us both." Her grip tightened on Victor's hand. "Everything is fine. I brought Alice Turner up on the stage and I made an announcement to the audience that Alice and Richard became betrothed, earlier today. They are to marry in Midleton next spring."

"Alice? Where does Alice fits in?" a bemused Victor asked.

"She has travelled with us for months as my companion and they have fallen in love. I do not love Richard. He loves Alice!"

"However, if you will allow me to speak –" Victor was about to say something again, but closed his mouth.

"I love you, Victor. I don't love anyone else!"

Victor stood up, shock evident on his face as Margarita

stepped towards him and put her arms around him.

"Aren't you going to kiss me?" she asked, as she put her hands on his face and gently brushed away his tears.

But he just held her closer until she broke the silence.

"Victor, do you still have Fleur's pocket watch?"

Victor nodded, as he touched his heart.

"Always keep Fleur close to your heart. She gave you a precious baby. Victor, I want only another part of your heart. Remember, I also loved her and don't forget that we both love Rosita."

Victor again held Margarita close, but he couldn't answer. He just continued to hold her, as his tears flowed freely for the first time in his life. He felt that at this moment he was finished fighting his demons. He believed that he had the chance of recovering, with the love of another good woman.

Alice and Richard returned many hours later to the hotel and were both shocked when the receptionist told them that Margarita was sitting in the library with a gentleman caller. When they entered the room, they saw Margarita and Victor, holding hands.

Alice rushed across to them and immediately knew that Margarita's happiness was assured. As she embraced them, she knew that today all her wishes had finally come true.

Hours later, as the warm glow of early dawn peeped through the window of the hotel library the four occupants could be seen eating an early breakfast and all wondered why none of them was tired enough to need sleep.

In was five days later before the carriages arrived in Liverpool to catch the boat back to Ireland. They had stayed on in London to meet their relatives again and to impart the good news that Victor was returning. He had gone with Richard to the Hatton Gardens jeweller to purchase an engagement ring for Margarita with a size and style recommended by Alice. He would ask her father for her hand in marriage as soon as they returned to Beconsford House.

Victor felt reborn, rejuvenated and relaxed during those heady days in London. He had sent a letter to his doctor in Vienna with grateful thanks for his advice. Letters had been sent to Ireland and there was much joy in Midleton, especially because of the fact that Victor was finally returning to his home.

It was a warm and gloriously sunny day when the two carriages, filled with the four smiling occupants, arrived outside the front entrance to the big house in Midleton. A welcoming party stood on the steps.

Deborah and Isaac were each holding a hand of Rosita, who was jumping up and down, with her pink frilly dress bouncing around. Jack, Eliza and Molly stood next to them and in the background Richard's family had already started clapping their hands excitedly, as soon as they saw the carriages appear in the driveway.

Margarita had earlier explained to Victor that Rosita called her "Mama", but only because she couldn't say Margarita. Victor had kissed her when she told him and said he knew that Fleur would have been happy with that.

As the footman opened the carriage door and Margarita stepped out, nothing would contain Rosita any longer as she dragged Deborah and Isaac down the steps and ran towards Margarita shouting "Mama, Mama!"

As soon as Rosita had jumped into her arms, Margarita turned to Victor.

"This is your dada, sweetheart. He has come home to help us care for you. Now give him a big hug and say, 'Welcome home, Papa'."

As Margarita handed the child to her father, Rosita looked at him shyly and said, "You cry, Papa."

"I'm crying because I'm so happy to see you and to be home. I've been sick, my love, and now I'm better and can help to take care of you."

As Rosita put her arms around his neck to hug him, everybody shed a tear of happiness, thankful for his safe return.

The evening was filled with revelry. Victor had got Jack's permission to marry Margarita and the kitchen staff had prepared a banquet fit for a king.

Margarita spent much of the meal time glancing at her exquisite diamond ring with three red diamonds surrounding the raised white diamond in the centre. He told her that the red diamonds stood for Love, Passion and Joy. He also acknowledged that Alice had a hand in the sizing! She loved it and knew she would have it on her hand for her lifetime. The party lasted into the night and for a second time Rosita was brought from her bed to hear Margarita sing, but this time the child was in the arms of her father.

Chapter 47

Christmas 1840

The marriage of Margarita and Victor would take place on Christmas Eve, in the estate church. They had both already acted as bridesmaid and groomsman during the marriage in the spring of Alice and Richard, which was held in the same church. They had all joked that it was a good rehearsal for the big wedding, except on this occasion Rosita would be a little flower girl throwing delicate red rose petals in the path of her beloved mama, as she walked up the isle to marry her papa.

On the eve of the wedding the excitement was mounting in Eliza and Jack's house. Everyone seemed to be there except Victor, who was dining quietly with Isaac, Deborah and Rosita. Alice was the chief dresser and Ann Marie was on hand for last-minute repairs. Molly, as ever, was making endless cups of tea. People kept calling with gifts for the bride. As they were ready to sit down and relax, Ann Marie answered the door to her cousin Hilda Bowe, who now worked full time in the Big House. She entered the kitchen carrying a large package, apologising for the lateness of the hour. Her youngest daughter Esme was by her side.

"I was delayed leaving Rosita earlier – she's so excited but isn't fully sure of what is happening. I have a silver spoon that I bought for Margarita, but this parcel is for you, Eliza." She handed it to the surprised Eliza, as she continued, "It's a patchwork cover for your bed that myself and the children made over the past year. The day that Rosita was born, I was at a low ebb. I had just lost my baby at birth and my husband couldn't work because of a weak chest. I could never have imagined that any good would come from the loss of my baby, but after you asked me to nurse Rosita, I saw her going from strength to strength and it was a privilege to be part of that. My husband Alfie is a good man and since then he's cared for the children, while I earned the money. As you know they are all getting their schooling, including Esme and this is to thank you, Eliza."

Jack got up from his chair and gave Hilda a hug, as he said, "We have to thank you. Our new grandchild is healthy, thanks to you. We will never forget that."

As Eliza opened the parcel and saw the delicate stitching and myriad of colours, she was humbled by the time and effort the Bowe family had put into its making. As Jack and Eliza glanced at each other, they both knew that Hilda realised that poverty was on the increase in the town.

Jack and Isaac had long conversations about the issue. Isaac told him of his worries because poverty was increasing everywhere. Jack felt the problem in Ireland was more troublesome, due to the Irish Poor Law Act of 1838. Unfortunately, it allowed support for the destitute to be given only through entering the Workhouse system. As Jack had said to Isaac, the Parliament did not seem to understand the psyche of the Irish race. The majority would rather walk the roads until they either emigrated, or died, than bring their families into the Workhouse. Jack knew of many families who now went to England in search of a better life and the number of sons and daughters who had gone to America in the hope of earning enough to send help home was growing weekly. Sadly, for these families, they knew in their hearts that they were never likely to see their children ever again. The idea that he might never see his daughter again made Jack shudder. He was one of the lucky ones and he knew it. On this wonderful night for his daughter, Jack had to remind himself that Eliza and he would always be most satisfied in life when they helped in any way to alleviate the burden of those less fortunate. He knew he would continue to do that while he still drew breath.

After everyone had admired the gifts, they all sat down and had tea together. Jack and Eliza reflected later that it was probably one of the last ordinary nights that Margarita would have, but they knew that she would never stray from the values she grew up with in her home on the estate. Jack knew, also, that his family would never stop their fight to educate and support those in need. He knew that his daughter was marrying into a family with similar values.

On the day that Margarita and Victor married, the sun shone brightly, as the frost glistened and crunched underfoot. The Midleton children's choir sang at the wedding ceremony, while Master Johnson played the organ. Jack Ryan was a proud man as he walked his only child up the aisle and handed her over to Victor Beconsford. Margarita wore a tiara that was worn at Beconsford marriages throughout the centuries. Her locket, as always, was her jewellery of choice and her dress of white satin was covered with silver sequins that shimmered in the winter sun which shone through the stained-glass windows. A white cashmere stole kept her warm on this winter morn. To Jack, she looked the most beautiful bride ever.

Richard sang, much to the delight of the invited guests and the Midleton school choir sang as if they wanted to raise the roof of the chapel. When the service was over, everyone waited in the town for the wedding carriage to drive through, as promised, after the ceremony. After all, Margarita was one of their own. Money had been given to Mrs. Sexton and the Haven Inn to feed all the townsfolk on Christmas Eve and as a further gift to the town from Isaac, every family was provided with a Christmas gift parcel to help them celebrate the occasion by feeding their families adequately.

385

As the carriage returned to the estate somebody shouted, "*Welcome to the next Lady Beconsford! It's great that you're one of our own!*"

Margarita had turned and laughed at Victor before realising that they were speaking about her. Victor silenced her with a kiss and then told her that he hoped there would be many more Honourable Beconsfords arriving in Midleton in the near future! His new bride answered by giving her husband a lingering kiss.

Epilogue

1843

Change arrived on the Beconsford estate in early autumn. The now elderly Lord Beconsford, who had returned from London with his wife Ethel, came down with a fever. His neurotic wife took to her bed as she was afraid of catching it. A nurse sat with him in an effort to keep him cool but on the morning of 20th of September, as the sun rose, Edward Beconsford lost the fight and he died without his wife at his side. Within two weeks, Lady Ethel developed similar difficulties with her breathing. On the 30th of the month, Ethel also died of the same fever and she was buried by his side in the family vault in the grounds of the estate. At the funeral service, before they were both laid to rest in the estate graveyard, the new Lord Isaac Beconsford remembered only the good aspects of life while they were alive. Anyone in the town with long memories of Lord Edward did not mourn his passing. Isaac reminded those present at the funeral of the good work his father carried out in the English parliament and that he now knew that great joy and hope had returned to the big house after the marriage of his only son Victor to Margarita Ryan.

"The marriage of Victor and Margarita has more than anything contributed to a closer bond between the estate and the local town of Midleton."

Victor sat with Isaac on a couch close to the fire. The parlour was warm but Victor felt cold. He held a hot teacup in his hands and his father put his arm around him.

"I'm so proud of you, son. You have come through very hard times in the past and tonight will be wonderful," said Isaac, as he prayed to anyone who would listen and make it so.

Upstairs Deborah and Eliza were in the main bedroom of the big house overlooking the Secret Garden. It was nearing midnight on the 8th of June, 1842. Eliza was holding Margarita's hand, as the midwife spoke to her soothingly. She was now in the final stages of labour.

Doctor Kearney stood looking towards the window. He too prayed that everything would end well on this night.

He had told Margarita a few months previously that she could produce twins but, as she knew how this news might cause anxiety for Victor, she shared it only with her mother Eliza who was sure that she was indeed going to have twins.

Margarita was a strong young woman and the doctor knew it should all be fine, but he wanted nothing to go wrong tonight. Nurse Janet, who loved her work in the Big House was now Rosita's nanny and she had become a great friend of Margarita's over the past years. Her bright and breezy chatter eased the tensions in the room. Margarita had been in labour for some four hours and they all knew that they just had to let time take its own course.

Jack joined the other men in the parlour, having gone for a walk in the fields. He couldn't bear to sit still in a room but had returned as midnight chimed. He knew there was no news. He started to pace the room but sat down when he realised that Victor was getting agitated. Suddenly they heard loud noises from upstairs. Victor put his head down and covered his ears with his hands.

Jack and Isaac looked at each other. They both made to run for the door, but it opened before they reached it.

It was Deborah, with the biggest smile getting wider as the tears poured down her face. She practically fell into Isaac's arms.

"She had a boy and she had a girl, and they are both fine and she's fine!"

Victor ran past his parents and took the stairs two at a time. He raced to the bedroom and Dr. Kearney met him at the door.

"Your wife had a second child, which I suspected some months ago, or else she was going to give birth to a very large baby! But no. You are the father of twins, Victor. A boy and a girl. They are all in good health and your wife had a straightforward easy birth. They are a good enough weight not to require any special treatment. Congratulations, lad, I couldn't be more pleased for you."

Victor hugged him fiercely.

"Go in, your wife and children are waiting."

When Victor entered the room, Margarita was sitting up, looking exhausted but smiling, one baby in her arms. The nurse handed the other baby to Victor. He held the red-faced little boy, with a head of thick blond hair, just like his father. He kissed his head believing that he was the most adorable baby he had ever seen. He gently returned his son to the nurse and then took his most precious little girl from Margarita. The baby's head was adorned with the same black hair as her mother. She too was perfect.

The nurse put the baby boy in Margarita's arms and left the room quietly.

Victor sat on the bed, his little girl in his arms, and kissed his wife.

"Well, that puts paid to either Victor or Victoria!"

"I still want to call this little boy Victor," Margarita said. "Maybe we can call him Young Vic!"

"Our daughter will be called Elizabeth Deborah after my mother and yours." Victor laughed. "We can also add Sheila or Molly, but I think we should keep those names for our next two girls!"

Their happiness was complete when Rosita was brought in by her granny Deborah to look in wonder at her new brother and sister. Victor smiled at Rosita, then leaned over and kissed his wonderful wife and the mother of his twins.

His only thought being how lucky he was to have come out of such a dark place in his life to now being the proud father of three wonderful children.

It was nearing dawn when everyone had drunk to the good health of the babies and mother. Jack and Eliza decided to walk home to their own house to sleep. As they sauntered down the gravel path, Jack suddenly took his wife's hand and pulled her into the field below the Big House. He held her close and looked up at the stars sparkling in the sky as the moon shone its light on the fields.

"Over a quarter of a century ago, I looked up at a sky far out at sea and dreamed of watching the stars, while standing surrounded by the four green fields. Tonight, that wish has come true again for me. Firstly, I married you, then we had Margarita. Now, I have two more stars that we both need to guide along their way. Tonight, Eliza Ryan, I am the happiest man in Ireland. We may meet challenges in life down the road, but I will face anything with you at my side. I love you so much. You are the brightest star in the sky!" Before Eliza could reply, he held her close again and kissed her as if he would never leave her go.

The End